Glass Hearts

Renee Lovins

Bad Ash Publishing — Powder Springs, GA

Bad Ash Publishing
Powder Springs, GA 30127
www.badashpublishing.com
www.reneelovins.com

Publisher's Note: This is a work of fiction. Names, characters, places, and incidents are a product of the author's imagination. Locales and public names are sometimes used for atmospheric purposes. Any resemblance to actual people, living or dead, or to businesses, companies, events, institutions, or locales is completely coincidental.
Cover - http://www.bigstockphoto.com/image-38393620/stock-photo-blonde-girl-with-silver-mask-looks-in-to-the-lens
Licensed 10/29/2015
Ccontributor - **Copyright:** photoCD

Book Layout © 2015 BookDesignTemplates.com

Glass Hearts/ Renee Lovins -- 1st ed.
ISBN 978-0-9905182-2-8

Dedication

To my husband, Ash, who thinks I'm sexy even when I'm not.

Acknowledgements

As always the number of people to thank for helping to get any novel off the ground is enormous. First my husband, who even though he doesn't read romance, has always had faith in me. Melissa, Amy, Leslie, who reviewed, found flaws and kicked my butt to fix them. Erica Ellis, my wonderful editor, who points out the rest of my flaws.

Thank you, for making my work readable.

Also by Renee Lovins

Fairy Modern Series

Ink Deep

Sign up for News & Tidbits at www.reneelovins.com

CONTENTS

Chapter One

Ember moved her body to the pulsing music, the flashing lights creating snapshots in time. She danced alone in a room full of people. When she stopped being pulled by the beat, she turned, but the people she had come with, fellow students, had all drifted off to find their own end to the graduation celebration.

Shutting off the feeling of being isolated, she focused on the feeling of being free, of her dreams about to become reality. Sweat gathered at the nape of her neck, and thirst drove her from the dance floor. Bars just weren't her style, and she would have rather been celebrating with her family. But that would be later this weekend. For now, she might as well dance. But first she needed a drink.

A quiet place didn't exist in the club, but at least at the bar she didn't have to shout to place an order.

"Water and two fingers of whiskey." She didn't visit bars often, but at least she didn't try to order a fancy drink at one.

The bartender glanced at the stamp on her hand and nodded, reaching for a bottle. Ember stopped him.

"Tullamore Dew, please." The bartender flashed a smile and reached for that bottle.

Looking around the floor, she realized she didn't fit in. But for the moment, it didn't matter. The knowledge of the scholarship, her excellent grades, and the general atmosphere of the club elevated her mood. Anyway, anything would be more fun that spending the evening packing and cleaning. Although, this just put that activity off for a few hours. Ember rocked, waiting for her drink, unable to keep from moving a little with the music.

The image of Belinda being here flashed into her mind, and she knew the men would be draped all over her. Ember thanked her stars Belinda had just turned fifteen, and it would be her mom's job to deal with that nightmare. Belinda possessed beauty, brains, and attitude, and she had qualified for Olympic swimming trials, which was the primary thing she talked about right now. Boys were a distraction she didn't care about.

Ember laughed at the mental image of Belinda and all her suitors. She pulled out of it when the bartender set her water and whiskey down in front of her.

"From the gentlemen." He nodded to two guys smiling at them a bit further down the bar.

Ember sighed, adjusting the dress, which suddenly felt too tight.

"Why would anyone hit on me? I'm not even playing the fat friend tonight." Her voice got lost in the noise as the bartender drifted away. Confused, she looked at the drink, wondering about the motivation behind the offer.

Ember grimaced as she looked out over the mass of twenty-somethings on the dance floor, mentally comparing the sleek bodies and enhanced features to her overflowing bosom and abundant curves. Her dress hugged every curve, something that made her even more uncomfortable. She lifted the shot, taking a mouthful, then swallowed, enjoying the smoky burn.

"I'm impressed. Most women don't drink whiskey, and when they do they look like they're gagging, not savoring something exquisite." A low male voice spoke the words over her shoulder, his breath ghosting over her ear.

Startled she turned to look at the speaker, so focused on the whiskey she hadn't seen him approach. He must be the mysterious benefactor of her drink, the cute one. A smile crossed his face, and he didn't have the normal, "I'm taking one for my friend" look.

"Um, yeah. My dad is big into it, and when I got old enough to drink, he taught me what to appreciate." She grinned. "At least old enough in his opinion. The law might have had a quibble or two about that."

The smile grew, and she found herself mesmerized by his green eyes and hair the color of Ceylon cinnamon, her favorite spice.

"Smart man. Educate you now, for someone else to enjoy the skills." His eyes locked on hers as he spoke.

The blatant flirting had Ember ducking her head, discomfited by his attention. Other women garnered attention, not her. On the rare occasion that she found herself in a social setting, Belinda and her mom tended to be there also, drawing the attention. Gathering up her courage, she lifted her head to find him still watching her.

"Wanna dance?"

His words caught her off guard and all she could do was nod. A strong, callused hand grabbed hers and led her out onto the dance floor. Her pulse, already pumping from the earlier dancing and the shot of whiskey, spiked as he pulled her close and began to move.

Neither of them were expert dancers, but he focused only on her, his hand in the small of her back, always touching her as she moved.

She wanted to have a last fling before she started her career, her dream. Why not make it something to remember? Mental walls dropped and she gave herself to his hands, the music, and her own desire. Ember laughed with joy at feeling sexy and wanted.

Dancing and feeling his eyes on her body set her blood on fire, and she wondered if he tasted like cinnamon. That thought made her blink and pull back. He looked at her, a touch of disappointment on his face.

"Break?" she offered, trying to get control of both her

heart and her breath.

He nodded and followed her off the floor. Before they got back to the bar, he snagged a small booth and pulled her into it.

"Stop me if you don't want this, but I've been dying to know if you taste like whiskey since you drank that shot."

A thrill of elation shot through her, and his mouth moved towards hers, giving her plenty of time to pull away. She leaned forward and captured his lips with hers.

He tasted of salt, smoky whiskey, and ginger, another favorite spice. She deepened the kiss, marveling at her own impetuousness.

Hands wrapped around her waist, pulling her close to him, her breasts smashing against his chest. Well as much as her supportive lingerie would let them.

The sweet burn of need made the kiss even better. When the ache in her lungs, which begged for oxygen, overwhelmed the pleasure, she pulled back.

Looking up into his dilated eyes, she felt the rapid rise and fall of his chest. Ember smiled. It felt different on her face. She felt confident, sure of herself. Sure that he wanted her. And she wanted him.

The temptation to ask why hovered on her tongue, but she pushed it away. No sense in ruining her enjoyment.

"You taste like ginger."

His grin revealed nice teeth, one of his front teeth slightly chipped. She'd have to remember to explore that with her tongue.

"I was sucking on a ginger candy before I came into the club. You have good taste."

"Yes, yes I do." Her eyes slid over his jeans and shirt, and the desire to know what scents wreathed his body outside of this overly scented environment intrigued her. Ember didn't know if it was the alcohol, the look in his eyes, or the fact that she was leaving the country in a few days, but courage and wildness, unlike her normal safe attitude, grabbed her.

"I'm not going to claim I'm a virgin." She wrinkled her nose at the memory of a very forgettable lover. "And I never do this. But I want to do this."

His grin widened a bit more. "Do what?" His voice had dropped an octave and she shivered with pleasure as he looked at her.

"Go to bed with someone I just met in a bar."

He responded by kissing her again, hard, and she dove into the kiss. She felt like a sex goddess from the intensity of his attention.

"Jordan. Yo, Jordan."

She whimpered as he—Jordan—pulled back, and they both turned to look at the friend he had come with.

"Jordan, me and Lexi here are going to go party some more. Steer her around some curves. You coming?"

The gorgeous blond woman on his arm gave a perfect plastic smile, and Ember cringed back, self-doubt flooding her.

"Nah, Clay, I think I'm staying here." Jordan's voice threw up a dam against her fears as his hand ran down her leg. Her throat hurt; fear and excitement mixed into a swirling ball of need. "I think I found something else." Jordan didn't move his eyes from her face as he talked, and she closed her eyes to savor the feeling of total focus. Paris wouldn't have anything to match this.

"Okay, have fun you two. Don't do anything I wouldn't do."

"There isn't anything you wouldn't do." Jordan's retort made her smile, but he just looked at her. A look that made her wet her lips as need spiked.

"So true. So very true. Enjoy."

Ember ignored them leaving, watching Jordan and focusing on what she wanted. Taking something for herself, something that wouldn't hurt anyone

"So now what?" She knew her voice trembled a bit, but what could she expect?

"Nothing you don't want to do, nothing you aren't eager to do." That rough voice made her very eager. He frowned. "You are sober enough to know what I'm asking, right?" There was a touch of worry in his voice. Her knees were going to melt if he kept this up.

"Oh, believe me, I'm sober enough to know I'm crazy. But, dammit, I never do anything wild or unplanned. And I deserve something before I leave."

Jordan frowned a bit at that but before he could say anything, she leaned in and kissed him again.

When they pulled apart, she struggled to breathe evenly, and her hands slid up under his shirt. Her pulse kept pounding as she saw his matching reaction.

"Come on." His voice was rough as he stood, pulling her down the hallway. Ember waited, wanting to see where they would end up. Sex in a public place had never sounded exciting before, but right now she thought she might be willing to just do him on the tables with everyone watching. That realization made her squirm even more. Who knew being bad could feel so good?

She had zoned out on internal thoughts, so when he exclaimed, she stumbled, trying to catch back up to the reality around them. A storage closet marked "employees only" hadn't quite latched closed and he pulled her into it, shutting it behind them. The door wasn't framed well, and he cast a glower at it, but the light crept around the edges and lit up the room enough that she could see boxes of alcohol stacked around them.

Jordan walked her backwards, and with a lithe move that startled the daylights out of her, picked her up and set her on a box. Just the fact that he could pick her up and didn't seem to notice her weight flipped the last little switch she had. Ember opened her legs and pulled him between them, kissing him like it was her last chance to ever kiss anyone.

Her hands undid the buttons on his shirt, pushing it down, revealing chest muscles and a smattering of hair riding over his pectorals and thickening as it went down to his belly. All restraint gone, she licked his nipple. His sudden shudder and moan gave her a wave of power she had never felt before. She continued to pay attention to his body with her mouth as her hands fumbled with his jeans, working to free the very interested part of his body.

Cool air brushed across her back as the dress fell off her shoulders. Gentle hands tugged her backwards, and with a moan of protest, her lips released his nipple. As her supportive bra went the same way as her dress, he laid her back, as his lips captured her nipple, sucking it into his mouth.

Her nipples had felt good during sex in the past, but more as an "Okay, you've touched them, now get to the good stuff" sort of thing. This time, the feeling of his lips on her areola and the gentle suction sent forking branches of desire and need through her body, and she cried out in pleasure. He raised his head to look at her, the shadows in the room making him into a mythical creature as he smiled and went back to her body.

Time disappeared as the rest of their clothing fell away. The beat of the music in the club, the moans and whimpers from the two of them, the crinkle of foil as protection slid over him, guided their actions. Sitting on the boxes, he kissed her as he slipped into her, filling her, stretching her, as he swallowed her moan. No words were needed as their bodies communicated.

The sex should have been fast and frantic, with both of them desperate to achieve satisfaction before anyone found them. Instead, he took his time, bringing her to the peak then down, over and over, until Ember begged.

"Please, oh please, Jordan, let me come. I want to see your

face as you come inside me."

He shuddered at her words and began to thrust hard into her, his eyes locked on hers. Even in the low light, she saw the flare as he began to peak. After all the teasing he had done, it sent her over the edge with a scream she didn't care if people heard.

He leaned against her, sweat beaded on both their bodies. She kissed his cheek, the taste of salt a reminder of what they had just done.

"Thank you. For a night I'll never forget."

He looked at her, eyes dark with passion. "You're incredible. I want to see you again. You're like no one I've ever met."

Ember began to pull her clothes back on, her heart aching with the insane desire to throw away everything and stay. To have a relationship with this man who thought she, Ember Verre, was a sexy goddess.

"I would. Oh, believe me I would. But, I leave for France in a few days for the next year or so. This is my dream. My future." She felt a wistful smile on her face, and shook her head. "If only we'd met sooner."

He looked like he would protest, but then he pulled her close, kissing her again.

"Then let me buy you a bottle of champagne to celebrate your dreams. I'd never want to stop anyone from achieving them."

She figured her smile would crack her face, but she nodded. "I'd like that." The urge to leave itched at her, but he held her hand.

"Don't leave. Let me enjoy what little bit more time I get with you."

Her throat went tight, and she had to swallow past the lump. She nodded, incapable of speaking.

They slipped out of the room, ignoring the wink of an

employee that walked by, and found a table in the corner.

When the champagne arrived, he raised it in a toast. "To your dreams. May they all come true."

"To dreams." She drank to the toast. Both of them avoided the topic of the future. Instead, they danced and talked about inconsequential things. When it was time to leave, the kiss he gave her sent her home with a smile.

Chapter Two

The next day, the fire and passion of the woman he had met still haunted Ring Jordan. The thought of seeing her again tugged at him, even as Clay continued to twist his arm to go out again tonight.

"Ring, come on. You never can tell whom you'll meet. The blond last night was a blast, but tonight I might find someone better." Clay's voice echoed a bit in the club. "You said you'd meet us here."

Ring shrugged, focusing on his computer. A one-night stand was a new experience for him. One he still didn't know how he felt about. His amazement at Ember wanting him warred with horror at the knowledge of sleeping with a girl he didn't know. He didn't even have her phone number. His mother would beat him if she knew.

"I said I'd think about meeting you there. Clay, I'm not in the mood. Besides, I have work to do."

"Wow, she must have been something in the sack to keep you this focused on her."

Ring's voice went cold. "Yes, she is an incredible woman and if you want to keep your tongue in your head, you'll never imply anything so crude again."

There was a pause on the other end of the line. "Got it. Sorry. You know me; I always speak before I activate my brain cells. Look, you said she was leaving the country, so come out and see what you are missing. She isn't the only fish in the ocean. And I hate running solo." Contriteness filtered through the line and Ring felt his irritation ebb. Clay spoke his thoughts and then processed what he said. It landed him in hot water on a regular basis.

"I thought Greyson was with you."

"No. He decided finishing up his paper was more important. If you weren't locked in your room, you'd have noticed he's in his."

The three of them shared a rental house near the college, three bedrooms and two baths, plus a dining room, living room, rec room, and kitchen. They rattled around in it, and only pulled it off because Greyson's parents had bought it as an investment. For now, they did the maintenance and some small remodeling around the place as rent.

Ring sighed. Clay could wear down the patience of a saint. "Fine, yes. I'll meet you at the bar. Give me an hour. I need to finish this thesis outline. It's half my grade, and I like my 4.0, thank you very much, Mr. I-Have-Rich-Parents."

A snort of laughter from Clay emerged from the speaker of the cell phone. "Hey, my GPA is 3.9. Just because I got a B+ in art appreciation." The suppressed laughter on the other side brought a smile to Ring's face.

"You mean just because you were busy chasing Linda? As you wanted in her pants more than you cared about the class?"

"Well that too. And I succeeded." Pride rang in Clay's voice, causing Ring to roll his eyes.

"You're a horndog, a rich horndog. As such, getting in pants is never very difficult."

"True, true. I'm rich, smart, and good-looking. You're right. Who needs a 4.0 when you have all that?"

"Okay, the BS is getting way too high." Ring laughed. "I'll be there in a bit. I need to concentrate on this. So go away."

Clay laughed. "No problemo, Ring. See you in a bit."

With a snort, Ring hung up on Clay. "Show off," he muttered, a smile still on his face. Rich didn't quite cover Clay. Youngest son of the Texas Hangdon family, his parents owned half the oil derricks in Texas. The thing that made him tolerable, and one of Ring's best friends, was his down-to-earth attitude and caring personality. Horndog he might be, but he cared about everyone, at least when he used the head above his shoulders. Having parents who made you do chores like the rest of the world and work your ass off at the bottom rung of the company helped.

Turning back to his computer, Ring frowned as he looked at the spreadsheets. He had based his thesis on taking a cattle ranch with no viable grazing land and converting it into another successful business. And he was struggling to come up with an idea that wasn't too far-fetched. The land surveys he had been given didn't indicate any mineral or oil reserves, so that idea had gone up in flames. His degree and his future lay in coming up with a workable idea, at least on paper. He had to make his dad proud of him, to earn that smile of pride. The idea of disappointing Luke Jordan was worse than failing.

He rubbed his eyes, aching from staring at the screen. There had to be a creative idea that the assigned budget could pull off, but where?

Blowing his brown hair off his forehead, he slipped the glasses back on and focused on the information on the computer screen again.

The ringing of the phone distracted him, and he answered without looking at the caller ID. A wistful hope flashed through that maybe Ember had called him, but she would need his phone number to do that. But he knew it would be Clay. "Clay, I'll be there. Just let me get some more done on this."

"Ring?"

The muffled feminine voice surprised him; the tone in it struck a chord of fear deep inside.

"Mom?"

His mother cleared her throat and then spoke a bit clearer, though it was still rough and thick.

"Yes. Ring… I have some news."

Her voice quavered, and his mother's voice never quavered. Raised in England, her voice was always crisp and matter of fact. The thickness in the tone made the hair on his neck rise.

"Mom, are you okay? Is something wrong? Where's Dad?"

Monica Jordan's words shattered his world. "Ring, your dad had a massive heart attack this evening and died on the way to the hospital." She bit off a sob. "He's dead, Ring."

"He's what?" Ring couldn't process the words; they didn't make any sense at all.

He heard her sniff hard. "He's dead. Luke is dead. My husband is dead." Sobs broke out again as he sat in his chair, trying to understand how his heart had just shattered into dark gray shards.

"I hate to ask, but I need you to come home, Ring. I can't deal with all of this myself. I'm sorry."

The apology, from a woman who had never asked him for anything once he became an adult, shook him out of his daze. "Don't you dare apologize. I'll be home as soon as I can."

He glanced at the clock, doing the math for driving from Stanford to his home near Encinitas. It was 9:00 PM now. He could get out of here in the next hour. "I'll be there as soon as I can."

"Ring, don't drive like a maniac." Her voice sharpened. "I know your lead foot. You can't change anything, and if you get hurt too, it would destroy me. But, thank you."

"Mom…" The thank-you hurt, and he wanted to be there so badly to pull her into a hug and try to make it all better. He suspected flowers or chocolate, his standard way of dealing with upset women, wouldn't make it better this time.

"Love you. Come home, Ring." He sat holding the phone to his ear even as she hung up. What did he do next? How could his father, the indomitable Luke Jordan, be dead?

Clothes, email, Greyson, Clay, car, in that order. He had a niggling feeling that it might be a while before he returned.

It didn't take him long to pack. Nausea swirled in him as

he put his dark suit in his bag. Sitting at his computer, he looked at his business plan, and it seemed so stupid and shallow now. One of the things he learned while getting a MBA with a double major in Project Management and Entrepreneurship was that you never burned your bridges. Pulling up his email program, he found the email address for his professor. Taking a deep breath, he started typing.

Professor Schueller, I have had a family emergency and have to leave. I don't know how long I will be gone. I am attaching the rough draft of my proposal for my master's thesis. I will let the university know my status once I am able to assess the situation at home. Please contact me if you have any questions or concerns.

He typed his name and provided his cell number.

Shutting down the laptop and packing it, Ring stood motionless. What did he need to do now?

The buzz of an incoming text to the phone in his hand jolted him and he looked down.

Waiting for you. 2 hot chicks. At fav bar

Ring looked blankly at the phone and then half smiled. Clay could find sexy women regardless of where he was. Well, tonight, he'd have to deal with them himself.

Family emergency, driving home. Talk later.

Bag in his hand, he walked down the hall and pounded on Greyson's door.

"I'm on the other side of the door. A knock would work just as well. It's open." The calm, soothing voice of his other best friend helped pull some of the pieces in his chest together. Ring pushed it open as Greyson turned to look at him.

In one motion, Greyson stood to his full six-foot-three height and walked over, concern clear on his face. "Ring, what's wrong? Is Monica okay? Luke?"

Hearing his dad's name made him flinch.

"Dad died. Mom called. I'm headed home." Each pause

between the words, he fought not to scream, not to deny this reality.

"I'll go with you. Monica is going to need you," Greyson responded before he could finish his final word.

"No. Let me get there and see what the situation is. I'll let both of you know when I do, okay?" The offer helped, but right now, he couldn't stand the sympathy. Ring wanted to be home, to hug his dad, something that would never happen again.

"Are you sure? I can come." Greyson crossed his arms, looking at Ring, his dark grey eyes, his namesake, boring into Ring.

"Thanks, but no. I'll call."

Ring headed out, unable to stay another minute without letting loose all the pain that circled what remained of his heart.

He flipped on his drive app, just to avoid the calls and questions. Talking did not sound attractive right now. He just wanted to get home and hope his mom had made a mistake.

Please, let her be wrong.

Ring drove in a weird Zen state. The coolness of the late-night California air didn't soothe his stress. Putting on some AC/DC, he concentrated on not speeding. The heavy beat of the drums matched the anger and fear he felt at losing the man he loved and had wanted to prove himself to. Now he never could.

Chapter Three

Sunday afternoon, Ember looked over her apartment, at her life packed in boxes around her. Glee bubbled up inside her. She had sold everything she wasn't storing at her parents' house. That left her ten boxes to contain twenty-two years of life. Hefting a box up into her arms, she headed to her car to stack it with her suitcase and her trunk. Everything she needed for France and her life as a Cordon-Bleu trained chef waited in that trunk. Once she finished her training - in Paris no less, on a full scholarship – her dream of running her own restaurant would be one step closer to reality.

Ember fought down the desire to dance down the stairs, instead making sure she didn't trip. Breaking a leg now would be the worst thing ever. She slid the box into her Honda, which she was giving to Belinda as congratulations on her Olympic trials qualification. Ember had known she would qualify. When Belinda swam, dolphins looked slow. Who could ask for a better little sister? Three more trips and everything would be in the car. Another few hours to clean the apartment, get her deposit back, head over to her parents' house for few days, then Paris, where she would finish her training and start her dreams. Another smile forced its way across her face.

In the middle of scrubbing down the bathroom, she heard her phone ring. Shrugging, she let it go to voice mail while she finished with the bleach and cleaners. Later she saw her mom had left a message. Listening to it made her smile. Leaving her mom would be the hardest part. How did you function without your best friend?

Cleaning the entire apartment took longer than she'd thought, and when Ember finished, her phone showed well after 8:00 PM. She wouldn't be to her parents until well after 1:00 AM, and that was speeding all the way. However, she would be leaving the place sparkling; the deposit return would not be an issue. When her phone rang, it startled her. She didn't recognize the number.

"Ember Verre?" asked a voice. She tucked the phone under her chin as she put the cleaning material back in a bucket.

"Yes." Distracted, expecting a telemarketer, she didn't pay much attention.

"Miss Verre, are you the daughter of Sabrina and Richard Verre?" She didn't recognize the voice, so serious and formal. It stopped her in her tracks.

"Y-yes," she stuttered a bit, confused and off balance. Her stomach felt like a blender churned in the middle. Instinct made her straighten up and grip the phone tight.

"My name is Jorge Svenson. I'm the ER director for St. George's Hospital. There has been an accident involving your family, and you're listed as their emergency contact. We need you to come down to the hospital immediately."

The churning stopped, and her stomach contents gelled into a hard lump sitting in her stomach like waterlogged dough. Ember fought to swallow, her throat so tight it hurt.

"A-are they…" She cleared her throat. The phone clenched so tight in her grip, her hand hurt. "Are they o-okay?"

"Miss, I need you to come down here, please." The neutral, professional voice scared her more than anything else.

"Okay, I'll be there as soon as I can. I'm not close."

"I understand. Thank you. Please go to the front desk and ask for me."

Ember repeated his name and hung up, her mind in a daze. The bucket of cleaning supplies dragged down her arm. The spotless room had lost its joy and suddenly seemed cold and barren. Ember picked everything up and moved to the door, shutting off the lights and locking it behind her. Fear gibbered in the back of her mind, but it couldn't break through her shock. She dropped off the key, put the last bit of stuff in her car, and headed to the hospital, all on autopilot.

Still in a fog of shock, she drove the speed limit, her mind blank. No thoughts formed in the hours that made up the drive, just emptiness as she pulled in and walked into the hospital. Her reflection in the glass doors as they opened told her she looked a wreck – hair falling out of her ponytail, pale blue eyes wide with stress, stained clothes that were a bit too small, no makeup, and no emotion on her face. Part of her knew she should be freaking out, but she just walked through on automatic, everything blocked out by the fear and panic swirling around on the outskirts of her mind.

A nurse looked up at her as she walked up to the desk. The nurse looked immune to the swirling chaos. Ember envied that isolation.

"My name is Ember Verre. Jorge Svenson asked me to come down. Said there had been an accident." Her voice remained flat and uninflected as the panic started to crack through the walls of her shock.

Something flashed across the nurse's face, but Ember couldn't place it before it disappeared.

"Of course. If you would follow me, I'll go get him." Another nurse appeared to take the desk as the first nurse guided Ember away.

She found herself ushered into a small room with three chairs, light blue paint, and three boxes of tissues. She sat and waited. She wanted to rant and scream, but she kept it all at bay, waiting for the blow she sensed was about to fall.

A light knock at the door as it opened turned her attention to the man walking in. Older, professional, his face bore a look of formulaic sympathy.

"Miss Verre?"

She nodded in response and he sat down.

"I'm sorry to be telling you this. Your parents and sister were in a car accident earlier this evening."

The world spun a bit as Ember felt the blood drain from her face.

The doctor waited until she nodded for him to continue, his voice low, sympathetic, but detached.

"Your mom and sister are still unconscious. They both were seriously injured. We are waiting for some tests to come back, but at this point we have no reason to believe they won't both make a full recovery."

A bit of the panic faded, but the doctor still looked at her, waiting for something?

"And my dad?"

"I'm afraid he died at the scene." He hesitated and then continued. "From what I understand, he was driving and he struck another car. The occupant of that car died. The police will want to speak to you at some point to get contact information and clarify information about your family. Right now..." He paused and again gave her a professionally sympathetic smile. "We will need you to come verify his identity as your mother will not able to for some time."

Ember felt herself shatter, and tears ran down her face. "He's dead?"

The doctor nodded. "Yes. You don't have to identify him right now, but we will need you to when you are ready. Please take all the time you need. When you are ready to see your mother and sister, let the nurse know. Until then you can stay here. Would you like some water or a soda? Or is there someone we can call for you?"

She shook her head, trying to wrap around the idea that her dad, the man who had been her biggest support all her life, was dead. He would never see her graduate from Cordon Bleu or see her open her restaurant.

"Here." A box of tissues appeared in front of her. "I am very sorry for your loss." He left her alone, the door closing with a soft snick.

For a period of time, Ember gave in, soaking tissues with tears of rage and sorrow, letting it out. But at the back of her mind was the knowledge that her mom and Belinda were okay. That knowledge let her get up, clean her face the best she could, and walk out of the room, tissues still clenched in her hand.

A nurse guided her to a small office, where the doctor looked at her with the same distant smile on his face. "Are you ready to see Sabrina? I understand she is your stepmother?"

Ember forced a smile on her face; at least she still had her mom. "Yes, she and my dad married after my mom died. She's my mom though. In all the ways that count."

It felt like she was walking through mud, emotions weighing her down, but she still walked in, anxious to see her best friend and biggest fan.

The first sight of her mom slapped her in the face. She lay there, pale, bandaged, with IVs attached to her. Bruises covered the part of her face that was visible, and all the vibrant joy that usually surrounded her like a halo was missing.

Ember turned to the doctor. "How bad was the accident?"

"Pretty bad. They had to cut your family out of the car. I don't know the full details, but I am sure you can get them from the police. They are waiting to talk to your mom and sister."

The repetition of the words helped her to remember them; it just hadn't seemed real until she'd seen her mom. She was about to ask another question when a murmur from the bed pulled her attention away.

"Oh, good, she's waking up."

Ember frowned. There seemed to be a bit more relief with that statement than what made her comfortable.

The doctor moved over to the bed. "Mrs. Verre? You are in the hospital. You were in an accident. Can you understand me?"

Tension wracked Ember's body as she waited, her throat tight as she kept her eyes locked on the bruised visage of her mother. So much of her was swathed in bandages, she didn't know where she could touch and not risk causing pain.

Emerald eyes were revealed by lids that pulled back in stops and starts, closed and opened again. Her mother's eyes first focused on the doctor, then Ember.

Relief rushed through her as her mom's expression signaled recognition.

"Hi, Mom." Her voice cracked a bit as she whispered the words.

"Mrs. Verre, do you recognize her?"

She nodded her head slightly, her eyes never leaving Ember's face.

"Good, that is very good. Can you tell me her name?"

The voice was croaky and harsh, not her mom's normal, soft, slightly nasal East Coast tone. "My ugly, worthless stepbrat. So glad I didn't waste an egg on her."

The pain that exploded across her heart, made her knees buckle, and she had to grab the wall to not collapse.

"Mom?" The sobbed word had the doctor's head whipping towards her and he helped her out of the room to a chair. Ember fell into the chair, new tears, tears she couldn't stop, streaming down her face as she looked at the doctor, trying to comprehend the pain in the unexpected words. The other leg of her support system collapsed.

"I'm going to assume from your reaction that those words were not normal for your stepmother."

"No." She blurted out the word. Ember had to swallow hard to try and not start bawling. "She's never said anything like that to me. What's wrong? What happened to her? That isn't my mother." She tried to deny what had happened, what could not have just happened. Tears welled in her eyes, and her jaw shook so badly she had to clench her mouth to keep from chattering.

"Damn." The whispered comment from the doctor as he bent his head to review the medical chart didn't help at all. He lifted his head to look at her. "Due to the way the airbag trapped her, her brain was without oxygen for a while. We weren't sure how long, but when we got her vital signs stabilized, I had hope. But, given this information, I suspect the brain damage was worse than we thought. This sort of personality shift, while not common, is not unheard of in anoxic brain injuries."

Injured, her mom was injured. That is why she said all that. Ember tried to let the hurt flow away, but the deep-rooted insecurities about never being as pretty or smart as her younger sister made her mom's comments hurt more than she should let them.

"So how does she get better?"

Dr. Svenson shrugged helplessly. "I'm not sure, to be honest. I'm a trauma doctor; you're going to have to work with a neurologist and get some specialized treatments. I can tell you there isn't going to be a pill that will make her better. It is going to take a while, and even then, she might not ever fully be the person you remember."

Mom, changed forever? The idea horrified her. She wanted her mom back. Dad was gone, and now she had lost mom? A scream locked at the back of her throat, burning to be released, but she refused to let it free, at least not yet. Sabrina was her mom, the only mom she'd ever had.

"What about Belinda? Is she going to be like this also?"

The doctor smiled, an honest smile. "I sincerely doubt it. She was hurt pretty badly. She wasn't wearing her seatbelt and was thrown from the car. She hit her head and broke her leg. But the odds of this sort of injury affecting her also are astronomical. If anything, I expect some memory loss. From the CAT scan, there is significant bleeding and swelling in the area of the brain controlling memory. She probably won't remember the accident, maybe even the day of the accident. We've performed reflex tests and everything looks good. Do you want to see her?"

Nodding in relief, Ember stood, a bit surprised her legs would hold her. She followed the doctor to another room, where a nurse met them outside.

"She's awake. She remembers her name and birthday."

Looking at Ember with an understanding look, the doctor asked the nurse, "Temperament-wise, how is she?"

With a slight frown, the nurse shrugged. "Nice enough. Confused and a bit scared. Disoriented, of course. She doesn't know what happen and wanted to know where her parents were. She seemed nice enough. We didn't talk much besides some basic questions."

Relieved, Ember smiled at the nurse, aware her eyes were still red from crying. "Can I see her?"

She caught the motion of the doctor nodding his assent before the nurse answered.

"Yes." The nurse turned and led her through the curtain to see her sister laying on the bed, one leg in a full cast, and Ember flinched as the meaning of that sunk in.

"Belinda, your sister is here to see you."

Green eyes matching her mothers' turned to look at Ember and widened. "Ember, thank god you're here. Where's Mom? What happened?"

Ember explained about the accident, and Belinda listened, then full coherence snapped into place. "Dad is dead?" Her eyes never left Ember's, and something broke deep in her eyes as she shook her head, tears running down her face unheeded. To Ember's surprise, she focused on her leg.

"Wait, my leg is broken? What do you mean my leg is broken?" An edge of hysteria coated her words, even as she cried.

The doctor provided the information Ember didn't have. "You broke it in three places. Luckily you don't need pins, but it will take some extra care to heal correctly and get all your strength back."

"No, no, you don't understand, it can't be broken. I have my trials for the Olympics in two weeks. My times are five seconds better than my closest competitor." Her voice pleaded, as if trying to prevent all of this from becoming real.

Ember tried to help, but as the words slipped out, she knew she should have stayed quiet. "I'm sorry, Beli. Maybe you can try again in a few years."

Belinda looked at her, shaking her head back and forth, even though she winced with the movement. Ember recognized Belinda avoiding reality, shifting blame to anything else. It was her least attractive quality, and Ember and Sabrina hoped she would grow out of it. But the words still hut.

"What? Are you insane? They're only held once every four years, remember? I'll be nineteen in four years. This was my chance. This is your fault. If you had been there, you could have driven, not Dad. You know you drive better than Dad. So this is your fault he's dead. You ruined my chance."

She turned her head toward the wall, still crying, and refused to even look at Ember.

Everything pulled out of Ember's control. Stifling another sob before it could turn into a wail of terror and agony, she pushed her way out of the room. Once outside, she slid down the wall to sit on the floor, her head between her knees. The doctor followed her out and pulled up a chair. He gave her a few minutes. When she raised her head to look at him, he started talking.

"She is just upset, and the odds are she has latched on to the aspect that hurts the least. Her leg. She can't deal with losing her dad, so your sister is blaming you. I know this sounds funny, but don't take it personally." He smiled at her wryly. "You going to be okay?"

A weak laugh escaped her clenched jaw. "I don't have a choice. They need me." Tears welled up in her eyes and she blinked them back furiously. She had cried more today than she had in the last two years.

"True. Do you have any other family you can call? Good friends?"

Ember sat and thought out loud, "My grandparents have been dead since I was little. Dad was getting ready to retire so they just sold the house. They were going to travel while Belinda stayed at a training compound for the Olympics and then move to Arizona and buy a house at the end of July. And there is a great swim coach there, so Belinda would be training with him. Mom has a sister, but she is traveling right now, and I don't know how to get a hold of her. We have a few family friends, but most of them..." She trailed off. How did you call a friend and say, "My dad is dead, my mom isn't my mom, and Belinda thinks I ruined her life"?

The doctor took a deep breath. "I'd like to tell you it will all be okay. But the accident was your father's fault from what I've heard. That means legal issues that might take years. Insurance will only cover so much, and then only if you keep up the premiums. Young woman, you've got a hard road ahead of you even if they recover quickly. Every person is different, but neither of them are going to recover without intensive medical support. Belinda just needs physical therapy, but your mom..." He trailed off.

This was it, time to grow up and face reality. Ember mentally prepared herself. Her life had changed. The question was, could she adapt and deal, or would she break? The thought of letting down her mom, her best friend, made her physically sick. Her sister, always the star of every party and so much smarter and more gifted than Ember, needed her now.

She didn't have a choice; she wouldn't let them down. A wistful thought of Jordan flashed through her thoughts and then faded like a pipe dream.

"Thank you." She stood up, steeling herself, and wiped her eyes with the tissue the doctor handed her. "I need to get ready for them to come home. How long will they be in the hospital?"

"Oh at least another three to four days. They still need some medical care, so you have a few days."

A sigh of relief slipped out. "Good. I'll need it. Now you said there were some officers to talk to me?"

"You sure you're ready for that?"

"No. I'm not. I'm never going to be ready." She felt her lips trembling again and forced it down. "But my family needs me, and this is the first thing that I need to do to take care of them. I'll have to manage."

With a calm that belied the storm of emotions raging in her heart and mind, she headed out to talk to the police and tried not to focus on the impossibility of the task ahead of her.

Chapter Four

Ring arrived at his parents' house early in the morning, finding his mother still up. Without any words, he pulled her into his arms and let her cry. The knowledge his dad wouldn't come walking in made the house seem empty and dark.

Monday morning, they headed back to the hospital. The doctor had requested to talk to them. Sitting in the doctor's office, Ring held his mother's hand. He had to move forward now, since he couldn't wake from this nightmare, and having it not be real wasn't an option.

"Mrs. Jordan," the doctor said, walking in with a file folder in his hand. "You must be Ring?"

Ring nodded and the doctor half smiled, sitting down.

"All the tests have been run. The final verdict is advanced heart disease complicated with diabetes." The doctor paused, and Ring glanced at his mother. Her face had the same look of shock that he felt on his own face.

"I'm assuming from your reaction that he hadn't told you about this?"

"No." Her voice cracked and Ring squeezed her hand tighter. Monica cleared her throat and replied again. "No. He said he wanted to eat a bit healthier and had cut back on the snacks. But he never said anything about this. I—" she swallowed again and pushed through. "I assumed if there was anything wrong he would have told me."

The doctor sighed. "If it helps, it looks like it was only diagnosed a few months ago. Lots of people have problems telling anyone, feeling like their body betrayed them. I'm sure he would have told you soon."

Ring could see his mother struggling with that and he leaned in, trying to distract her and needing to get past this torture.

"So what now?"

The doctor tried to smile sympathetically, but it didn't work. "The hospital should be contacting you for funeral home information and they will deliver his body there. You bury him, and try to learn to live without him."

The words, so blunt, felt like a two-by-four across his heart, and he flinched, but this blow he couldn't avoid. He drove them home, both of them silent. When they got home, his mom shut herself in her room for two hours, and when she emerged, her eyes were red and swollen. Ring felt lost and didn't know how to help her.

The days leading up to the funeral were a blur of bureaucracy, forms, paying for the oddest things, dealing with family and friends, coping with anger, and grieving. Ring still struggled with the idea his dad was dead. Even seeing him laid out in a coffin for the service, it still didn't seem real and he kept expecting his dad's hearty laugh to boom through the room. Or to hear a sarcastic quip about why did everyone look like someone had just died. His parents' house seemed emptier with him gone. Clay and Greyson had come down to be there for him, bringing a few other friends.

The service went as well as any could, full of tears, questions they couldn't answer, and disbelief. Afterward, Clay and Greyson cornered him in the den, his dad's favorite place.

"Sit, Ring," Clay ordered as he walked over to his dad's liquor cabinet and grabbed the Gold Label Johnnie Walker. The bottle that, if Ring had touched it, even after he turned legal, his dad had threatened to beat him. A threat he had believed. With his dad's husky build, even twenty years later, he still looked like a football player.

Clay poured all of them a finger of whiskey and handed a glass to Ring and one to Greyson.

"To Luke Jordan, a great man and a great father."

The three of them raised their glasses silently and sipped. Clay took one of the chairs and the room filled with a companionable silence. Greyson broke it before it became uncomfortable.

"So what now? You're a week behind in classes, but it shouldn't be an issue to make up what you've missed."

Ring shrugged. "We still have to get some paperwork taken care of, but I'm figuring maybe Wednesday I'll be able to head back."

Clay nodded, his sharp eyes looking at Ring and showing the caring that so many never saw behind the joker facade. "Are you going to be okay? Do you need help with anything? Money, time, more Gold Label?" He raised his glass to Ring with a half-smile.

Ring chuckled. "I think Dad would approve of this use. No, I think we'll be fine. Maybe have to make a few changes at the hotel, but I don't know of any issues. So, see you back at school in a few days?"

The boys agreed and took their leave later that evening, chasing the few remaining people out with them. It had been great to see everyone, but at the same time, when it was over, the food packed away and the house cleared, he was relieved to have the house empty, with just him and his mom.

Ring looked around the room two days later, his duffle packed. He should be able to head back to college tomorrow. He hated to leave his mom alone, but there wasn't much he could do to fill the hole his dad had left. He walked through the house looking for her and found her in the office, which was really just a small desk area that the business paperwork had taken over. His dad had purchased a restaurant and hotel in Santa Monica thirty years ago. He had built it up into a good business. Ring remembered him muttering something about not doing so well of late, but he couldn't pin it down.

"Hey, Mom. What are you doing?" When his mom looked up at him, worry wormed into his heart at the expression on her face.

"Mom, is everything okay?"

"I think I might dig your father up so I can kill him again."

Ring blinked. Each word had been bitten out, and the grief that had shadowed her for the last few days was gone. Instead, rage made her hands shake. He couldn't remember ever seeing his mom this upset. Not even the time he had decided to use the washer as a nursery for his tadpole colony.

"What's wrong?"

Monica looked at him and grabbed a ledger, a bunch of paperwork, and a calculator. "Come on, and tell me I'm wrong."

He followed her to the dining room table where she spread out all the information.

"You've been going to school for this stuff. So please tell me I'm being stupid and don't understand something."

Not sure what his mom meant, Ring sat down and started looking at the information in the paperwork. But he found it hard to believe his mom might miss something; she wasn't stupid. She had been a partner in an image consulting business for as long as Ring could remember. She understood business concepts and how to handle accounts. So what was going on?

Sitting at the table, he started flipping through documents, comparing numbers, and it didn't take long before he saw exactly what his mom saw.

"He's in debt, and from the terms on these loans, he's about to lose the hotel and restaurant."

"Damn him." His mother's mouth compressed into a tight line. "I asked if something was wrong. He started acting off, but he just told me it was some stress with the restaurant. I didn't pry. It's always been his baby, but I would have helped.

You know that." The look she cast at Ring was beseeching, and he responded by squeezing her hand.

"Do you know what happened?"

"No. I suspect, now, his heart had been bugging him. Maybe that is why he wasn't paying attention to this stuff. But, you know how he reacted about medical issues. He didn't want to talk about it, and he was an adult so I trusted him and didn't pry. Why didn't he tell me? Why? Did he think I wanted to lose him?" Tears welled up in her eyes as she looked around the house. "Why didn't he talk to me?"

Ring pulled his mom into a hug and just let her cry as he ran scenarios through his mind. When the tears had faded, she pulled back from him and gained some composure.

"I'm tired of crying. I guess I sell it for a loss. I don't know enough about running a hotel or a restaurant. That was his joy." Her mouth twisted even as she said the words, and Ring knew she didn't want to sell, to see what his dad had worked so hard to build just get thrown away. Anyone who bought the place would tear it down and build something else. It was in a prime location, and they had received offers for it before, but as far as he knew, his dad had never been tempted to sell.

The idea of letting his dad's legacy fade made him sick. He spoke before he could think it all the way through.

"I've got an idea mom. You won't like it, but I think it's what I should do."

Wiping her face with a tissue, Monica looked at him. "And that would be?"

Ring took a deep breath and let go of his dreams. "Because of the scholarships and me working, I still have about two hundred thousand in my college fund." He shrugged as she shot him a surprised look, "I practiced my investing with it. I did pretty well."

Pulling out a piece of paper, he started writing out the various loans, overdue bills, and past due taxes. "That is just enough, with a bit left over, about ten thousand, to pay everything off. I suspect the place needs to be updated and I see Dad noted a bunch of minor things that need to be fixed. I can do that. I guess me working construction during the summers is going to pay off. Another piece of paper with all the fixes and repairs that needed to be done was attached to a building supply bill. Most of the things on this list, I can do. I'll drop out and spend the rest of the spring and into summer getting this back up to a profitable situation. I can pick up classes again next year."

"Ring, I will not ask you to give up your education because your father was an idiot and didn't tell me what was going on." Monica snapped at him, but Ring smiled at her, unable to fail his father.

"I'm not looking for permission. This is my legacy as much as it was his dream. If there is anything I can do to salvage it, I'm going to." He shrugged; he had to do this. It was his last chance to make his dad proud. That need drove him more than anything else. His dreams could wait; salvaging the hotel would be his final gift to his father.

Monica sat and looked at him for a long time. She must have seen his resolution because she leaned back in the chair and nodded. "Okay, what do we do first?"

He shrugged. "Spend money. What else?"

Weak laughter filled the room, but it was laughter.

Ember cried herself to sleep each night, the impossibility of her father being dead tearing her apart. She struggled to deal with the overwhelming number of details involved in death. She sat in her parents' house and wanted to scream, get ragingly drunk, or just throw a fit. She didn't do any of them;

instead, she went through the mountain of paperwork and tried to make sense of the information in front of her.

With her dad dead, a thought that caused tears to well up again, health insurance would stop in another twenty days. They had signed for and received the money to sell the house and they had to be out in three weeks. Due to the legal issues of her dad's probable DUI and the civil suit filed against him, the state had put a lock on all accounts with his name on them. Her mom had one small account with about fifteen thousand dollars. COBRA for Belinda and Sabrina was non-negotiable. If she went with new health insurance, their co-pays and premiums for the level of coverage she needed would be astronomical. With dad's insurance, even though the COBRA payments were high, the coverage was better than anything else she could get on the market. She couldn't even skip it for herself. Ember had been carrying the minimum for a while, but it would have been nice to get that two hundred a month back.

Calculating the amount, she cursed again. For the three of them it would be twelve hundred dollars a month. She had to keep it up just for basic coverage that didn't include any of the specialized therapy her mom and sister needed. Plus she had to find a place for them to live and a way to pay for the basics. Once the legal case was solved and all the accounts were unfrozen, she would be better off, but right now, her options sucked.

Swallowing the wave of self-pity, she started on her list. She needed to deal with the funeral, find new housing, find a job, and get access to her mom's accounts. That one threw her for a loop, but she didn't have a choice. Her mom's mental abilities were fine, she simply treated Ember the way you would an unwelcome burden. Would she be able to convince her mom to let her pay the bills with the money in that account? Or would it be another battle, one she would lose?

She had avoided visiting her mother or sister yesterday; it

hurt too much to see them. Her mom's vitriol and Belinda's anger tore her apart. The doctor agreed that the personality change, drastic as it seemed, indicated brain damage but probably not mental incompetence. She needed her mom's help to get through this, and that battle would hurt.

Once all the papers that needed to be signed, including the signed contract on the house, were all organized into a travel folder, Ember headed to the hospital, dread pooling in her stomach. She had a funeral to schedule and she needed her mom capable of going. Anything else would be unthinkable.

The nurses smiled at her, sympathy in their gaze. She knew they had all heard her mother's rantings, and she thought most of them understood the transformation that had taken place, though one or two still looked at her with doubt. It didn't matter. This had to be done. She would do anything to get her mother back and help her sister heal. They would be released in two days, so she didn't have time to avoid any of her responsibilities, no matter how good running away sounded.

Her soft knock garnered a response from the room, "Enter."

Mentally girding herself for the confrontation to come, she walked in, a pleasant smile firmly on her face.

"Morning, Mom. How are you feeling today?"

The look of contempt on her mom's face hit with the crack of a whip against her heart, but she didn't falter in her smile or calm front.

"Oh, it's you. Why did I ever agree to raise such a waste of space as you?"

Ember forced the smile a bit wider and replied with a joking tone, "Just lucky, I guess. Not everyone has someone as wonderful as me in their family."

Sabrina rolled her eyes. "Please. Next time let me lose the lottery, if you're the prize. What do you want? And I know you want something. You always were a greedy child. Unlike my daughter."

The unfair categorization hurt. Previously, she had always talked about how Ember had been a quiet undemanding child, unlike Belinda, who was an overly active child who found trouble everywhere.

Her hands clenched tight, relaxed, clenched, and relaxed again before she controlled herself enough to place the paperwork on the table tray near her mom's bed. "I need your help with this. They are releasing you tomorrow, but you sold the house and we have to be out in twenty-one days. Plus, because Dad was apparently drinking and driving when the accident happened, all his accounts have been frozen. So I need your help to pay for COBRA and figure out what to do before the end of the month."

Surprise flashed across her mom's face and she frowned for a minute, but then the sneer was back.

"You are useless, aren't you? So cancel the contract, pay back the money. I am not moving."

The stubborn aspect of her mother's personality surfaced in full force. Ember fought back a sigh. "I can't. Because the money was deposited under Dad's name, I can't pay back what they've paid. Per the legal team, there won't be access to anything in his name for a while. At least not until all the legal issues are hammered out"—she swallowed—"and the lawsuit has been settled. That is why the accounts are locked. The other driver's family filed suit immediately and requested all accounts be locked so we couldn't clean them out."

A sharp glance from Sabrina skewered Ember. Sabrina snatched up the papers and started to look them over, a sneer still on her face.

"Fine, I'll authorize payment for the health insurance from my account, but only for Belinda and myself. Slackers pay their own way. And I'm not moving. They will have to evict me."

Ember fought a sigh. She'd never expected her mom to pay her portion. "Thank you. But you need to consider where we are going to move because the purchasers have already let me know they will have us evicted if we aren't out the day that was agreed to in the contract. I'll get things packed up and either sold or put in storage."

"You little wench, get your grubby hands off my possessions. Don't you dare sell a single thing or I'll have you up on charges." The snarl of rage, while expected, still hurt.

"I'm going to dispose of things that you had marked as garage sale. I'll work on getting everything else in storage, but, Mom, I only have what is left in my school fund. Do you have some other money that can help with this?"

A calculating look entered her mother's green eyes, something Ember had never seen in those normally loving eyes. It made her sick all the way to her soul.

"About time you paid us back for what we had to put up with. But I suppose that if I don't want my possessions damaged, I might have to help as, obviously, you can't solve any issue by yourself."

She grabbed the checkbook that Ember had brought and wrote, in her strong clear hand, a check to a local storage and moving company. "After all, if I made it out to you, you'd just waste it, probably on junk food. Look at you, fat and a slob. How did I get stuck with a stepwaste such as you?"

The forced smile trembled at the edges. "Thank you, Mom. I'll be here to get you tomorrow and arrange for the movers to come a week after." She forced down a swallow. "The funeral will be in three days. I can't find your address book. I need to let people know. Do you remember where you put it?"

A look of intense grief flashed across Sabrina's face. "The funeral," she murmured, and then the contempt flashed back. "Well I guess you're going to paw through all my things, anyhow. Look in the credenza near the bedroom; I usually put it in the top drawer. We have plots purchased. You'll find the information in the legal file with his will. He—" Her voice cracked and the grief crept back in. "He wasn't supposed to die this soon, so we didn't make any other plans yet. So, make him proud. You've already failed me." The venom in the voice hurt less than the grief that had snuck in.

"Okay. We also need to think about moving. Do you have any idea where we can move? And some way to have some money coming in after that?"

"How should I know? I'm stuck here, remember? Call Seri, she can help."

"I can't." Ember hurried to explain as she saw anger flare in her mom's face. "Remember, she is travelling in Asia. I've sent her an email and gave her my number, but I don't have a response yet. And even if she sees it immediately, it will take her days or even a week to get here. And if I remember correctly, she put everything in storage and let her apartment go while she traveled."

"Oh yes, her exploration of her inner self." She sneered as she said it. Then she quieted, brow furrowed, and Ember forgot for a moment the change in her mother.

"She'd been saving for years for this. Remember how giddy she was at her going-away party?"

"Don't you correct me, bitch." The words slapped across her face like the heat from an oven, and Ember had to close her eyes to resist pulling back. "I know, and it's just like her to not be here when needed."

"So anyplace I can look, or someone you think might be able to help?"

Sabrina sank back into the bed and turned her face away, staring out the window. "Do I have to do everything for you? Surely even you can solve this problem. Now get out; you're contaminating my air."

Ember nodded her head and gathered up the papers and the checks and slipped out of the room. She leaned against the outer wall trying to control the shaking that rippled through her whole body. One of the more understanding nurses came over.

"You going to be all right, dear?"

The sympathetic voice pushed her emotions over the edge and tears slipped down her face as she struggled to not let her knees buckle.

"I miss my mom. This so hard, and she isn't here. Why did this happen to us?" The words came out in between sobs, and the nurse handed her a tissue.

"Oh, child. I wish I knew. All I can say is at least you are trying. She will get better. The traumatic brain injuries I've seen go up and down like a roller coaster. I'm sure that someday the mom you know will look out those eyes at you."

Unspoken was the possibility that Sabrina might not get better. The doctors had been blunt that while proper treatment could reduce the damage, in some cases it was irreversible. The sooner she got the specialized treatment, the better her chances. With no access to money, there would be no specialized treatment.

Ember sighed and stomped on the self-pity. She didn't have time for this. And she still needed to go see her sister.

"Thanks for the tissues. Belinda in her room?"

"Yes, they finished the last set of X-rays and did a permanent cast. She is looking forward to going home tomorrow."

"Yeah, I expect that will change when I start packing her stuff." Ember shook her head and pushed off the wall. "I guess I'll see you tomorrow when I get them out."

The nurse nodded and headed back to her duties as Ember headed to the floor where they had put Belinda. She stopped outside the room and gave in to the need to remember who they were. Pulling out her phone, she hit play on the voice mail. She listened to the laughing voices of her mom and sister. Their love and caring washed through her, soothing some of the sting. Saving it carefully, she took a deep breath and walked into Belinda's room to deal with her.

Chapter Five

The trip back to school let him stew about his choice. Did he want to give up his dreams for his dead father's dreams? For that matter, what were his dreams? Ring honestly didn't know. If you had asked him a month ago, he would have muttered something about creating his own business, but now that he had one, he didn't know if he wanted it. The hotel had been what Luke Jordan lived for, and Ring had many memories wrapped up in that place. He remembered going to work with his dad and exploring the nooks and crannies of the hotel as a child. As he got older, he went up there less and less; it became his dad's workplace, not the place of daydreams. His dad's death changed everything, and the idea of seeing this dream crumble into cinders made him sick.

The whole drive he struggled with this choice, leaving him no closer to the answer in his heart than when he started. The hotel had fascinated him as a child. Now the idea of running it both terrified and thrilled him. Still, this had to be done. He had to prove to himself he could live up to his dad.

Walking into their house, he flinched. Clay and Greyson were both sitting in the living area, waiting for him.

"Hey, guys. Thanks for coming down to the funeral. But why aren't you in class?"

Clay frowned at him. "Of course we came, Ring. You're my best friend. I would have come if I'd had to fly in from the moon. Your mom called. Told us you were coming back up today."

"Did you think we wouldn't show?" Greyson asked,

arching a brow at him in silent rebuke.

"No, I guess not. Just there is a world of difference being friends during the fun, easy stuff and during the hard stuff."

"No there isn't." Clay's voice was firm. "The hard stuff, that's what makes the easy stuff worth it."

Ring had to duck his head and cough. Men didn't cry. It just wasn't done. He focused on something else. "My mom called you?"

"Yeah." Clay drawled out the word watching him. "Said something about you making a decision she wasn't sure about. So what's the plan now? You don't look like you're ready to go back to classes," Clay commented. Both of them watched him with the intensity of a lion scoping out its prey.

"I'm dropping out and going home to get dad's hotel and restaurant all fixed back up and profitable." Ring left out how badly he had raided all of his accounts to pull that off. No need to stress them out or make them feel guilty.

"Wait, what? I thought everything was fine with the hotel." Greyson tensed up watching him.

Clay looked at him like he'd grown a second head. "Dude, you are two months away from getting your master's. You can't drop out now."

That reminder made Ring flinch, but he'd made his choice. "I have to. Right now it's a month away from all falling apart. Mom can't wait two months for me to finish. If I don't do something now, we will lose it all. So, I come back later and get it then."

With a growl, Clay leapt to his feet, stalking in the small open area. "This sucks Ring. So how can we help?"

The offer caught Ring off guard, and he looked at them confused.

"Help with what?"

"Rebuilding, fixing, redoing what needs to be done. You don't need to do this on your own."

Greyson's calm logical voice made Ring question his

decision. Their help would make this so much easier. But then they would drop out also, and he could never live with himself if they did that. Not to mention their families would be out for his head. Locking his jaw, wanting to take the easy way out, Ring shook his head.

"I'll be fine. You two need to finish your degrees and go back to your families. I know they are both waiting for you to take your places in their businesses. What I need help with right now is packing. I need to talk to professors and the school, and try to save as many credits as I can. But I'm planning on being out of here by Friday."

"Jordan, did you lose your mind as well as your dad?" Clay tried to joke, but Ring could see the seriousness in him. "We aren't bailing on you. Friends don't do that."

"You aren't bailing. But this is my problem and something I need to do. I'll be fine. I will." Ring didn't believe himself, but it was up to him to fix this. He'd figure it out somehow. That's what you did when you were an adult. Then when it was all said and done, he'd decide what he wanted.

Clay looked like he was about to protest more, but Greyson shook his head, and Clay sagged a bit.

"Fine, we'll help you pack. But don't expect me to be happy about this." He grumbled under his breath, looking around the room. "You got boxes?"

"Yeah. I brought a bunch with me. Everything should fit into the truck."

"Fine. But tonight we are going out. If I'm losing one of my best friends, I'll be damned if I let him go without a sendoff party. Besides, there might be some hot chicks there." Clay grinned at him, and Ring forced a smile, even if the hot chick he wanted resided in France. The image of Ember on the boxes flashed through his mind, and a bolt of need shot through him. It turned out to be a good thing she'd left. He wouldn't have wanted to drag her into this mess.

"Don't count on that... the hot chicks, that is. You aren't losing me. Life just got in the way a bit sooner than we thought it would. I'll give you a call when I have the place spiffed up, and you can come down and see what I pulled off."

Greyson just arched an eyebrow again but stood up and helped Ring pack. The next three days were going to be busy, and frankly, he wished they would never end. If he looked deep in his heart, he'd have to admit that he didn't know if he could pull this off. Much less pull it off alone. But asking for help would make him seem weak. His dad had never asked for help, so neither would he.

"What do you mean we have to leave?" Her mother all but screeched it at her, and Ember tried to control the trembling in her hands. They had buried her dad yesterday, and she couldn't put off what was happening any more than she could prevent milk from souring. And she didn't even have anything to make pancakes with.

"Mo-Sabrina, we went over this. You sold the house and already accepted the money. So we have to move." This wasn't her mother, not anymore, and for now, it made it easier to think of her as Sabrina.

"Wonderful. The child who was forced upon me can't do anything except give excuses. They can't have it. I'm canceling the sale."

She took a deep breath, hoping it could calm the shuddering in her heart. "They refused. I tried a couple times, but they had already moved out of their house and the money they paid us is locked up in Dad's accounts, so they want the house. We have to move, and fast."

Her mother whirled and threw a book at her. Ember just

stood there as it flew by; her aim was atrocious. Tears welled up in her mom's eyes as her whole body sagged. "I'm sorry, I'm—" she broke off and stood up straight. "Fine, but don't expect me to help you solve this. I didn't create this problem, so I won't be responsible for fixing it."

Sabrina stalked off, her body held rigid, and Ember closed her eyes, remembering the soft look that existed for a moment, a moment of getting to see her real mother.

"She won't tolerate living in an apartment and neither will I. This is all your fault, you know. If you had gone to the party with us, and not been so selfish, Dad wouldn't have drank and gotten himself killed." Belinda sneered the last part as she hobbled by on her crutches, her whole leg encased in the cast.

It still sounded strange to Ember. She couldn't ever remember her dad drinking much, and never when he was the driver. But at this point, that was one more thing she couldn't change.

Ember turned to say something, but Belinda was gone, leaving her alone, wondering what to do.

With a heavy heart she turned back to the computer and phone. With Aunt Seri still somewhere in China, very out of touch, she struggled to find any help. Ember's grandparents had died when she was young, and her dad had been an only child. Resisting the urge to throw things, Ember sent one more email to Seri's email address, begging her to contact them. Once more she laid out everything that had happened and provided cell phone numbers.

The funeral director had been a miracle worker. She'd assisted with the funeral arrangements and had given her clues as to what to do. Ember had never regretted being so insular as she did now. Her few high school friends had faded away as everyone went on their own paths. Focused on food, she never took the time or energy to create any more than casual friends. Besides, she had her family, who were the best friends anyone could have.

Dammit, family and friends were supposed to be there for each other. Their family had dwindled to just Seri, and she had found out all too well how insubstantial her dad's friends had been. Even people she had thought were close friends showed their true colors right and left. They gave a little money and lots of "Sorry, I just don't know how I could help." It turned out most of them hung around for social or business reasons, and the pall of the drunk driving accident had created a barren landscape of people who might help her. The funeral had hurt as she only had ten people there, mostly people whom she barely knew. Her tears had dried up – too much pain in the last week – but still, as they lowered the casket into the ground, her heart ached with the hollow spot where her dad had been.

She took a deep breath as she looked at the remaining person she hadn't called. What little pride remained prevented tears as she received rejection after rejection. She learned a long time ago, you never showed that it hurt. As soon as people spotted a weakness, they would pounce on that. More than one round of childhood torment about her weight had proved that.

The last person left to contact was Cecil Patin. More a friend of her grandfather than her dad, but he had been friendly every time he saw them. Expecting yet one more rejection, she dialed the number.

"Hello?"

The voice reminded her of eggshells, strong yet incredibly fragile.

"Mr. Patin, I don't know if you remember me. This is Ember Verre? Richard Verre's daughter?"

"Oh yes. How is Dick? I haven't heard from him in ages."

Sorrow welled up in her again, but the pain was familiar by this point. "He was killed about a week ago. We buried him this morning." Even the words seemed to come out distant and not immediate.

"What?" Shock filled the voice. "I am so sorry to hear that. Why wasn't I notified?"

Ember swallowed. "Mom was in the car accident with him and is having issues. I didn't know everyone to notify. I didn't mean to leave anyone out, but..." She trailed off, unsure what to say.

"But you were overwhelmed and did the best you could under the circumstances." Understanding laced his voice this time. Perhaps if she didn't mention the drunk driving, he would help. No, she had to mention it. Otherwise, the entire reason for asking for help didn't make sense.

"Thanks, but I'm calling to beg for some help." She refused to cry, and she would crawl on her hands and knees for her family. Begging sacrificed her pride, and she could live without it.

"Why? What is wrong?"

The kindness, the actual caring that seemed to be missing from most of the other people she had called cracked the shell around her and it all came tumbling out. A place to live, and either a lot of money or a job until everything unfroze was paramount at this point.

"Ouch. *Liebchen*, you have had a bad month. I don't have the sort of money you need, and right now I live in a nice one bedroom, but still it is just a one bedroom. But, from what I remember your father says, you're very good in the kitchen, right?"

"Yes. I am." She left it at that. Why talk about dreams that had been shattered?

"Well, I have a friend with a bakery in Encinitas and if I remember correctly, he has a two-bedroom apartment above the bakery, and he is desperate for some help. He's got some medical issues that require him to step back severely from working for a while, but he doesn't want to sell. Let me call him and see if I could swing this for you."

"Oh, please. Anything for my mom and sister, just to keep us afloat until all the legal stuff has settled down would be a blessing."

"I don't have a magic wand or anything, but I have friends I've made over the years. Let me get back to you, but it might not be until tomorrow."

"Thank you. It's more than I have now."

Thin hope, but it was more than she had possessed an hour ago. Holding that close to her heart, she focused on packing everything up that was going into storage, which meant more battles with her mother.

"Mom, everything has to go in storage but your clothes and what you can't live without."

"I can't live without any of this. Do you want me to be destitute?" She ran her eyes up and down Ember's form. "Just because you dress like a homeless person doesn't mean I will. I can't live without all of this."

Ember didn't even bother to explain she had on her oldest, ickiest clothes because she had been cleaning and packing all day. Her hair was twisted in a tight knot, and her face was covered in sweat and dirt.

"I know, but it needs to go into storage. You get one suitcase of clothes and one suitcase of possessions you want to bring with you."

"You're going to sell it all behind my back, I know you are. Belinda? Belinda, where are you?" Sabrina turned hard eyes back on Ember. "I don't know why I ever agreed to keep you. I should have insisted on boarding school. You're stabbing me in the back. I refuse to live on the streets."

"We won't. I'll find something. I promise. Remember, the house is sold. The movers are coming tomorrow for everything we aren't taking with us, to put it in storage. You have to pull out what you need. Hopefully, the lawyers will get it all straightened out in a few weeks."

Sabrina forgot things, or chose not to acknowledge them

until Ember reminded her, but sometimes that was what it took to get any compliance from her. At this point, any battle she could resolve was a win in her book. Though she made a mental note to bring up the short-term memory issues to the doctor the next time they went in. The knowledge that the longer it took to get some good treatment, the more likely this would be permanent, ate at her.

"Thanks. Remember we're going to do a lot of walking, and we won't have any parties to go to for a while, so you won't need many dresses. But I'd pack a few bathing suits. And beachwear."

That made Sabrina's face light up, and Ember hoped that wherever they were they could get to the beach. Her mother had loved the beach, and it would help. She hoped.

Girding herself for the next battle, she headed up to Belinda's room. She sat on the bed, playing games on her laptop.

"Okay, tell me what you want to keep, and what you want to box up." She had stacks of boxes next to most rooms and had grabbed one as she walked in.

"All of it. This is my stuff. I'm taking all of it."

Ember knew screaming wouldn't solve anything, but it sounded wonderful.

"I know. But I still don't know where we are going to end up, so it may be a hotel for a short while." A very short while. She didn't have funds to make it last more than a week.

"I don't get why we can't just go buy another house. Why can't we get the money? And what about my therapy?" A hint of panic filled her voice. "I have to get my leg strong enough to compete again." She still shied away from any mention of their dad dying and had focused on her phone through the entire funeral, disappearing into her room the minute they got home.

"I know. And all I can say is rules and lawyers. I'm hoping

it'll get cleared up soon, but Beli, I can't promise anything. So for now I'm working on the worst-case scenario."

For a minute she thought Belinda might let down her walls and cry, but they snapped back up and the bitchy teenager appeared. She pulled herself up on crutches.

"Do whatever you want. If I'm going to be a prisoner no matter where we go, what does it matter if I have anything? Just don't destroy anything else. I think getting Dad killed is enough for one year, don't you?"

With that bit of snark, she left the room. Ember tried to ignore the words said in anger and pain, but still they caused a few more cracks into her heart.

Her cell phone rang and the recently added contact of Cecil Patin popped up on her screen. She couldn't stop the hope that flared up.

"Hello?"

"Good afternoon. Ember. I do hope you are doing better."

Ember looked around her sister's room and forced a laugh. "As well as could be expected, I guess. Did you have any luck?" She reserved her ability to be patient for Sabrina and Belinda.

"I did. He is interested in having you run his bakery for a few months."

"How few are a few?" Ember ran through the calculations in her head. Given the estate issues, mixed with the criminal case and the fact that the lawyers for the other driver had everything locked up so it couldn't be touched, she figured she needed six months, a year at the worst.

"At least six months. Possibly more. But the reason I think this is perfect for you, beside the baking aspect, is that he will include the two bedroom, one bath above the shop. He'll throw that in plus salary. It won't be much but it should cover what you need as utilities, and all you can eat in baked goods would be included."

Ember sat down before her knees buckled. The answer to

her needs. "So what next?"

"He'd like to interview you tomorrow. If he is happy with you, we'll figure out where to go from there."

"Okay and how do we do that?"

"Hmm, tell you what. I need to come pay my condolences to Sabrina and Belinda, so I'll provide transportation, and we can go over to Ernie's. If nothing else, it will give you some moral support, something it sounds like you've been lacking as of late."

"Thank you." The words were heartfelt, though they couldn't express the depths of her gratitude.

"Wonderful, then I will see you at 4:00 PM tomorrow, *Liebchen*."

Chapter Six

Driving back to his mom's house felt odd; it didn't feel like going home. Torn between two worlds, he didn't know which one he wanted to be in. No matter what, he failed, either his education or his family. In the long run, he figured he could survive failing school better than failing his family.

His mom waited for him at the front door as he climbed out of the truck and walked up to her.

"You sure about this?"

No, he wasn't, but telling her that would be foolish.

"Sure." The smile felt half-true, but he pushed on. "It should be interesting to put all the stuff I'm learning to work and try to get the Del Mar back to the jewel it should be."

She frowned but walked into the house with him. "If you say so. You going to live here?"

"I was hoping I could dump most of my stuff here but stay in one of the rooms at the hotel while I am working there. Get a better feel of what is broken in the hotel and how to fix it. Not to mention shorten the commute and save money. I checked and we have three rooms currently closed, as they aren't rentable right now. I figured I'd take one of those."

"Why aren't they rentable?" she asked with a worried look. "What *is* wrong with the Del Mar?"

Ring slumped into a chair. "Mostly minor stuff like damage done to the room by the occupant. At least for those we got compensation for the repairs. A few are plumbing issues, one that needs the toilet replaced and new toilet seats and such. Let me go through the numbers again. I know I paid off everything, but something has been eating at the back of my mind."

Monica sighed and shook her head. "Okay, I'll let you run with this. But really, ask for help. I know how to run a business, and I know at least something about the hotel business. I can help."

"Nah, I'll be fine. I'll treat it as my senior thesis or something." Ring injected his voice with assurance he didn't feel.

"You already did a senior thesis." Her voice was deadpan, and he could tell she wanted to jump in and help, get him to ask for help, but he resisted.

"Fine. My Masters project, or something. It doesn't change my point. I can do this, Mom. Trust me."

She blinked at him and even he could tell her smile was forced. "Okay, then I'll let you get to it." With that she headed out, and he started unloading his truck.

Ring crashed early in his old bedroom; he planned to start figuring out exactly what needed to be done with the hotel in the morning.

Morning sun found him at the table, paperwork everywhere, a huge mug of coffee in his hand, and curses turning the air blue.

"And you kiss me with that mouth?"

He jumped at the voice behind him, turning to see his mom walking towards him. "Do I dare ask what is wrong?" She poured herself coffee while he marshaled his derailed thoughts.

"Bottom line? Never look at financials while in shock and grieving." Ring tossed the papers down, his shoulders slumped. "So I thought we would have plenty of money to hire some people and get this place done up right. But either I can't add, or I just wasn't thinking clearly." Both were possible. Trying to do that and arrange a funeral would go down as not one of his smarter ideas. "But we don't. We've got enough money for the supplies to fix stuff, but not for the labor — maybe one or two people. I had thought we had enough to run a small crew and I'd just do the little stuff and work as foreman." He snorted. He knew this would be work, but he hadn't realized how much work it would be.

"I see." She sat down a bit heavily in the chair. "So what do you suggest?"

His traitorous mind flashed to the summers with Clay and Greyson working for their respective fathers, but he shied away from the idea of them helping him. He had to do this himself. Ring pushed the papers away with a heavy sigh.

"I think I can get all the repairs made with what I've got left, even if I have to do the majority of it myself. I'll need an electrician for some of it, but everything else I can do with one or two other people. I'll see if there are some highly skilled day laborers that want a longish-term work assignment." He frowned as he stared at the statements.

"But?"

Ring met his mom's eyes. Those eyes the color of his own drew the words out of him. "The income predictions suck, to be frank."

She smiled at him, as always cool and collected. "Why?"

"This is a Pueblo-style hotel and restaurant. It's dated, and the food at the restaurant is fair at best. We've got an awesome location." Tapping the map showed they were a few blocks from the beach. "We aren't upscale enough, and we don't have anything to draw in the volume we need. The hotel manager is damn good, but the restaurant." He shrugged. "It isn't bad, but it isn't good. And we need it to be great to give people a reason to choose us over the other options."

Monica nodded. "All obvious issues now that you've mentioned them. I know I should have kept more abreast of what was going on with the hotel, but it was his baby. Since we were making money, I let it go unless he asked for input."

Ring snorted. "Which, knowing Dad, would have been

about decorating and nothing else. He always was a bit prouder than he should have been."

She arched her eyebrow at him. "Pot, kettle?"

He ducked his head in acknowledgment. "And yes, I'm just as bad. But none of that changes the current issue. What do I do, beside repair the damage, knowing the status quo isn't enough to keep this place afloat?"

She looked down into her coffee cup, thinking. "I don't know. Let me think about it and do some research. Check out the current trends."

"That would help if you don't mind." Ring felt a bit guilty asking her to help, but he reminded himself, this belonged to her also.

"Oh, please. Like looking up travel magazines and the current trends in hospitality will be so difficult. Let me do that. You do the repairs so at least we can rent out all the rooms."

With that decided, he headed to the hotel, his laptop and a notepad with him. Driving up to the hotel, the general state of shabbiness struck him like a blow. He parked in the furthest parking lot and walked around the hotel property, growing more confused as he explored. He remembered a bright shining hotel, not a second-rate motel. The landscaping needed attention with new plants added and the paths needed to be patched. The whole place looked rundown. In today's market, the pueblo style screamed old and dated. Remodeling would be mandatory if they wanted to compete. The gleaming memory of how it looked to him as a child surfaced and he vowed to get it looking bright and welcoming like that again. This hurt too much.

Walking in, he looked at the worn lobby, aged furniture, and window treatments that had been there since his childhood. Cringing at everything he saw that would require more money to fix, he headed to the desk. The hotel manager, Serge Lansky, stood talking with the restaurant manager, Lee

Thompson.

"Ring. It is good to see you. I'm so sorry about your dad. How are you feeling? How's your mom?" Serge asked, a look of concern on his face.

He flinched. Ring didn't know how he felt, or how Mom was doing. They were both faking it; they didn't have any other options.

"We'll be okay. You two are the ones I came to discuss business with."

They both tensed up and looked at him, wariness on their faces. It threw him off guard.

"So, can we talk?"

"Sure. My office." Serge led the three of them back to his office. On the way, three other people stopped Ring to offer their condolences, each one slapping him again with the knowledge his dad would never walk back in the door. Getting to the office, dragging in another chair for Lee to sit in, and shutting the door gave a sense of relief. At least he would have a few minutes of no condolences.

Ring looked at the two men, who seemed to be bracing themselves for an attack. He had no idea what was up with those two, but right now, he didn't have time. If they didn't get the income coming in sooner rather than later, the entire house of cards would collapse.

"So, Monica and I"—it felt so weird referring to his mother by her first name, but calling her Mom would have been ridiculous—"paid all the vendors. A bunch waived the late fees, and we – well, I'm going to be making repairs to fix all the outstanding issues. But I suspect there are more items than what I found on the list that Dad"—he had to swallow and force himself to keep going—"was working from. I was hoping, Serge, you could help me get a punch list of items that need to be repaired started, so I know what I'm dealing with?"

Their faces relaxed, and a smile appeared on Serge's.

"I'd be happy to. I know I've been making lists. I tried to

convince your dad for ages we needed a handyman, but he was sure he could do it. Needless to say, he never managed to get to everything."

"That doesn't surprise me. I'll be your go-to person for now, but long term, yes, we need a handyman, someone who can handle most of the issues. Do we have an additional punch list of what needs to be done so I can compare?"

"Yes and no," Serge replied. "I have what was started, but in all honesty, we need to go through every single room in this place and note what needs to be fixed. Anything short of that and we might as well not bother."

Ring stifled a sigh, worry eating at his mind. Had he bitten off more than he could chew? He pulled himself up, trying to look assured.

"Okay, before we get started, do we have a landscape company? I didn't remember seeing an invoice for them."

"No, Luke never wanted to pay one, so he just cut the grass himself."

Another bill. Landscape made the initial impression and making this place shine required good plants and someone to care for them. One more thing to think about when they started the remodel. He mentally saw the small cushion they had get even smaller.

"So punch list time? Serge?" Ring stood, grabbing his notepad, and leaving the laptop in the office.

Serge grinned, grabbed the master card, and printed out a current list of which rooms were occupied. They spent the next few days going over every single room and making notes as to what needed to be fixed, repaired, touched up, or just plain replaced. By the time they were done, the list was over two thousand items long. The night they finished, Ring sat and looked at it, feeling completely overwhelmed.

He knew he could do this, but first he had to break it down into manageable parts. He needed at least one good helper who could patch and paint at a minimum. Then he would break this into things he could fix and stuff he needed to hire out… primarily anything with electricity. Putting in a light fixture was one thing; fixing wiring was not something he could do.

Three days later he thought he was ready. The local temp agency had found him Daniel Tall Bear, a local handyman who had skills like crazy and was trying to save up money to start his own handyman firm.

They would start the next day. He would need caffeine and some sugar to make it through the day. He spared a thought for his last minute of normality and a sexy woman in a club, one he still wanted. Ring sighed and pushed the thoughts away. One more thing he couldn't have right now.

The doorbell rang at 4:00 PM on the dot. Ember had pulled on her most professional clothes. They fit a bit better around her hips and chest than they had for a while. It seemed that stress and working like a servant caused you to lose weight. Who knew?

She opened the door to a bird of a man. He had a white crown of hair and a smile that pulled an answering one from her. Dressed impeccably in a violet oxford shirt and slacks that seemed to have been made for his frame, his hands never quit moving, and he perched on the verge of exploding into action. Memories sprang to the forefront of a few holidays as a child and this man being in the background, an adult who had little to do with her as a child.

"Ember. It has been a while. As much my fault as Dick's." He hugged her. The simple gesture meant more than he realized, and she had to resist squeezing too hard, aware that she might break him. She felt like a giant to the man that couldn't be more than a few inches above five feet compared to her own five ten.

She let go of the hug, scared at how much that simple touch had meant. "You want to talk to Sabrina?" Ember offered, curious as to how that meeting would go.

"Of course."

Ember led him through the disaster of a house, boxes and half-packed possessions everywhere. Sabrina sat in her room, looking at the piles of stuff everywhere, and Ember had to take a deep breath. Every item ended up being a fight, and at this point she would just tell the movers to box everything left behind.

Cecil walked in, hands outstretched. "Sabrina, my dear. I am so sorry for your loss."

Her perfectly coiffed blond head jerked up, and for a minute Ember thought she would crumple into tears, but the sneer appeared as her mom stood.

"I see you couldn't bother to show up to his funeral."

Ember cringed, expecting to see this fragile man crumple in the face of her mother's attitude.

"Sabrina, don't be a diva. You know I have no patience for them." He went over, and took her hand in his, sitting down next to her. "Ember, be a dear and give us a few minutes. I'll meet you back out at the foyer."

Even though she was curious about what he might say, she simply nodded and walked out of the room. Ember spent the next few minutes making sure she had remembered to grab everything she might need.

Cecil walked out of the bedroom, that smile and calm front still present. "Ready to go?"

"Yes."

He led her out to an old Aston Martin, and while Ember never drooled over cars, even she admitted it looked nice.

Once they were driving, he spoke. "I see there have been some changes in your mother. How is Belinda? I didn't see her."

"Angry, and lashing out. She won't talk about Dad at all. He seems to have disappeared from our lives. And I miss him so much." She blinked back the tears, not wanting to ruin what little makeup she wore.

"The same for Sabrina, though this is an aspect of her personality I had not seen in a long time." He sounded pensive.

"What do you mean? I never remember her like this."

"Your mother is a kind, generous, and loving woman. And she loved Dick with all her heart. But heaven help you if you betrayed her or wronged someone she loved. She would unleash sheer cruelty to hurt you three times as much as you hurt the one she loved. She mellowed with age, but when she was younger. Ah, spitfire didn't begin to cover it."

That information gave Ember food for thought. She pulled out of her pensiveness an hour later, as they pulled up to a nice house a few miles outside of Encinitas.

"Here we are. I'll introduce you to Ernie, and then it is all in your hands."

Trying not to focus on her desperation, she forced a smile on her face and walked on up. A man opened the door as they walked up the path. He had a florid face, bright green eyes, and a shock of red hair that brought to mind adobe powder.

"Cecil, thank you for this. You must be my lifesaver. Please come in both of you."

He limped his way into the house and into a small library filled mostly with cookbooks. Her fingers itched to start flipping through them.

"Cecil, go see Joann while I talk to Ms. Verre here. She has some tea for you."

"Good luck, *Liebchen*." Cecil disappeared into the house as Ernie waved her to a seat.

"As you might have figured, I'm Ernest Baumberg. If Cecil didn't mention, I need to have hip surgery, which means no working for quite a while after that. Leading to my need for someone to run the bakery for me while I recover. So tell me about you and why you think you can do this."

Ember laid out her experience, her willingness to work, and admitted she had earned a full ride to Cordon Bleu.

Ernie looked at her in amazement. "Why would you want to work for me then?"

She swallowed and walked through the minefield. "There was an accident and my father was killed, and my mother and sister severely hurt. Due to various issues, money is tight at the moment, and we have to leave the house almost immediately. So I need a way to make it through the next few months until legal issues have been cleared up. At the same time, I have to take care of my family."

He gave her a long soul-searching look and then nodded his head in a sharp motion. "You'll do. Though I warn you, the apartment is in rough shape. I lived in it years ago when I first opened the place, and it has been vacant for close to a decade now. Most of the time I forget I even have it. But, it is yours if you want it. I'll pay you five hundred dollars a month, all utilities, and any food you want from the bakery. That should help a bit." He paused and chewed on his mustache, then haltingly offered. "And a thousand to help get the place up to livable standards. I figure I'll make it back via renting it out after all of us get back to normal. Heck, maybe I'll convince Jimmy to live there." At her curious look, he elaborated. "My son. He helps out at the bakery but lives in his own apartment."

Ember all but collapsed in relief. "Thank you so much. You won't regret this, I promise."

"Of that I have no doubt."

They both looked up at a soft knock on the door to see

Cecil standing there.

"Ah, your timing is perfect." Ernie dug in his desk and brought up a key. "Cecil, are you busy? You willing to take Ember to the bakery and see if the apartment will work for her?"

"Why not. It has been a while since I've been down there and it is an excellent day for a drive."

Ernie scribbled out a check and handed it and the key to Cecil. "If she takes it, give her this and that should help get the place into a more livable status."

"And I'll see you Monday morning, Ember, 4:30 AM."

"Thank you, again."

Cecil led her out and headed towards her new home, she hoped. He filled the drive talking about her father, stories from Richard's childhood years. Just talking helped, and while the accident still made no sense to her, some of the pain of losing him lightened just a bit.

They pulled up to a small strip facing the ocean, a walkway leading over the dunes to the beach.

"Nice location."

"Yes, he purchased it years ago." Cecil drove behind the strip to a small amount of parking, and Ember saw that the majority of the stores had something above them, be it an apartment or something else.

Cecil opened the door with a key, and they entered into a small area with a door directly ahead of them and stairs to the left. Steep stairs.

"Ooh. That might be difficult for Belinda for a while." Ember chewed on a wisp of hair while she looked. "Well, maybe I can use the money Ernie gave me to get someone to put on double railings. It would make it safer for her to get up and down."

They climbed up the stairs to the apartment. A musty scent filled it, and dust covered everything. Holes in the walls, cabinets falling off the wall in the kitchen, and lack of any color made it look drab. She wandered through – two bedrooms, a full bath, galley kitchen, and a small living area. Just to get it tolerable would take a lot of work. To make it livable she'd have to spend every second here. The amount of work ahead of her forced her eyes closed as she took a deep breath. She didn't have any other options and time ran away from her no matter how fast she moved.

Working things out in her head, she looked inside the rooms. Decent sized, but for one person not two. There was a small linen closet in the bathroom and closets in both bedrooms.

Chewing on her hair more, she fretted. Belinda right now would not react well to sharing a space, and Ember hated the idea of taking anything else from her. Another door caught her eye and she opened it to find stairs leading up to the attic space. Following them up, she found a small garret finished with two dormer windows. This might work. She could put just a mattress up here, and she could set up her small desk in the other space for her computer. There was room for a chest of drawers and a rod to hang clothes on. It would be small and there were just two places she could stand up, but it would work.

Relief made her giddy as she trotted back down the stairs.

"I'll take it."

Cecil turned to look at her, concern on his face. "Are you sure, *Liebchen*?" He looked around, doubt on every inch of his face. "This place makes some storage areas seem pleasant."

"I know. But I think if I clean it, paint it, and use the thousand to repair some of the bigger things, like the holes in the wall, then we should be fine. Not happy but fine."

"If you are sure." He handed her the key and the check. "Let's get you some stuff to clean with and paint. My treat. We can leave it there, and then I'll take you home."

"Thank you." She wished she had better words, but they

were all she had to give.

Chapter Seven

It took three days of hard work to get the unprepossessing apartment habitable; Sabrina and Belinda harangued her the entire time. Ember moved everything she could to the apartment – linens, cookware, spices, anything she could get in there, especially anything to make her mom and sister's life a bit nicer. She often got fewer than four hours of sleep a night, trying to do everything. The movers were a godsend. They finished packing everything she had left and made two stops, the first to get the small amount of furniture she would keep into the small apartment and then taking the rest to the storage unit. The money Ernie had given her added rails to the stairs, repaired the drywall, and got the kitchen fixed. One small blessing had been that their existing refrigerator and dishwasher fit. So at least that worked out in her favor.

If she weren't naturally a calm person, she would have snapped, between the time pressures and the venom hurled her way by the two women. As it was, she fled as soon as she set dinner on the table late that Tuesday night. She ended up sitting on a weathered dock looking at the sea and trying not to cry.

The rhythms of the waves calmed her and she focused on her mental list. First day of work tomorrow. Only the fact that she had been working in restaurants and loved baking had gotten her the job. The money was enough to cover travel costs, car insurance, and food, but not much else. But she reminded herself constantly that this was short term. Six months, a year at the most, and the money would be freed up, her mom and sister would get better treatments, and she could follow her dreams again.

She suspected she lied to herself; the hope of Sabrina getting better seemed further and further away each day. But she didn't want to accept it might not ever get better. The thought of that distant tomorrow kept her sane.

When her emotions had settled, she walked back to the apartment. It was about a half mile, but she enjoyed the exercise. At least the bakery covered her breakfast and lunch.

Getting back, she found both Belinda and Sabrina had gone to bed, and relief let her breathe easier. Making her way up to the small garret room, she collapsed on the mattress on the floor and barely remembered to set her alarm before she fell asleep.

Said alarm went off at 4:00 AM. She pulled herself off the mattress and, after a quick shower, walked down to the bakery, standing in front of the still dark door by 4:20 AM.

"Morning, Ember. Good to see you."

A cheerful voice carried from down the street and she turned to see Ernest Baumberg walking slowly up the street, with his limp on the right more pronounced than it had been when she had seen him last.

"Good morning, Mr. Baumberg."

"Oh, please, call me Ernie." He held out a hand to shake when he got up to her. "You ready to start this adventure?"

In reality, she needed more sleep and a week's vacation, but she knew that would not happen, at least not anytime soon.

"Sure am. This should be fun."

"I hope so. I love this place. You'll have help during the days. My son, Jimmy, works here." He rolled his eyes with the comment. "He's more interested in flirting with the young ladies that come in than learning the business. I need someone to keep this place running, and everyone I found wanted more than I made in profit here. So frankly, if you keep the place standing and break even, I'll be happy."

He opened the door and led her into an open area in the

front full of small tables and chairs, a bakery display unit, and a register. As they moved behind the wall, the ovens and prep area were exposed.

Ember nodded. "I think I can do that. All my restaurant management classes were rather thorough, and as for the baking, not an issue. I love to bake. If you've got the place set up so I can just keep it going, we should be good."

"Wonderful. I'll be available via phone, and I'll place all the orders. Just keep in touch via email on what you're running short of." By this time, all the lights were on, and he had the ovens heating up. "You ready to see how to run this place? Jimmy usually will come in about 5:30 before we open. He knows the cash register and deals with the coffee. I'll make him show you, but the rest is up to you."

Ember smiled. The place smelled like her idea of heaven, and she could see he had everything set up in an efficient manner.

"I can't wait. Let's get going."

He smiled at her and they started to work. Ember caught on quickly and before she knew it, the morning crowd arrived and she kept busy getting new muffins, scones, and other pastries out. She never had time to be bored, and though exhausted, she enjoyed every minute of it. Jimmy popped his head in and waved when he got there. Ernie introduced the two of them but didn't have time for anything more. Jimmy had the same shocking color of hair as his dad. Her two-second opinion of him centered around the quick smile and wink he gave her before he got to work.

When the crowd died down around ten o'clock, Ernie looked around. "Okay, now it's Jimmy's job to clean up and get everything set up for the next rush. Do you hear me, Jimmy? I won't have her calling me saying she had to do it."

"Yes, Dad. I get it." His tone had a long-suffering aspect to it, and Ember had to fight a smile. From what she had seen,

Jimmy acted laid back, though he worked with efficiency and purpose. She didn't think she'd have any issue working with him.

Ernie continued. "We stay open until about 1:00 PM for the later workers, but we don't serve any lunch-specific food. Bread gets a rush around noon for people buying it for their dinners. So now is prep time for all the work we did this morning. Getting bread in the oven and getting all the other stuff ready to bake in the morning.

With that they were off again, and she absorbed all the information like a sponge. This reflected her dreams, running a real restaurant with her name on it. But for now, this job came pretty damn close.

At one o'clock, Jimmy locked the door and turned off the "Open" sign.

"Last part is cleaning and shutting everything down for tomorrow. You have to remember to shut off the ovens; letting them run is a fire hazard. Usually I'm in the back for another hour or two mixing up things for the morning and seeing if anything was particularly popular."

He went through it with her and it all made sense. Both of them finished up their work about three.

"Okay, today is Monday, and I'll be here the rest of the week to get you in the groove, but then next Monday I have surgery. Are you going to be able to handle six days a week working close to twelve-hour days? Sundays we'll be closed for now. It was always my lowest earning day so I don't think there will be any issues. And you will need the break." Ernie had a worried look on his face as he spoke.

Ember thought of what was waiting upstairs, and the knowledge that at least Sabrina would approve of this.

"I'm good with this. Better to stay busy than focus on things I can't change."

"Too true that. Well then, go home, and good job. I'll see you in the morning." He showed her the keys to get in via the back door, which would make it easier to get to work, and safer.

She climbed the stairs, tired but feeling good. This experience would do her good if she ever got to run her own restaurant someday. She needed her own place, where she got to make her own decisions. Ember entered the apartment to Belinda throwing a fit.

"I don't want to stay here. I hate this place, I want to go home."

Ember forced a smile on her face. "This shouldn't last for more than a few months, six at most. I'm sure the police will let us know when everything is settled. Though I do need to contact a lawyer like they suggested. I just haven't had time."

"Sure, but you have time to do things you like, like cooking." Belinda sulked, and it served to highlight her beauty. Ember fought an internal sigh.

"Beli, I'm working. It is what I have to do to keep this place and food on the table. Again, it should only be for a short while."

With a sigh implying world-ending suffering, Belinda hobbled off to her bedroom, and Ember cast a silent thank-you at Sabrina for staying in her room.

Deciding not to push her luck, she dished up food for each of them. Plating hers, she knocked on each door, letting them know dinner was on the table. With a sigh of relief, she escaped upstairs to her little garret.

The stifling air, though unpleasant, felt better than the atmosphere downstairs. Opening the windows to get some of the fresh sea air in the room, she curled up at the tiny desk, eating and looking at her finances, hoping this time it would be different. Time disappeared and the ring of her cell phone yanked her out of her mire of despair. She looked at it, not recognizing the number on the caller ID.

"Hello?"

"Ember?"

"Yes?" She didn't recognize the voice, though it sounded a bit familiar.

"Hey, it's Jimmy. Ernie's son." The food she had just eaten roiled in her stomach.

"Yes." She couldn't stop the wariness in her voice.

"Ummm, there's been an accident. Dad fell at home tonight, and he broke the hip. They've rescheduled his replacement surgery for tomorrow. So, starting tomorrow it is just you and me."

"What?" Her voice cracked in panic. Granted, she still had a job, but she had only been there a day. She couldn't run the place. Her mind began to spiral. He'd close the shop, and he would kick them out. Trying to stop the spin of panic, she focused on Jimmy's words.

"Yeah. Dad swears he has everything written out at the shop. And in between bouts of unconsciousness – man those drugs knock him out – he's been telling me everything he remembers. I've written it all down, but I can't tell you how accurate it is. I'll be there first thing tomorrow and try to help. Just remember, there's a reason I work out front." He chuckled a bit. "Besides the fact that this isn't my dream job."

Ember didn't know what to say. Her throat was dry. But at least she hadn't lost everything.

"So he isn't going to close the shop?"

"Hell, no. You impressed him. And I think we'll be fine. I'm not a complete idiot with what he does, regardless of what he thinks. Just a partial one." The humor in his voice went a long way to calming her nerves.

"I, well, okay. I guess I've got to make it work. Though I hope he knows I'm going to make a lot of mistakes."

The grin in his voice on the other end of the line helped settle her stomach. "I don't think he is worried about that. Mostly I think he doesn't want to lose all his customers and doesn't want it to burn to the ground. Anything in between should be fine."

This time she laughed. "I'm pretty sure there is a lot of room for middle ground there. I'll see you in the morning then."

She hung up and forced herself to finish her meal. Running the place by herself? Next time she'd be more careful about what she asked for. Falling asleep that night, she distracted herself with memories of a night with a man who made her feel sexy and beautiful.

Monday morning – the first day of his race to get the hotel back to a profitable business. Ring yawned, stumbling into the shower at 5:30 AM, letting the stinging heat wake him up. He'd moved into a room near the back, the one that needed the most work. It made it easier to work the long days he had ahead of him not to have to drive back to his parents' place thirty miles away. Which, given SoCal traffic, could be forty-five minutes or two hours.

Marginally more awake, he decided caffeine and sugar had risen to mandatory status. He'd grab some for David Tall Bear, his day worker for the foreseeable future. Ring figured he might as well start off their working relationship on the right foot. If Ring wanted to pull this off, he'd be depending a lot on this man. This bakery had been there as long as he could remember. It was about a fifteen-minute walk from the hotel to its location near the beach. Maybe the walk would loosen him up for the day ahead.

The salty, crisp air of late spring felt good on his face. Soon enough, it would heat up and only the breeze from the ocean would cut the heat.

The bakery bustled, matching his memories of it being popular. He slipped in, letting the scents of fresh-baked bread, cinnamon, and coffee rejuvenate him. A smile of anticipation appeared as he made his way to the front. A young man who looked vaguely familiar worked at the counter. He must be the owner's son. Ring nodded hello as he walked up to the counter and saw the nametag "Jimmy."

"What can I get you?"

Ring glanced at all the various things, but he had known what he wanted the second cinnamon had hit his nose.

"Can I get two large coffees, and two of those huge cinnamon rolls?" He frowned, as he didn't see them in the case, but his nose told him there were some in the store.

"Sure, if you can wait a minute. They're being pulled out of the oven now and should be up here in a minute. Name? And I'll call when I've got them packaged up for you."

"Jordan. Thanks." His last name slipped out, a habit of using his last name to pick up orders.

The man handed him two cups and pointed to the coffee makers; Ring went over, filling his cup and making it to fit his tastes. David's he left a bit of room for cream and grabbed some of the to-go creamers and some sweetener. If those rolls tasted as good as they smelled, he might be coming here regularly. What else did the bakery make?

Busy looking at the coffee supplies, he missed seeing the cinnamon rolls being put in the display case until the man called his name. "Jordan."

A woman dressed in an apron, and with more than a bit of flour on her whipped around and looked right at him. Her pale blue almost gray eyes caught his, and the image of a face glowing in ecstasy, light from a club making her look like an angel, blossomed in his mind.

The name tumbled out of his mouth before he could think. "Ember?"

Her eyes widened, and a smile started, then it fell and she

shook her head. "Later," she mouthed at him, and then she turned and disappeared into the back.

"Here you go. Come back soon." Jimmy's voice pulled at him, prompting a response.

"Oh, I will be," he promised as his eyes still looked for a trace of her curves to come back around. The funny look from the employee reminded him he had someplace to be. With a low growl of frustration, he headed back out, grabbing the two cups of excellent coffee. He let the walk back up to the hotel cool him off.

Tonight he would find out why she had lied to him, and why she wasn't in France. The happy look held joy, and he didn't remember any guilt when she told him that night, but he wanted to know the details. Of course there was the fact that she had met him when all he had to worry about was school and this was a ways from that... a world away in fact.

David sat on the tailgate of his Dodge Ram, waiting for him. He nodded at Ring as he stood up. Ring would see today how well he worked out, but already he earned bonus points by being early.

"Hey, got us coffee and a treat. I at least need some sugar to start the day."

The other man nodded. "Thanks." He sniffed the air. "Not much for sugar but that smells good."

"Yea, why I bought it." He handed David his coffee and the extras. Turned out David took his coffee black with sugar. Ring filed that bit of information away.

"Heard about your dad. Sorry for your loss."

"Just don't, okay?" Ring snapped, and David arched a brow at him, making him instantly feel like an ass. "Just can't handle any more sympathy, okay? Nothing anyone says will bring him back. And I'm not ready to deal with him being gone." He snapped at people too much, but that one spot had worn thin.

David looked at him for a long moment and then nodded. "Understood."

Ring pulled out the cinnamon rolls, each individually wrapped, and handed one to David. He unwrapped his, the smell of cinnamon, sugar, nutmeg, and something else he couldn't put his finger on. He took a bite and moaned. David jerked his head up to look at him, but Ring didn't care. The cinnamon roll had chopped almonds in the middle, and he was sure the dough had almond extract in it. It might have been the best thing he'd ever eaten.

"Okay, might become a fan of this in the mornings. It's incredible. Coffee's good too," David commented, his mouth as full as Ring's.

Ring just nodded his head, not wanting to take enough time to clear his mouth to speak. They both stood there in silence as they finished the rolls, and both of them licked their fingers clean.

"I knew they'd taste good, but wow. Now if our restaurant would cook food like that…"

"Don't know anything about restaurants. But I won't turn down one of those, ever." He half smiled at Ring. "So we ready to get this going?"

Ring sighed and cast his eyes at the hotel, comparing it once again to his memories. It came off looking so neglected. But there had to be the bones of something that could be great.

"Yeah. I still don't know what I'm going to do to remodel and make this pop again, so for now we're just fixing all the things that don't work." He pulled out the punch list. "So, first thing. The hot tub isn't getting above 90 degrees. I started it draining last night, so we should be good to get going on it."

"Got it." David turned and grabbed a different box of tools. It was one of the things that had impressed Ring. He had different toolboxes for different jobs: one for plumbing, a different one for carpentry/general repairs, and a third for tiling and hanging dry wall. That and his apprentice-level rank at the plumbing union.

As they walked to the fitness area of the hotel, his mind split into two parts. One focused on ways to update the hotel and bring guests in. The other part was on the woman he had seen in the bakery. Why was she here? And did he have the energy or the time to follow up on something now? A month ago he would have jumped at half a chance to get to see her, to date her.

The sheer amount of work kept him occupied, but also showed how he had gotten lazy the last few months of doing nothing except schoolwork. Real hands-on work left him exhausted.

After three he called it a day. "David, I'm dead. I didn't realize how rusty I am."

David snorted and pulled out a bottle of water, taking a deep drink. "Probably more that we worked through lunch and we've been working at a non-stop pace all day. I'm wiped out too. Pick it up tomorrow?"

Ring blinked, realizing they hadn't stopped. At least maybe that meant he was in better shape than he thought.

"Sounds good. Coffee and roll?"

"Yeah. Was good." With that David packed up his stuff and headed out.

Ring stood, indecision warring in his head. Time and energy were two things he lacked at the moment. The idea of trying to juggle a girlfriend on top of this whole mess made him cringe. But he knew down to his bones that if he passed on this chance he'd always regret it. He had to go talk to her. Moving as fast as his sore body would allow, he headed back to his room and took a quick shower. After pulling on clean clothes, he headed down to the bakery.

The walk down the hill stretched out some of the soreness, but he knew he'd need some aspirin tonight. He got there a little before four. The open sign was off, but he could see her moving about inside, and he knocked on the window.

Her head jerked up, and an interesting array of emotions crossed her face. She nodded, apparently to herself, and headed over to the door, opening it.

"Hi."

He focused on her, eyes hungry to see the woman who haunted his memories and dreams. She looked as tired as he felt. She had flour on her face, circles under her eyes, hair slipping out of her hair net, and clothes that pulled too tight in some spots, and bagged in others. And he knew he could look at her forever. How had this woman gotten so under his skin? And why now when he already juggled more than he could handle?

Chapter Eight

Jordan stood there looking at her, his eyes taking in all of her, and she still didn't know if she felt excited or something else. Emotions were hard right now. It felt like anything other than treading water was more than she could handle. Another person wanting something from her might kill her. Not to mention that her score at finding real friends resided at zero.

"Hey." His voice was soft as his eyes met hers. She felt self-conscious. No makeup, hair in a bun under a hair net and sweaty from the ovens, not to mention the flour and other things. She reached up and yanked off the hairnet – no need to look like a complete dork. At least she smelled good. If you liked baked goods. But if he didn't like cinnamon and nutmeg, they would never get along.

"Wanna come in?"

"Please." He followed her in and she locked the door behind him. She turned to watch him, his body as nice and tight as she remembered, as she had dreamed. That night fueled her dreams and may have kept her from killing her family.

He took a chair from one of the tables, setting it down on the floor, and then slumped into it, watching her. "So what happened? I thought you were headed to France."

She tried not to sound bitter, but it slipped out anyhow. "Life. It kinda exploded in my face." Ember shook her head. If she started talking about what she would be going home to when she left here, she'd start crying. "What about you? Why aren't you at school?"

Jordan started to reply, then stopped and thought about it.

"Pretty much the same. Life exploded in my face." Looking more than a bit uncomfortable, he offered. "Do you want to talk about it? I could listen."

"God no." The words exploded out of her without having to think about them. "I'm living it. I don't want to talk about it. You?"

He snorted a bit, smiling, "Same here. Talking about it isn't going to change a thing. And just brings it back up. I'm just tired of people asking me about it."

They both fell silent, looking at each other.

Ember broke it. "So, what do you want? Cause, honestly, I like you. And that night has given me more smiles than anything else around me." She felt her face heat and knew she was blushing, but she pushed on. "But right now? A relationship? I don't think I could handle it. I've got so much stress going on right now. One more thing might break me."

Jordan nodded. "I know how you feel. I'm working construction now up at the hotel." He nodded up the hill and Ember realized he must be talking about the Del Mar. "And as it is, I'm worn out. I just don't think I could take much more until some other things get settled or cleared up. But, Ember." He paused and leaned forward, looking at her. "I enjoyed that night just as much. And I wished you weren't going to France. But not like this. Dreams shouldn't be shattered."

Again silence fell, but she could tell he was thinking about something. He got this adorable furrowed brow as he looked off into space. She reminded herself she couldn't afford another needy relationship at this point and time. Her mother and sister were providing too much "love" in her life as it was.

"I've got a crazy idea, if you want to hear it," he blurted, making her jump from her distracted thoughts.

"Sure. Listening is free."

He chuckled a bit, and she closed her eyes to just enjoy feeling human for a fleeting moment.

"I need something not associated with the drama and stress

going on in my life. It sounds like you need the same. Someone that you can relax with but not feel the need to talk about the past, or family, or the life that is driving us crazy. A safety valve, friendship, drinks." He grinned. "Maybe sex if you want. But no strings. Just both of us using the other as our oasis from what is going on in our lives."

Ember sat back against the chair, looking at him. Someone to talk to that wasn't a doctor, her family, a customer, a cop, or an ex-friend. A friendly face that wouldn't ask how her mom was doing, or avoid asking because they didn't want to face the guilt of walking away from the help she cried out for. Oh hell. The chance for a repeat of that night, something to escape to? The idea caused her throat to tighten in want. Moments that her mom couldn't tarnish because neither her mother nor Jordan would ever know the other existed. At the same time, it sounded a bit silly, but silly didn't mean bad.

"I, I kinda like the idea. But let me think about it. Basically we give each other an outlet? And the rules are no talking about our lives right now? Just living for a moment without all our... baggage."

"Exactly. I know I could use that. Someone that won't ask questions they don't want to hear the answer to because it would make them feel guilty when they don't help"

"Oh god yes." She slapped her hand over her mouth, and then giggled. "I want to say yes. But let me think about it. That night was me being wild and spontaneous, something I almost never am. Come by tomorrow?"

"Oh hell yes. Those cinnamon rolls were incredible. If nothing else, even if you decide you don't want that, you're going to get a friendly face every morning for that alone."

She knew it was fishing for a compliment, but she did it anyhow. "You liked them? They were my twist on the recipe."

"Ember"—his voice dropped an octave as he looked at her—"they were almost as good as I remember you being."

She had to swallow hard again as the image of him thrusting into her and making her world explode in spice and light sprang to the forefront of her mind.

"Well then, try them tomorrow. I'm adding orange essence to the dough and the icing. It should come out pretty good."

"I'll be here. But either way, if you need a friendly face, if nothing else, I'm here."

"Thanks. You too."

She stood and let him out. "I'll see you tomorrow?"

"Yep."

With that he left. She locked the door and leaned against it. Who would have expected him to walk back into her life?

Shaking her head, determined to think about it later, she finished prepping for tomorrow and then cleaned up the prep area, made sure everything was turned off, and headed out the back. Still smiling, she headed up the stairs and opened the door.

"About time you got home. What, cleaning ovens more exciting than your family?" Her mother's voice greeted her as she walked into the apartment. Sabrina dropped her eyes to Ember's empty hands, hands she clenched in guilt at that look. She'd forgotten.

"And I see you couldn't even be bothered to bring home the bread you said you would. Why do I bother?" Sabrina sneered and pointed at Belinda. "She has an appointment tomorrow afternoon. You will remember to take her, or have you decided that we aren't worth your time?"

Ember ducked her head and bit her lip, hard. "No. I let Ern.. Mr. Baumberg know I would have to take both of you to the doctor on occasion. I'll be back up to take her." She lifted her head, the tears having been diverted by pain. "So how about hamburger soup for dinner?" She headed into the kitchen to get dinner ready, trying to ignore the glare from two sets of eyes.

"Really? Hamburger again? Why can't we have steak or

salmon? The omega 3 from the salmon would be better for me." Belinda put a whine into her voice, and Ember didn't have to turn around to see the petulant look. It appeared clear enough in her mind's eyes.

"I agree. All this red meat and chicken can't be healthy for either of us. I think we should have salmon."

Stiffening her back, mentally and physically, Ember turned. "I'd love that. Do you have some money that I can use to go get us salmon for dinner tonight?"

"My daughter would have saved enough to be able to get us at least decent food. I always knew you were worthless. Thank god you aren't mine. I'm not hungry. Good night." Her mother turned, but for a moment, she saw tears in Sabrina's eyes, and a half flicker of the woman who had praised her skill in the kitchen and been her biggest fan.

"I'll make it anyhow and put it in the fridge. You can eat it later tonight." Her offer fell into the empty kitchen as Belinda hobbled off to her room to listen to her music.

Ember made dinner and convinced herself the onions caused her eyes to water. Once she and Belinda had eaten, sitting like strangers at a shared table, Ember escaped upstairs. She looked at the list of things she needed to do: find a lawyer, call Cecil, send her aunt another email, follow up with the police department, pay the COBRA, follow up with the makeup work for Belinda's school.

Belinda, while she resisted everything else, at least did all her homework and turned it in on time, per the agreement with the school district when all of this fell apart. Ember realized Belinda must be bored to tears being stuck in here all day unless someone helped her get down to the beach. One more thing for her to feel guilty about. Just more stress added to all the things she needed to remember at work. She knew she was missing things, trying to do it herself with minimal training.

The list of things she need to do, to remember, to deal with was overwhelming. She needed a refuge, someplace to hide where all of this didn't exist. Ring's idea popped back into her mind. To act as an oasis, someone who didn't know what was going on and wouldn't ask how everyone was in that fake tone, never planning on helping. She shoved it away. It would never work; he'd find out and leave her too.

Taking a deep breath, she picked up her phone and dialed a lawyer that had been recommended. The conversation ended with, "While we can file an injunction on your behalf, it will still be about two months before there would be a decision on it. And you would have to pay our retainer of two thousand upfront to hire us."

She stammered and ended the call. If she could pull up a spare two thousand, she wouldn't be in this mess. Ember pulled up the voice mail icon and stared at it, not even hitting play. She replayed it in her mind, letting the memory of the love it represented surround her.

Someone who didn't know any of this, who wouldn't ask about it, sounded like heaven. His idea popped back in to her mind, and this time she didn't push it away. It sounded like a life preserver, and she made up her mind. At least then she'd have one person who couldn't use this as a reason to abandon her. She wouldn't tell him, and if he kept the agreement, he would never ask.

Ring still didn't know what insanity had prompted him to suggest the deal. Even that might be too much for both of them to handle right now, but for some reason, he couldn't turn away a chance to see her, even if just for drinks and a bit of conversation. Ring found himself at the bakery at six thirty this time, and he tried to convince himself that he didn't know if the food or Ember provided the main attraction. But the need to know her answer prodded him more than anything else. The shop welcomed him this time with scents of coffee and apple. He wrestled with the idea of getting whatever created that smell instead of the cinnamon roll. He headed up to the counter and Jimmy smiled at him.

"Hey, back again. What can I get you?"

"Two large coffees. And Ember told me to try the cinnamon rolls this morning. But what smells of apple?"

Jimmy looked at him with an odd expression. "You know Ember?"

Ring shrugged. "We'd met before. I was surprised to see her here."

"She's pretty cool. Quiet, good at her job, and don't tell my dad this, but I think she's better than he is. The apples are fresh apple turnovers she made this morning. I've already had two. I couldn't resist. So two cinnamon rolls?" Jimmy handed him the coffee cups as he looked at Ring waiting.

"Please." Ring gave in to his nose. "And two of those turnovers."

Jimmy grinned. "Coming right up." He stuck his head in the back before heading to the baked goods. Ring watched, needing to see if she would say anything.

Ember stuck her head out and half smiled. "Tonight," she mouthed and held up six fingers. He nodded, and she disappeared into the depths.

A few minutes later, he headed up to the hotel, a coffee in each hand, and a bag that was driving him crazy with the smell. He even caught one or two of the other early morning risers give a sniff as he walked by.

David sat in the same place as the day before as Ring walked up.

"Morning."

"Hey. I brought us food. I'm becoming a bit worried I'm

going to have to add hours to my workday to burn off what I'm eating." Ring dug out the turnover and saw David's nose twitch.

"Apples?"

"Yeah." He handed one turnover to David and one roll. Then he bit into the turnover. Flavors hit him, and he closed his eyes. Apple, salt, cheddar, savory spices not sweet. It was like nothing he had tasted before, and he thought he might be able to eat these forever. When he opened his eyes, only crumbs remained of his turnover and David focused on licking his fingers.

"Stuff is damn good."

"Oh, hell yeah." He looked at the cinnamon roll and then wrapped it. "I'll save this for lunch. If nothing else it will guarantee we stop."

David chuckled. "Good. Yesterday was rough."

"True. But today won't be any easier. Ready?"

"Yep." David didn't talk much, but he sure earned every penny Ring paid him. Work grabbed their attention, but mentally he counted the minutes to this afternoon.

Focusing on the idea of that roll ensured they took a lunch. Even a bit dry, the cinnamon roll still tasted as good as he had remembered. The orange essence added a sharpness to the flavor that made the sugar richer. If their restaurant served food like this, the line would be out the door. He'd ordered room service for dinner the last few days and, compared to these baked goods, the food managed passable and not much more.

They got back to work, and hours later he sent David home. Another room could now be rented out as they had repaired the damage to the Sheetrock and repainted the room. Another two items off the punch list, but it still wasn't enough. He needed to move faster, or come up with a brilliant idea to make the Del Mar shine.

Ring enjoyed the hot shower, letting it pound out the

soreness in his muscles, then he wandered down to the bakery, his mind bouncing between trying to come up with an idea to revamp the hotel and wondering what she had decided. Either way, he could at least get a glimpse of her in the mornings — but only because of the food. If it weren't so incredible, he wouldn't bother. Probably.

The lights were off when he walked up. Ring shrugged and sat down on a chair near a table outside, looking up at the hotel sitting on the hill. What could he do with it, without giving in or undoing all the work he and David were doing now?

"Sorry I'm late."

He turned his head to see Ember walking up. She looked exhausted. It was on the tip of his tongue to ask what was wrong. He bit off the comment and smiled.

"I'm glad you wanted to meet. So are you going to throw me cruelly to the wolves out there or rescue me with some intelligent conversation and companionship?"

She sagged in the chair, propping up her head with one hand on the table. "I don't recall us talking much that night about anything real. I might disappoint you and not provide anything intelligent."

"Well, you did mention you had earned a scholarship, and that was why you were going to France. So you can't be too stupid."

She let out a low chuckle as she shook her head. "To be honest, all I remember clearly is you making me feel like the sexiest thing on the face of the earth, and giving me pleasure I had figured existed primarily in romance novels."

"Well, you are sexy." Ring gave in and let his eyes travel over her curves. Even with no makeup on and exhausted, she lit up when she smiled, and he had loved the feeling of those hips in his hands, the soft skin giving as he held her. Her skin, already flushed from a day at work, just made him wonder what she would look like in full light where he could see her reactions. He shook his head to get his thoughts off of Ember naked in his bed.

She blushed, shaking her head. "I look like crap. I'm exhausted." She lifted her arm and sniffed the crook of her elbow. "But hey I smell like cinnamon and apples."

Ring burst out laughing, her action so contrary to all the girls he knew. Somehow it made her even more real.

"So, inquiring minds wanted to know. Your decision?"

"Yes?"

"You don't sound sure of that."

"Oh, I'm sure I need something besides the bakery and..." She paused then shrugged. "Life. So yes, I'm just not sure how to go about it. Seriously, regardless of that night, I don't DO that. So, I feel a bit awkward."

Ring wanted to dance with joy. If nothing else, he had the option to be with her again. Even if neither of them could handle a full relationship right now. Hell, how would he find the energy to be with her and not hurt her? The idea of hurting her caused a primal revulsion in him.

"Let's start small. What do you want to do right now?"

"God, I want a drink. A huge, pain numbing, senses blurring drink."

That he could handle. Standing, he held out his hand, "Let's go. The local bar is just a few blocks away."

Ember shook her head at him. She took a deep breath and looked right at him. "I'm broke. I'm beyond broke. What little money I have has to be saved for necessities. And regardless of how badly I want,—need, a drink to help keep me sane, it doesn't qualify."

The answer surprised him. She hadn't worried about money that night, but he looked at her and the bakery and figured it came hand in hand with the life that had smacked her down.

"No worries. I can buy. I'm not rich but my—" He paused.

The last thing he wanted to do was explain that his mother gave him an allowance because she felt guilty he had spent everything he had on paying off the bills, and he now worked for free. Shaking his head, he shrugged. "Let's just say a few drinks, or many drinks, isn't going to affect my budget that much. Now, you want a new car, and I might have an issue." He smiled, holding his hand out to her, urging her to take it.

Pale eyes looked at him for so long his hand started to fall to his side, when she reached out and took it. "I might not like charity, but I've had too much up-close evidence of how many people don't practice it, beginning at home. Thank you. I'm not going to refuse anything that will help keep me sane." She heaved a sigh. "And help ensure I make it through."

He didn't ask what she needed to survive. Right now he understood how your heart could feel like fragile glass, all too ready to shatter at the next blow. If he could help and have a safe place at the same time, he'd grab it with both hands. They held hands as they walked to the bar, neither talking. Ring just savored being with someone that understood how life could kick you in the teeth, someone who wasn't handing him platitudes, or worse, asking if he felt okay or wanted to talk.

Pushing inside, they grabbed a table and a waitress came by.

"What can I get you?"

"I'll take a whiskey sour and a platter of wings." He shot a look at Ember. "Hot, medium, or wuss?"

She snorted. "Medium, and a Long Island please."

"IDs"

Ring froze, glancing at Ember, who with no makeup on looked closer to twelve than old enough to drink. She didn't blink, pulling the ID out of her phone case as he handed the waitress his.

"Thanks. I'll have your drinks out in a moment, and your wings."

"Wuss? I don't think that is an actual term for the spiciness of the wings."

Ring shrugged. "Maybe not, but it's accurate, isn't it?"

Ember just shook her head at him. "So the rules are no talking about what sucks about life. Obviously, if you are here, you aren't at school. What were you going for?"

Ring flinched a bit, but answered. "A master's in business. Was halfway through my final year. Had to drop." He tried to shrug as if it didn't matter, moving shoulders tense with stress and exhaustion. "Should be able to pick it up later. They let me finish the midterms remotely. So hopefully in a year or two maybe I can finish my degree."

He paused to let the waitress set their drinks down and grinned as Ember drank the first three inches of hers.

"Oh god, that tastes good. I needed that so badly. At least you can go back. So that is good, right?"

"I hope so. What about you? You said you were leaving for France, not why."

She took another sip, "Having dreams shattered sucks, you know that?" He nodded in agreement. "I had a scholarship to Le Cordon Bleu in France. A full four years. I was one of three people in the US that earned it. So much for that now. I had to let them know that, well, that my plans changed."

"Any chance of going back in a year or so?"

"I don't know. Haven't thought about it. Hurts too much. I'll deal with it maybe when most of this is resolved."

"Well, from my point of view, you don't need to go. That turnover this morning was insane. I can't wait to see what you are going to do tomorrow."

"Not much else unfortunately. I'm kinda limited to the ingredients I have on hand. So I can tweak a few things, but not get anything new."

"Hmm, that's too bad. Cause so far what you have is impressive."

They munched on the wings that appeared and chatted

about movies, both wanting to stay on safer topics for a bit.

She focused on her drink for a bit, then lifted her head and sighed. "I'm exhausted and still have things to deal with when I get home. So how do we meet up? Me coming out each morning will both be obvious and involve time I won't always have."

Ring frowned. "You ashamed of me?"

"Not. But right now there are people I can't let know about you." She paused as if she might say more, then she shook her head. "Back to that life sucks thing."

"Ah, understood. So we use texts to stay in touch, meet up when we both have the energy and time?"

"That would be nice. If nothing else to ..." She trailed off and shook her head. "It doesn't matter." He watched her shrink into herself and then shake it off. Ember pulled out her phone. "Number?"

He read it off and she entered it, then texted him. "There, now you have mine. For now let's assume evenings only. You know where I am during the day. If one of us can't make it just text back, busy, no guilt, no strings, right?" She looked at him, her worry clear on her face.

"If you can't make it, you can't... same for me. We both have this life that is going to throw wrenches on a regular basis. We'll both take what we can get."

"Agreed. See you later, Jordan."

She slipped out, and he had never had a chance to kiss her. And why did she keep calling him by his last name?

Chapter Nine

Work and family kept Ember busy for the next few days. The memory of drinks with Jordan gave her something to smile about. Friday evening, she sat in her tiny room and worked with money, or more accurately, the lack of it.

"Dammit, between COBRA, copays, and what little I make, the money I have left in savings isn't going to last until this is all over. Hell, at this rate, it isn't going to last more than two months." She muttered to herself as she tried to figure out a way to get a few more thousand to see them through.

COBRA alone took up the bulk of her available income. The law said she had to have insurance for herself, though the temptation called to her. With her yearly income below the poverty line, she should get off without a fine.

"If I could get about another seven hundred fifty a month from Ernie, I could cover everything and keep us afloat until Christmas. And if everything isn't settled by then, I might just kill everyone." Once again, the idea of her father drinking and driving jarred her.

Throwing herself backwards on the bed, she stared up at the ceiling and tried to come up with something. Sitting back up, she went through the motions on her laptop. She hotspotted it to her phone, then checked email, looking for the medical referrals, hoping Seri might have replied or that there'd be information about the legal case.

Feeling up against the wall and needing to vent, she called Cecil.

"Hello, *Liebchen*. How is life at the bakery?"

"Busy, hectic, stressful, but still good. You hear what

happened to Ernie?"

"Ah, yes. It is a good thing he found such an excellent person to cover for him, is it not?" His smug tone made her laugh.

"For both of us, I think. Can I just say I hate health insurance? It costs a fortune."

"You have no idea. Try getting old. You think it is bad now, you just wait." His humor and lack of condescension helped.

"You think you'd be willing to take Mom out tomorrow night? She needs a break from this place and me. She walks on the beach a lot, but she needs more, and I can't navigate the medical paperwork fast enough. I should be getting a new referral for another doctor, but I'm still waiting on it."

"That sounds delightful. I'll call and invite her out. There is a new restaurant I've wanted to try."

Ember smiled to the empty room, blessing the fact that her dad had paid for everyone's cell phones for a year in advance, with unlimited data and minutes. Right now it made all the difference. "Thanks, Cecil. You have no idea." A faint noise from downstairs had her sitting up, and her mother's yell explained it.

"Ember, there is someone at the door, and I am not the help to be answering it."

"Cecil, I have to go. Someone's here. Enjoy tomorrow."

"I will. Goodnight, Ember."

She headed downstairs. Door? Who would know they were here? Even Jordan didn't know where she lived. And with luck, he never would. She reached the main area and got to the door just as the knock sounded again.

She pulled open the door to a man in an off-the-rack suit with dark hair, dark eyes, and a badge hanging from his chest pocket, a police badge.

"Yes?" Was this a good or a bad thing?

"I'm here to speak to Belinda and Sabrina Verre." A statement, and no smile crossed his face.

"About?" Why would anyone have more questions? For a minute she didn't think he would answer. But he did.

"I'd like to talk to them about the accident that killed Richard Verre and Douglas Lawton."

Ember frowned, not recognizing the other name. Her mind spun until it dawned on her. That was the other person, the one her dad killed.

"And you are?"

"Detective David Richert."

She looked at him surprised, trying to figure out why he might be here. When she didn't respond, he spoke, his voice smug. "I could talk to them down at the station instead."

That would not work. Getting Belinda up and down the stairs to her doctor's appointments burned her nerves to the bone as it was. Doing it again while going to the police station? Ember knew she'd shatter.

"No, it's okay. Come in." She stood back and let him into the apartment, trying not to see it through the cop's eyes. Messier than it should be, as neither her mom nor her sister would clean up, and she hadn't had the energy. Embarrassed, she grabbed laundry off a chair and nodded at it.

"Give me a minute to put this away. Belinda, Sabrina, someone wants to talk to you." She headed into the bedroom to put away Belinda's clothes when the detectives' voice stopped her.

"I need to talk to all of you, actually."

"Oh. Okay." She dropped off the clothes and stuck her head in her mom's room. "Are you coming? There is a police detective here."

"What, you steal something? He here to arrest you and take you out of my sight?" Her voice, both scornful and loud, carried clearly to where the cop sat. Ember flinched but forced a smile.

"He'd like to talk to us about the accident."

"Well, not like I'm going to be any help. I don't remember anything after arriving at the party." Sabrina picked up her book, plainly not planning on leaving her spot.

"He said he'd talk to us here or at the station. I assume you'd prefer here?" She tried not to let her voice get too tart, but stress caused lemon juice to saturate her tone.

"Oh, very well." With a huff Sabrina threw the book down, tearing the cover, and headed to the living room, not giving Ember another glance.

Ember fought the desire to let her knees buckle and walked back out. Belinda had already seated herself, leg stretched out on the couch, using her big blue eyes and ability to pout to thaw the cop's rigid stance.

Sabrina seated herself on the other chair like a regal queen, arching a brow at the detective. "Well? What questions did you have to ask, young man? I don't have all day."

Left with nowhere to sit, Ember leaned against the wall.

"I'd like to know the events leading up to the accident."

"I'm sure I don't know," Sabrina sniped back. "Brain injury. Memory loss is part and parcel of that I believe."

He shot Ember a look and she just nodded. Writing quickly in his notebook, he moved on. "And you, Miss Verre?"

"Oh, call me Belinda." She smiled her professionally whitened smile at him, batting her eyes as she ducked her head. Ember bit her lip hard to not moan in annoyance. The detective on the other hand seemed to blush a bit, and he was at least fifteen years her senior.

"Very well, Belinda. What do you remember?"

"Well, it was a party. And..." She shot a glance at her mom. "I didn't hang with my parents. A few other teens were there, and we went and watched movies."

"I see and were you drinking?"

"Me?" Belinda's head jerked up like she had hot oil

splatter on her. "Hell no. I was in training. I was supposed to leave in a few weeks to qualify. I still would be leaving if not for her." Belinda glared at Ember and pouted again.

Ember had already heard all of this too many times and couldn't stomach hearing it again. She turned into the kitchen to check on the dinner in the crockpot and start some noodles to eat with it.

"Why do you say that?" His tone was eager, and Ember heard the chair creak as he shifted.

"Well, if she had been there, she would have been driving and not dad." Belinda sniffed a bit, real emotion, but not for anyone but her.

"I see. Did he drink a lot?"

She could still hear them, and she came back out when he asked that question and the silence echoed in the room. Belinda just shrugged, sitting there picking at her cast.

"No, he didn't. In fact, he wouldn't drink at all if he were driving. Dad had lost someone when he was young to a drunk driver. So I've always had problems with that scenario. But there's nothing I can do." Ember offered this up, as it still burned like lye in the back of her mind.

"I see. Well then why do you think this accident happened if he didn't drink?"

Sabrina decided to offer her two cents then. And Ember listened, her throat seizing up.

"For all I know my ungrateful stepdaughter sabotaged the brakes or something else to get rid of us." Spite laced each word and she smiled smugly at Ember.

"What? Why do you say that?" The detective jerked up as if he had been burned.

Ember tried to speak but couldn't, her voice locked in horror as Sabrina replied.

"She was leaving, going to Paris, and starting a new life, without us. Maybe she thought she needed more money and just wanted the life insurance. I wouldn't put it past her. She always was an ungrateful wretch. Too bad I couldn't have just raised my darling Belinda without taking on the burden of a worthless lump of flesh." Sabrina never looked at the detective once, just staring at Ember, smiling a smile that made her flash back to the evil witch in movies.

"That is very interesting." He made a couple of notes in his little book. "I came because there was some information that wasn't making sense. Maybe this will explain the contradictions. I'll look into this. Ember Verre, please don't leave town. I may be back to talk to you again."

He glared at all of them and then walked out the door, leaving Ember staring at her mother in horror. Even Belinda looked shocked.

"Mom, you don't think I did that. Do you?" Her voice stuttered and squeaked as she tried to comprehend what she had just heard.

Sabrina stood and flipped her hand in a dismissive manner. "Heavens, no. You don't have enough brains. Besides, if you did, obviously, you failed horribly. We're both alive. Just proves you fail at everything. I'm going to finish reading. Let me know when dinner is ready." She flowed from the room as if she was royalty and Ember was her servant. At her door she paused and looked back at Belinda. "Or, your sister's very clever and wanted to make sure she had us in her power." With that Sabrina slammed the door closed.

Belinda just looked at Ember, her face white and eyes wide, shaking her head in denial, tears streaking down her face. Turning, Belinda hobbled back to her room, shoving the door closed in Ember's face when she tried to follow.

Stunned, Ember leaned against the bedroom door, eyes burning, and her heart fled from the fire of grief. Moving as if she carried their hate on her back, she went into the kitchen, turned the crockpot off, put the al dente noodles in it, and then pulled her phone out of her pocket.

sex, alcohol, now?

A minute went by, and all she could do was hope he could make it. If he couldn't, she might kill herself, or them.

okay. My place, hotel ground floor room 50 - you okay?

no. Be there soon, just make me forget, please?

k, be waiting with whiskey

Gratitude and relief lightened the weight on her back. Without changing her clothes or even brushing her hair, she headed out the door, almost running towards her salvation, her heart cracking into even smaller pieces.

Ring sat looking at her text message, not sure if delight or concern filled him. Something major must have happened to spawn that, and he couldn't ask. He had wondered if she would want to do something tonight, but the energy had left him and he had fallen asleep, fully dressed, on his bed until the text woke him.

Stifling a moan he stood, rinsed his mouth out with some mouthwash, and pulled the whiskey from the closet shelf. Grabbing the ice bucket, he propped open his door, padding down the hallway to get ice. The walk woke him up, and a slow grin twitched at the corners of his mouth. She wanted to see him. Distraction maybe, but still, she had chosen him.

Back in his room, he stood and looked at the hotel room. Not really anyway to set it up for a seduction scene. With a disgruntled sigh, he flipped on some music. Hotel clocks that linked up to your phone and playlist, for the win. It wasn't much, but it was something.

He stood there, unsure what to do, when the knock on the door pulled him out of his reverie. How long had he stood there like an idiot? Moving to the door, he opened it and saw her standing there, tear tracks down her flushed face, hair falling out of the messy bun, and bleak despair in her eyes.

He wanted to ask, to find out what happened. But their agreement sealed his tongue.

"Come in." He stepped back into the room and poured her three fingers of whiskey over ice. "Here."

She had come in behind him, wordless, still a bit out of breath. How fast had she moved to get up here? Ember took the glass and gulped down about half of it. Eyes closed, she released a big shuddering sigh.

"I needed that."

"Bad day?"

"Bad life." She shrugged, looking around, suddenly awkward.

"Why don't you go wash your face, might help you feel better?" Those tear tracks aggravated him, and he couldn't ask to find out who had made her cry, who he should hurt.

"Oh?" She looked puzzled, but set the glass down and went into the bathroom. The soft "eep" he heard through the door made him smile as he topped off both their glasses.

A few minutes later she came out, face clean, back to her normal healthy glow. He looked at her, cycling through paint samples in his head, trying to match the color of her skin. Eggshell was too white. Whitetail matched the beauty of her skin. She needed more sun though. And he needed a hobby if he was matching skin colors to paint samples.

"Did I miss something on my face?"

"Huh? Oh no, sorry, mind wandering. Long day. You feel better?"

"Yeah, didn't realize I looked like such a hag. Surprised you didn't shut the door in my face."

A flare of anger swelled in him at how she thought of herself, but he forced casualness. "You looked cute. Tired, upset, but cute."

Ember rolled her eyes at him but grabbed the drink and flopped into one of the chairs. "So you live in the hotel you're remodeling?"

He chuckled. "No. Just decided it was easier to stay here and not have to commute. This was one of the worst rooms, so I'll save it until last." Ring watched her eyes track over the torn wallpaper, gouges in the drywall, and damaged dresser.

"That's a relief to know you didn't do all this damage to it. Made me wonder a bit."

"Not me. Most of it is cosmetic. So we'll match it up later. Not too worried about the color right now."

"What do you mean?"

Should he answer that? Technically, it was talking about what was going on, but it didn't hurt to talk about the hotel. His dad, yes, hotel no. This remodel, it was just work.

"We're still trying to figure out how to upgrade the hotel. Pueblo style is rather dated. But with money concerns, not sure how to remodel it."

"Ah. Didn't realize you were so high up in the decision making."

"My job." Ring shrugged, not wanting to get into the complicated situation. "I'll figure something out."

Ember drained the glass but shook her head when he stood to get her more. "I needed that but any more and I won't be able to think."

He looked at her awkwardly. "We can get a movie? I have the code for anything, or… you want a massage?" Offering sex would be a bit tacky, but with a massage he could touch those wonderful curves.

She laughed, and the sorrow in it made his heart twist. "I want sex. I want to be wanted. To feel like I matter and that nothing else exists." Pain laced her tone, and he wanted to do something, to make her smile and stop whomever hurt her.

His throat hurt and he walked towards her. "Oh, trust me. I

want you. I've got a box of condoms, and I haven't been with anyone since you."

"That makes two of us." Her eyes locked on his as she licked her lips.

She stood up as he moved towards her. Giving her plenty of time to change her mind, he kissed her.

Her lips were soft, and he deepened the kiss slowly, planning on taking the time to seduce her. She ruined all his plans by wrapping her arms around him and pulling him tight against her body. Her full breasts pressed against him, and he moaned, opening his mouth. She took full advantage and darted her tongue in, tasting of whiskey. His fingers weaved into her hair as he kissed her, feeling himself harden.

A whiff of drywall dust caught his nose and he pulled back. "I'm so sorry. I didn't think."

Ember blinked at him, her eyes dilated as she looked at him. "Sorry for what?"

"Let me jump in the shower. I should have done it while you headed up here, just didn't think about it. Guy, you know."

Her laugh sent frissions of want running up his spine.

"Okay, you first, but then give me a minute in there to wash myself a bit too. Working around ovens all day isn't a cool job."

"Ah, but I like the smell of you." He leaned in, burying his nose in her hair. "Nutmeg and chocolate today."

She blushed, and he had to kiss her again. Pulling back a few minutes later, his heart raced and he ached with want. "Ten minutes. I'll be right back."

"I'll be waiting."

He grabbed a fresh towel and rushed into the bathroom. Soaping his body, he stroked himself once, thinking of her, of getting to be inside her once again. Jumping out of the shower and drying off, he wasted a minute trying to decide about shaving. It was good enough. She didn't seem to mind stubble, and the marks it left on her pale skin were sexy as hell.

Ring walked out of the bathroom to see her lying on the bed, a light blue bra and panties on, lacy; they would look excellent on the floor. Her hair lay around her head, her hand tucked underneath the pillow. She looked like a painting by Botticelli... and she was sound asleep.

The humor of it made him chuckle, and he dropped the towel, pulling on a pair of boxers and a T-shirt. He lifted her legs and put them under the covers, and looked at her, sleeping, trusting him. A hard sweet emotion wrapped itself around his heart and he ignored it. Taking another sip of whiskey, he just watched her.

Trying to remember when she said she got to the bakery by, he set the alarm for 3:00 AM. Then he slipped into bed. Giving into temptation, he pulled her over to him, her head on his shoulder.

Ember murmured in her sleep but didn't wake. With a contented sniff of her hair, he flipped off the light and held her close as he fell asleep.

Chapter Ten

A discordant beeping pulled her from dreams of being wrapped up in a blanket in front of a roaring fire. Ember struggled awake. She couldn't remember the last time she had slept so deeply. She felt almost refreshed. Different, but nice.

The ceiling appeared too far away to be her attic room, and what beat under her ear? Memory bloomed in her mind, and she jerked upright, looking around.

Next to her, Jordan groaned and rolled over to shut off the alarm.

"Morning." His sleep-husky voice made her shiver in delight.

"I fell asleep?" Horror laced her voice. She had fallen asleep on this man?

"Yep. You looked like a painting by a Renaissance artist. Adorable."

Ember blessed the dark room because she knew her face flushed red. "And you just let me sleep rather than waking me for sex?"

"Hey." He sounded affronted. "I might be a guy and famous for thinking with my dick, but you were obviously exhausted. I'm not a dick. Besides, I kinda liked sleeping next to you."

She sat there looking at the shadowy outline of his figure, then leaned down, finding his lips with her fingers first, then her mouth, kissing him deeply, not caring about their morning breath. Her heart filled with joy at the tenderness he had shown.

"You're incredible, Jordan," she stated when she pulled

back. "Thank you. And I have to go." The red numbers told her she had just enough time to get home, shower, and get to the bakery.

"Why, yes, I am." The grin in his voice made her laugh and she crawled out of bed, finding her clothes on the chair where she had left them.

"You going to call me again?" His voice in the dark seemed to reach into her soul.

"If you don't call me first."

"Good. Be careful. I don't like seeing you hurting." His voice caught at the end and she froze, glancing towards the bed. If only... Her mind didn't know where to go. If her dad hadn't died, she wouldn't be here, with him now, but she'd give anything to not be here in this situation.

"I don't like to hurt. But right now, life seems determined to see what it takes to break me."

"Well, if you need shelter, I'm here."

The quiet words caused tears to spring to her eyes, but she blinked them away. "You too. I gotta go." She slipped out the door before he could reply, not willing to dwell on this man who seemed to have ignored all her walls and slipped underneath them. If she looked back, she feared her heart might crumble into dust.

She speed walked to the bakery, needing the adrenaline to clear her mind. Jordan she wouldn't deal with right now. Money, and how to make more had greater importance. There was no way to take on another job, and the odds of Sabrina helping were nil. Ember noticed that while Sabrina tended to be sugary sweet to Belinda, even to people other than Ember she was crueler, harsher than she had been before. Which meant even if Sabrina did get a job, she'd get fired in short order.

A smile tugged at her lips. For as bad as the evening had started out, waking up in Jordan's arms had been a very nice way to end it. Too bad she didn't have the energy to pursue a real relationship with him. But that brought her back to money.

Something niggled at the edge of her memory as she unlocked the door to the apartment and quietly got her work clothes, slipping into the bathroom. Washing up, it snapped into focus: Jordan commenting on her turnovers the other day, and her comment about limited ingredients. One idea after another stacked up. By the time she got into the bakery and had the ovens heating up, she knew she had to talk to Jimmy.

Six o'clock seemed to take forever to get there, but finally she heard his key in the lock. Making sure nothing would get ruined, she paused what she was doing and headed to the front.

"Jimmy, you got a minute?"

He jerked his head around, surprised. "Sure, Ember. What up? Can I work while we talk?"

"Yeah, this is a listen, not a do, conversation."

He smirked at her and started on his morning routine — coffee, chairs, getting everything ready for the morning crowd.

"So your dad has a set array of things he makes right?"

"Yea. Though I do like some of the twists you've made. Those apple cheddar turnovers were incredible."

Ember's heart leapt at that endorsement. "So, let me ramble a minute. He's paying me based on the assumption of basic income, just not wanting to lose money but not stressing about making a large profit."

Jimmy paused, scratching his neck. "I think so, but I always thought he made good money. However, I love my dad, and I'm doing this to pay for college. Baking and running a business never excited me, even if I know a bit more about baking than what I might pretend. I'm working on my degree in computer science, mostly late afternoon classes. So that sounds about right." He shrugged a bit, going back to making the coffee.

"Okay. Do you think he'd be open to me mixing up the menu, making different things, in exchange for me getting the extra money?"

"Hmm..." Jimmy kept working while Ember waited, trying to not bounce up and down, anxious for his answer.

"I can't see why not. Call him and ask. He came home last week. And I think he's already bored. If nothing else, you'll give him something to think on." Jimmy looked at her, eyes sharp. "Just remember, he is a business man, so if you present him with specific ideas and plans, you can win him over easier."

Excitement surged through her. "Thanks, Jimmy." She headed back to continue prepping, but her mind started working full speed. She had a chance, and right now that would do.

While the alarm had been a rude way to wake up, the kiss had more than made up for it. He didn't need a shower this morning, so he set his alarm for 6:15 and went back to sleep.

He made his normal run to the bakery once he got moving, but the place was busy and he never caught a glimpse of her. Dejection warred with the memory of the kiss as he headed to meet David with two coffees and two cinnamon rolls, though this time he thought he smelled lemon wafting from the icing.

The two of them enjoyed the treat then got started on retreading the stairs between levels. They were damn lucky an inspector hadn't caught that none of the cement stairs had any tape marks left on them. Easy to fix, but boring.

The idea of Botticelli kept drifting through his mind, and Italian villas. Not sure where his subconscious had decided to head, he let it go, drifting, thinking of the warm Italian sun.

Mediterranean summers.

Mediterranean.

He jerked straight up and slammed his head into the railing he had been working under.

"Ring, you okay? You trying to become a bell for some reason?" David's voice echoed oddly in the stairwell.

He rubbed the knot forming on the back of his head. "Yeah, I'm fine. I'll be right back." All but running outside, he grabbed a sketchbook from the pile of tools and started roughing out his idea. He stood outside and looked at the hotel with a stranger's eyes.

Discarding the memories and expectations of what had been, he looked.

"This could work." He sketched down some ideas as he headed back into the hotel.

"David, you're on your own for the rest of the day. I've got to follow up on an idea."

The man just nodded, working steadily on laying the tape.

"I'll see you in the morning."

"Yep."

Ring headed to his parents' place, alternating between speeding and holding up traffic as his mind tumbled ideas over and over on how to remodel the hotel.

As he pulled into the driveway, he realized he had no idea if his mother would even be home right now or out working at her own job. That gave him pause; she seemed to be working less and less. Did he need to worry about that? The garage door opened, revealing her car, and he sighed with relief mixed with worry. Keeping this bottled in, even for the drive here, had been almost impossible, and he figured he had rambled out loud most of the way there.

"Mom, you busy?" he yelled, coming in the kitchen door.

"Really, Ring. How old are you that you still need to yell coming in the door?" Monica half smiled as she saw him. "So what are you doing here? How are the repairs going?"

"Pretty good. Do you still get that travel magazine? I have an idea for the remodel."

She blinked at him and then sighed. "I'm sorry, you asked me to look for ideas. I forgot." She seemed to crumple inward.

"What's wrong?"

He watched her fight to get a hold of herself. "I found these." She walked over and pulled tickets off the desk and handed them to him.

Ring looked at them — a two-week cruise in the Mediterranean, prepaid. He glanced up at her, frowning.

"My best guess is they were for our wedding anniversary. Which would have been last week. Thirty years."

He didn't know what to say as she blinked rapidly, trying to keep back her tears, and failed.

Monica took big shuddering breaths, dashing her tears away with the back of her hand. "I don't know what got into me. I thought I was done crying. But every time I turn around, I find out another secret about the man I thought I knew. It is killing me. Why didn't he just talk to me? Though at least this secret was a good one." Her voice quavered on the last sentence, and she lost the battle against tears.

Ring didn't have an answer for her. He pulled her into a hug, trying to give her the same comfort she had given him as a child.

Eventually she got control and pulled away. "Give me a minute. I need to go wash my face, then we can talk."

He nodded, watching her walk away, grief and sorrow bowing her shoulders in a way he wished he could unsee.

When she got back, Ring looked at her, really looked. She had lost weight, and she looked older than he ever remembered her looking.

"Mom, is everything else okay? Why aren't you at work?"

Monica twisted her mouth into something that might have been called a smile. "I let myself be bought out." Ring just looked at her, confused. "After Luke dying, I just didn't have the energy to care. So my partners bought me out." He started to open his mouth but she held up her hand. "The house is paid off, and between the money they paid me, mostly in stocks and bonds, and what I have in my retirement accounts, I will be fine as long as I don't go buying a new Mercedes every year. Not enough to dump hundreds of thousands into the hotel but more than enough for me to help. Easily pay you some sort of salary. And I need something else to focus on, something to keep me from climbing into a hole." She smiled again, this time a bit more natural. "So what brings you here?"

Ring scrutinized her and then gave in, not knowing what else to do. He put his sketchbook on the dining room table. "Do you still have any of those travel magazines?"

The question made her blink and she thought. "I think so. Let me go look." A few minutes later she came back into the room. "Here, I have four issues I haven't donated yet." She handed them to him as he flipped to a new page in the sketchbook. Once he reached a blank page, he grabbed the magazine.

He rapidly flipped pages, stopping when the image of a white stucco, terra cotta tiled house radiated from the pages. "This. We redo the hotel in a Mediterranean theme. Bring the beach into the hotel, mimic this design style, and brighten the whole thing up. No more dark colors, but the white, blue, and green of the Med."

Monica reached out and flipped through the book, closing her eyes after each page. Ring paced back and forth, trying to see a flaw in his plan. There wasn't anything else like this in the area, and the white sand of the beach would mimic the colors he would choose.

"Ring, I think you're correct. This would be beautiful." She flipped a few more pages. "And I have ideas on how to make the color scheme work using our current decor as much as possible. But even with you doing as much work as you can and running the general contracting on it, we are still looking at about a hundred fifty thousand, two hundred possibly."

He couldn't stop the flinch. That number hurt. And he didn't have that much. He slumped into the chair, all the previous excitement draining away.

"I don't have that much."

Monica huffed at him. "I keep telling you, this is not all on your shoulders. I loved that place too; I just let your father run with it. Let's see what I can liquidate."

Twenty minutes later, the answer was still not enough. "Fifty thousand, best case scenario."

A deep breath, and the picture in his mind of what the hotel could be made him sit up straight. "Then I get a business loan. The property alone is worth more than that. If I put it up for equity, then we can do this the right way."

"Go for it. I'll cosign anything you think is good. I trust you."

The words meant more to him than he could express. Ring stood and hugged his mom, dropping a kiss on her head.

"Thanks. I need to finish our punch list, but then I can start hitting local banks and see what is available."

"Good. But tonight, have dinner with me? I've been missing having someone here." Her voice trembled a bit. "I'm still not used to the house being so empty."

The slam of guilt made him reel, and he dropped to his knees next to the chair. "Mom, I'm so sorry. It didn't occur to me. Do you need me to move back in here?"

She sighed, giving him a mock glare. "No. I'm fine. Just didn't realize how much I'd miss him." She swallowed back tears. "But I wouldn't turn away a few more visits than what you've had time for, what with all the work you're doing." He heard her struggle with the plea in her voice, and it added another fissure to his heart.

"Deal. Besides, who am I to turn down your home

cooking?"

"You've been living on fast food, haven't you?"

"Well, that and a bakery with the most amazing things."

Together they got up to start with dinner, though he took one minute to text Ember *family* then turned to enjoy learning about his mom, as an adult.

Chapter Eleven

Ember spent the lull between breakfast and lunch writing out ideas, ingredients, and profit thoughts. By close, she figured she had all the information she needed. Sitting at one of the tables in the quiet after hours, she dialed Ernie's number and tried not to hope.

"Yep." She recognized his voice, and fought a smile at the odd greeting.

"Hey, it's Ember."

"Ember. I'm glad you called. Jimmy's been keeping me up to date on the place and he says you're a rock star. His words, not mine."

A rush of warmth at even that little bit of praise almost made her melt. That realization froze the warm feeling in its tracks. She needed to get Sabrina's help if she didn't want to lose her own self.

"Well, I'm glad he thinks I'm doing a good job. I wanted to talk to you about the menu here, and your profit margin."

The pause on the other end added to her stress, but she heard him sigh. "Can't see why not to share it with you. After all, you're the one doing all the work. Let me pull it up. Wife bought me a laptop. This way I don't have any excuse to get up. I swear I'm dying of boredom."

He might be bored, but he still acted better than Belinda did. She heard the clicking of the keys as he muttered to himself, navigating to what he needed.

"Okay, here I am. Hmph."

"Hmph what?" This stress would kill her, she knew it.

"You're pulling in more than I thought. To be honest, I expected a decrease in sales. But if anything, they've gone up." She could hear the curiosity in his voice as she resisted doing a jig in her chair.

"That's great." Ember tried not to sound too relieved, but she figured she didn't succeed. "I'd like to make you a proposition."

"Girl, you might be great in bed, but my wife would kill me, and these old bones just can't keep up with a youngster like you. Jimmy would be a better person for that sort of activity. But not in the store."

Her mind froze as she spluttered, "What? No, that isn't what I meant, I wanted—" She heard him break out in laughter and she sagged back into the chair. "Ernie you are a very, very evil person."

Still chuckling, he replied, "Maybe. But you aren't stressed anymore, are you? I could hear it in your voice. So spill it, what is this idea of yours?"

Shaking her head in bemusement, Ember began to lay out her plan. "I'd like to take over ordering the supplies and change things up. Order different ingredients so that I can expand the offerings of the bakery. While I was pretty sure people had enjoyed the tweaks to the standards, your numbers helped confirm that. My proposition"—she stressed the words, trying not to smile—"is let me change up what is made. And if there is a jump of over 25% in profits, I get the difference after the vendors are paid. And I worry about what is being made each day."

"Hmm." Ernie stayed mostly silent on the other end of the line, but she could hear him tapping and muttering to himself a bit. "You've definitely proven yourself in the last few weeks. But while I can handle a small dip, anything major would hurt. So here is my counteroffer. I generate a decent profit, after all costs are factored in and salaries paid. So how about anything above a 35% increase goes to your paycheck, calculated weekly, with a two-week delay. I pay all my vendors, usually every two weeks. So it would mean when you decide to leave me for a better opportunity, you would still have two weeks' pay coming in."

But it also meant she had a full two weeks before her first bump in pay could even possibly show.

"I think I can handle that."

"However, if you drop below that average for the week, it comes out of your paycheck. So you could end up with nothing."

"Oh." Ember looked at her numbers, then glanced above her head where what was left of her family depended on her. Even losing ten dollars at this point might cause everything to fall apart. She chewed on a strand of hair, weighing the options. But there weren't any. She'd just better not fail.

"You have a deal. I'll call you every two weeks to see how the previous weeks did?"

"Sounds great. And good luck, Ember. I'm hoping you're as good as you think you are."

She hung up, hoping the same thing. But now there was a chance, if she could increase sales. Her laptop beeped, signaling a new message. The email from Ernie sat there, with the promised account information, but she also saw the referral for her mom's doctor. Finally. She called and took their first appointment for the next afternoon. Anything to get her mom the help she needed. That done, she started on the planning for the recipes and baked goods she wanted to make. And she tried not to hope too much. Right now, hope hurt.

Ring's mind bounced from thought to thought, trying to get the ideas fully fleshed out for the remodel and lining up appointments with banks. The last thing Ring needed was text messages from Clay and Greyson. They had allowed him two weeks of peace and quiet, but that morning his grace period ended.

Jordan how goes? need Grey and me yet?

You're missing Clay being an idiot. I can't deal with him on my own. I'll send him to you.

Yo, the parties rock, u missing out on chicks

Ring rolled his eyes as he scrolled through the text messages.

All we do is study, Clay hasn't gone out more than once in the last few weeks. I'm not sure if that is good or bad.

He laughed at that text from Greyson; even in text messages he used whole words. It seemed Clay was full of it as usual. He missed both of them, but he needed to fix the hotel, and if he pulled them into this mess, their parents would kill him. Not to mention it was his family, his responsibility, his project.

seriously, we'll help, y r u so blasted stubborn Jordan?

Ring flinched at that one and dropped the phone in his pocket. Doing this, proving he could do this, was important. But the reasons why were starting to slip away from him.

Ember awaited him as he walked in, a bag in her hand. "Made you something. Just pay Jimmy, but I need your opinion."

"If you made it, I know it's delicious."

Her face, already a beautiful pale peach from the heat of the ovens, deepened to rose as he watched. The urge to kiss her right there swept through him but he refrained.

"Dinner tonight?"

She twisted a strand of hair around her finger, thinking. "I think so. I've got an app— something to do this afternoon, but if that doesn't blow up, yes. Seven?"

"Works for me. I'll text if my life blows up."

Ember flashed him a smile and headed back to her kitchen. Fighting the urge to follow her, he went and paid, ignoring the smirk from Jimmy.

"Morning boss," David said. His face lit up as he saw the bag in Ring's hand. "What's it this morning?"

"Not sure. She said these were a test." He dug in and came up with two odd looking pastries. Handing one to David, he looked at his. The dough was like a croissant, but the middle looked like Ember had filled it with eggs and cheese. Biting into it let the richness of the eggs, mixed with cheese and spices, fill his mouth. It reminded him of eating an omelet.

"This woman sure can bake," David mumbled around his mouthful of food, and Ring just nodded. They ate in silence until every crumb was gone, and then he sighed.

"Okay, best part of the day is over. Guess we should get going."

"Still have coffee." David held up his cup and Ring chuckled.

"True. Ready?"

A text alert caused him to pull out his phone again to read the message from Clay.

call old roomies for help, we don't charge much

With an exasperated sigh, Ring silenced his phone. Clay didn't realize how hard he worked, and right now, dealing with his text messages distracted him. And he had enough distractions in the form of Ember. He thought about her, wanted to help her, and had no idea how to help, much less the energy to do so.

David nodded and they set off to whittle down the punch list. Ring saved the easiest job for last so they could call it a day once they were done. One of the rooms needed to have a cracked toilet replaced.

Shutting off the water to the toilet, both of them unbolted it and worked on the connections. Ring kept thinking about tonight and went through the motions of getting everything unhooked. Trying to disconnect one of the connectors, he cranked too hard, and heard a sickening crack.

Watching in horror, the crack ran down the pipe and into the floor.

"Ah shit." Water started to seep out, and he wanted to scream. "David, go shut off water to this floor, fast."

David headed out of the room at a dead run, and Ring cycled through everything he knew, and realized he didn't have the skills or the equipment to solve this. Swallowing down the bile at the back of his throat, he looked up a local plumbing contracting company and called for help.

Six hours, four relocated guests, and fifteen thousand dollars later, everything had been fixed, though the bathroom needed to be retiled and repainted.

Numb, he stumbled to his room, having kicked David home a few hours ago. He sat on the bed, the magnitude of the disaster hitting him. If he didn't get those loans next week, they were done. That little mistake had eaten up the working capital to get all the repairs done. At this point, he had enough to pay David for all his work, and not much else.

He teetered on the end of screaming, everything now balanced on getting the loans, and he gritted his teeth and stood up to pour some whiskey. The red numbers of the clock caught his attention: 10:27 PM.

"Ember!"

Ring wrenched the phone out of his pocket and sure enough there were text messages from her, Clay, Greyson, and two missed calls from his mom. Ignoring all of them, he called Ember.

"Yes?" Her sleep muffled voice kicked his brain back into gear. "I forgot." He crumpled back onto the bed. "I forgot our date, I forgot you would already be asleep, I forgot to check my phone. I'm useless." He wanted to scream, but at this point that took too much energy.

A low chuckle filled with sleep and her own sheer sexiness answered him. "Work?"

"Cracked a pipe. Water everywhere. Disaster doesn't begin to describe it."

"Everything good now?"

Not really, but the pipe worked. He on the other hand might be screwed. And not in the way he had hoped. "Yeah, we got it fixed."

"Good. See me in the morning?" She yawned and that ratcheted the guilt up.

"If you still want to."

"Silly. Yes. Night."

He hung up and stared at the phone. No anger, no recriminations, just understanding. If he had the energy, he'd date her in a second. For now, he'd settle for just friends. He tried to convince himself as he crawled into bed that he could handle just being friends.

Chapter Twelve

The ingredients were here. The shop closed for the day, Ember sat with her recipes and worked out how to use her new ingredients for the next three days. The urge to get in the kitchen and start mixing dough had her almost dancing as she mixed and bagged and tweaked everything.

Lost in the process with four different recipes going on, the pounding on the front door caused her to jump and drop a container of yeast on the floor.

"Dammit." She picked it up; about half had spilled out, so she should be okay. The pounding continued and she headed to the front. Ring would have texted her, and Jimmy and Ernie both had keys.

The figure of her mother standing outside the door caused her stomach to contract. Fighting her trepidation, she opened the door, and her mother launched into a stream of words.

"You must come right this instant. Belinda fell, and I suspect she hurt her leg again, as she can't put any weight on it. This is your fault; if you were here to help us she would not have tried to go down the stairs by herself. And why didn't you answer the back door when I knocked. I've been trying to get your attention for ages. At this point it might be too late."

At her words, Ember dropped her apron, pushed her mom out the door, locking it, and raced to the back entrance. "Why weren't you helping her? Why was she on the stairs?"

The stairs, while sturdy, were steep enough to make walking on them heart pounding. When you added in the crutches, Belinda required someone else supporting her to get up and down them.

She had made it to the stairs before her mother could reply, and Belinda sat half way up, face white as she held her leg with trembling hands.

"It hurts, Ember. I know I should have gotten help but I just wanted to walk on the beach. I was sure I could do it myself. I was wrong." Her voice shook, and Ember wanted nothing more than to pull her into her arms and just cradle her. But that wouldn't solve anything.

"Sabrina, come help me carry her down. I need to get her to the urgent care so they can look at her leg."

"Hmph, if you had been here this wouldn't have happened."

Her patience snapped. "Mother, I swear, if you don't get your ass up here right this minute and help, I will kick you to the curb and you can find someone else to freeload off of."

"Well, I never. Hmph." Sabrina sniffed, and looked horribly affronted, but she came up and helped get Belinda to the car with a minimum of shrieks of pain, worry clear in her mom's eyes even if her tongue remained sharp.

"Stay here. I'll get her there, and I can't deal with you also."

"Oh, I see how it is. I'm a burden and too much effort for you. Good thing I didn't feel that way when I agreed to treat you like family. How stupid of me."

Ember started to snap back but saw her mom's face, eyes locked on Belinda, still gray with pain, and Sabrina's wringing hands as she stood there unable to do anything.

"I know. I'll call and let you know what happens. Please just go inside."

Checking via the rearview mirror as she drove away assured her that Sabrina had headed back inside. Guilt tinted her thoughts, but even with the brain damage, her mom didn't need to be that much of a pain in her ass.

Ember pulled out the phone and called Jimmy.

"Hey, boss lady. What up?"

"Jimmy, I had an emergency and am rushing my sister to the hospital. I had to leave everything out. Can you get over there and clean it up and finish putting things away, or at least cover them so they rise properly for tomorrow?"

"Wow. Sure thing. I'll head over right now. She going to be okay?"

"I think so. Just need another X-ray. At least I hope that is all it is."

After arriving at the hospital, getting a gurney, getting Belinda admitted, and paying the upfront copay of one hundred-fifty dollars, which felt like a knife across her belly, Ember found herself alone and exhausted. Even in the crowded waiting room she felt isolated, and she curled in on herself more, trying to figure out what to do in the worst-case scenario.

She came to the conclusion that killing everyone then going on a multistate rampage eliminating lawyers and cops would be the best option, so the doctor coming out to talk to her was a relief.

"Miss Verre, could you come with me?"

Trying to hide her shaking, and glad doctors couldn't read minds, she followed the woman to a consulting room.

"Your sister is getting a new cast on her leg. She recracked her leg right where the previous break was. She will need some special physical therapy to get her strength back and intensive training if she wants to qualify for the Olympics in four years."

"She told you?" Ember glanced at the doctor, who wore a weary smile that Ember sympathized with all too much.

"Oh yes, and then some. Along with how evil you were and how this is all your fault."

Ember pulled back and hunched her shoulders, trying to disappear.

"Oh stop it." The brisk tone in the doctors' voice made

Ember jerk up.

"I have two daughters. One of whom just got out of this phase. She's being a little bitch. Don't let her get away with it. It's just been made worse with the death of your father and all the stress. She can't deal with that, so she is taking out all her grief and anger on you. But you're letting her beat you up for no reason. You didn't cause any of this; so don't take any of it seriously. Either slap her back verbally, or just ignore her. Either one will work."

Guilt that had been weighing on her cracked and flaked off, and Ember sat up straighter, feeling a bit more in control of her world.

"Good. Now, from the rambling, self-centeredness of your sister, I assume money is an issue."

"Yeah. There is legal stuff going on with Dad's death, and until it is resolved, all the accounts are frozen and can't be touched. Which leaves me struggling to pay what needs to be paid."

The doctor tapped her index finger on her lower lip and shook her head.

"I'll give you the address to the local Shriners Hospital. Explain it to them and they'll help. They'll ask for a donation once you get back on your feet, but they'll get her the therapy she needs, mental and physical, and they'll even deal with the transportation if you ask them."

Ember felt like a yoke had been yanked off. "They will?"

"Yes. That's what they are there for, and as your sister is under eighteen, she's eligible. Just pay it back in the future so it is there when others need the same help."

"Thank you. It seems like I've been doing this all by myself. Thank you." She couldn't hide the relief in her voice.

The doctor smiled at her. "You're doing good. Ignore your sister. And your stepmother," she said, her voice dry.

"Wow, did Belinda talk the entire time?"

"Pretty much. I'll have the nurse bring you the info and the prescription for her pain. She's already been given something, so I'd expect her to be very sleepy by the time you get home. Get the prescription filled tomorrow and she should be fine. Good luck, Ember."

She nodded absently to the doctor. The relief of having someone else, even a stranger, tell her she wasn't failing made everything seem more manageable. It meant more than it should, but she clutched it to her, drawing strength from it.

"Here you go, dear. She'll be out in a moment." The nurse looked like she was going to say something else but just shook her head and walked away.

Curious, Ember walked out and saw them wheeling Belinda down the hall in a chair, a new cast on her leg and a thunderous look on her pretty face. She put a pleasant smile on her face.

"Ready to go home?"

"Great, back to that hole in the wall, sitting there while my future is passing me by. Yeah, thanks." Belinda sneered at her, watching her with a calculating look.

"Okay. If that is how you feel. Where would you like me to take you? I have to go back to work. So I can leave you here, or let social services know I'm unable to take care of you properly. Or is there someplace else you'd like me to drop you off?" Standing up to her sister hurt, but it felt good at the same time. For the first time in a long time, Ember didn't bend.

Belinda sat there blinking at her, with her mouth open. "You, you can't do that."

"Sure I can. I'm not legally your guardian. And if I turn you over to the state, they'll take responsibility for you. Or, we can go back to the apartment with your own bedroom, and the therapy appointments, and you can quit being a bitch." Her voice never changed, nor the smile on her face. Peace spread through her as Belinda dropped the scowl and shook her head in a slow motion.

"No, I'll go home."

"Great. Let's go."

Ember ignored the smirking orderly, who had apparently been the victim of Belinda's tongue. He helped her get into the car and winked at Ember as she climbed into the driver's seat.

Belinda glanced at her out of the side of her eyes the whole drive home. Once there, Ember called Sabrina down to help them.

"About time. What? Did you have to drive to Seattle?"

"Mother. We are back. I need to get Belinda upstairs and then go finish at work. Belinda, I'll be setting you up with a specialist at the Shriners Hospital later this week. The doctor was pretty sure you could make a full recovery. But no more trying to go out by yourself."

Belinda just nodded and let them help her up the stairs. The pain pills were obviously taking effect from her glassy eyes. Ember left her on her bed, eyes struggling to stay open.

"I'll be back later, Sabrina. Don't wait up."

"Like I would waste my time on waiting for you," Sabrina snapped back at her and slammed the door to her room.

Rolling her eyes at the histrionics, Ember headed back to the shop and was pleasantly surprised to find that Jimmy had put everything away very well and she had another hour of work to be ready for the morning. The words of the doctor kept her smiling.

Finishing up, she pulled her phone out, and texted Jordan. *life sucks, but might be getting better*

Three days of going to banks, filling out forms, wearing suits, and not getting to see Ember made Ring grumpy and anxious. He stayed at his mom's, where his suits were, which meant he didn't get to visit the bakery in the morning, missing a bit of heaven in the form of food and a chance to see an angel. Sitting in the last bank, the one that had seemed interested in his proposal, he waited for the bank manager.

He could do this, he knew it, but he had to get the money first. And at this point, without the money, they might as well sell. Ring sat up straight as the manager came back in.

"You disclosed everything on this property?"

His face was blank, but Ring's stomach flipped inside out.

"Yes. We cleared all the outstanding debts, and while there is a mortgage, it is being paid easily every month."

"Hmm." The manager sat down, still looking at the form. After staring at it so long Ring was sure he would die of the stress, the manager turned it around and handed it to Ring. "Did you know there was a second mortgage that has now gone into default, and you're at risk of losing the property?"

"What?" Ring heard his voice crack but was too stressed out to care. "I don't understand." He read the information; his dad had taken out a second mortgage for seventy-five thousand dollar two years ago. But why hadn't they gotten notices? Up at the top he saw the address. "A PO Box. I didn't know he had one."

"I am sorry. But taking this into consideration, we can't take the risk and loan you any money at this time. That property isn't healthy enough to handle a third mortgage."

The bank manager's comment jerked Ring out of his morass of confusion. "No, I completely understand. I'll go get this taken care of. Thank you so much for telling me, and not just declining me."

"Of course. Have a good day." The tone was a bit wry, but Ring could tell he had been dismissed. Gathering up the piece of paper, trying to not throw a screaming fit in the middle of the bank, he headed home.

Monica looked up as he stormed in to the kitchen. "We didn't get it I take it."

"You could say that." He tossed the paper down on the desk. "Did you know he had a PO Box?"

"No." She grabbed the piece of paper, and growled softly. "I swear if he wasn't already dead, I might just kill him myself." Monica chewed on her lip for a minute. "I think I saw a key that might be to a PO Box with some of his odds and ends on his key ring."

She stood and went over to a desk, digging through it. "I didn't think much of it when I first saw it on his ring. You know your dad; he never removed a key he hadn't personally destroyed the lock for. Aha, here it is." She held up the familiar key ring, with a few lonely keys left on it.

"It has to be this one." Monica selected a small silver key.

Ring sighed, slumping on the dining room chair. "Great. Any idea where it is from and how to pay off that mortgage? For that matter what did he do with the money?" he sat up a bit, focusing on his mother.

Monica started to reply and then paused and walked over and sat down. "I think I know. He suddenly got a new truck, and added the sauna to the hotel, plus a new stove in the restaurant. I didn't think much of it, cause, again, it was his business." She sighed with resignation. "He put the appropriate amount of money in the joint account we held for bills. Damn you, Luke." Her tone held so much anger and sorrow that Ring flinched back from it.

Ring didn't know if crying or screaming would help. And right now either of them just seemed like too much effort.

"But hey, the key has an address on it. So that's probably where it is. It doesn't change the money issue."

"No. And somehow, I don't think our luck will work to having a hundred thousand sitting in that PO Box. Odds are it will be more bills."

Monica nodded her head with an expression of resignation.

"So, do we give in and sell?"

The very idea corroded his heart, and he just couldn't do it.

"I don't know. I can't see a way to do this at this point. Not without help."

"What is it with you and your father?" She threw her hands up in the air. "Asking for help doesn't mean you are a failure, it means you are trying to succeed. I swear that is half the reason we are in this mess. He wouldn't tell me he needed help."

Ring winced. On a normal day, being compared to his dad would have been a major compliment. Today, she might as well have slapped him in the face. The worst part was, she was right.

"Point made."

Monica rubbed her temples. "I'm sorry, dear. I know you're as frustrated as I am. Promise me, if you ever get married, share everything with her. This hiding crap doesn't work, and the ramifications are a bitch."

An image of Ember in a white dress, looking at him, made his heart clench. "Promise."

"I'll leave you to it then. Let me know if you need help. Right now I need a glass, or more likely a bottle, of wine."

She left, and Ring pulled out his phone, stared at it for a long time, and then clicked a contact.

It went to voice mail, and he almost hung up again. No, he wasn't his father. Not in this. "Guys, I give. I thought I could do it alone. I was wrong. Any ideas would be welcome. And yes, I am a stubborn jerk."

He disconnected and grabbed his keys. Right now, he had a PO Box to find.

The address seemed to match the local post office about two miles away. He headed in, searching the boxes for the number that matched. Sure enough, there was one. The key fit and unlocked a pile that made him slightly sick. He pulled out the bills from the mortgage company he recognized, a small journal that meant nothing to him, and a few other random bills. Looking at them, most of them seemed to have already been paid off, outside of one for a colonic cleansing that he just didn't want to know about.

Trying to not cuss at his dead father, he got back into his truck and saw his phone flashing a text from Clay.

we'll be there friday night. Talk then

He hadn't expected them to come down here, but he couldn't help but look forward to seeing Clay and Greyson tomorrow. Greyson was just as well off as Clay, but more studious and quiet. He and Ring had competed for top grades. He'd be winning now.

At this point, crashing at his mom's made sense. The emotional roller coaster had left him feeling like he'd been in a cement mixer all day and poured out. He pulled out the most recent bill from the mortgage company and dropped the rest on his dad's old desk. Looking at the journal just required too much energy.

"You were right about that key, Mom. It opened a PO Box that held all of this in it." Ring waved a hand at the mail.

"I keep asking why, and I'm not sure I'll ever know. I guess at this point it doesn't matter. We have to live with it. But I just keep feeling like there must have been something wrong for him to hide this stuff from me. I don't believe he ever did before. At least I don't think so." His secure, strong mom looked very fragile.

"We'll figure it out, Mom. Promise."

Monica just pointed to the lasagna in the oven. "I'm going to read and get drunk. I think I've more than earned it while I try to come to terms with my husband of thirty years keeping things from me. Lock the door when you leave in the morning, please. I'm sleeping in."

"Okay."

Ring served himself some lasagna and poured a drink. He

sat in the living room staring at the TV. He didn't even know what he had watched when the alert from his phone pulled his attention away. To his surprise it was dark out, and his drink was gone.

thinking of you. Hope your day didn't suck

A smile crossed his lips as he read Ember's message, and he regretted not getting to see her.

it did, but that's life. issues tonight, can say hi in morning

k, will keep something special for you and david

The idea of a treat made by her waiting for him made him smile more, and he headed to bed, setting the alarm early to get to the bakery and then work.

Chapter Thirteen

Jimmy signaled her when Jordan walked in the door, and she walked out around the counter with a bag in her hand.

"Morning, you."

"Hey. Here's the surprise I promised you. But you have to tell me what you think, an honest opinion, okay? It's what I'm planning on making for tomorrow."

"I get to be a guinea pig? I don't know, is it dangerous?" He grinned at her and she wanted to be alone with him, not here at work.

"Only to your taste buds." She smiled at him. "This is on me. I already paid for your coffee and this, so just let me know."

She started to walk away, when he stopped her. "Since I don't get to see you tonight, this will have to hold me over."

He pulled her into a deep kiss. It stole her ability to think or do anything else but wrap her hands around him and hold him close to her.

"Yum, chocolate and caramel. I'll let you know. Can't wait to get to see you again."

He smiled, removing his hands from her slowly, and headed over to the coffee, leaving her standing there hot, bemused, and more than a bit turned on. A few of the regulars winked at her as she headed back. She ducked her head, but the smile didn't go away.

The first day of her new recipes turned out to be a success. Or at least she counted it as one, given they were out of almost everything she made before the day ended.

"I don't know what magic you put in this stuff, Ember, but

if this keeps up, we're both going to be getting bonuses."

"Your dad told you?"

"Yep. But be prepared for him to quiz you mercilessly for your recipes when he's ready to come back. I might have been raving about them a little bit."

Ember grinned. "I can live with that. Thanks, Jimmy."

"No prob. See you tomorrow."

Ember grabbed some leftover bread and headed home, her mood lowering a degree with each step she took up to the apartment. She needed to grab laundry and get it washing. But that meant going through the front door. Steeling herself, she pushed open the door to a quiet apartment. The place had been picked up, and there was food in the crockpot. Confusion washed through her, and she moved over to Belinda's door and knocked softly.

"Yeah."

She pushed it open to see Belinda laying on the floor doing curls, her leg laying under the bed.

"Hey. Everything okay?"

Her sister shrugged, not looking at her. "I guess. I started some chili. Mom's been hiding in her bedroom most of the day. I turned in all my assignments, so I'm done for the year. They should be mailing you the results, but it better be an A." She glowered and then sighed. "You bring home any bread?"

"Yep. Sourdough even. His recipe though, not mine. Mine's still growing."

"Is cool." With that Belinda closed her eyes and started doing more curls. Ember backed out of the bedroom. She looked at Sabrina's door, gathering her courage, and then decided the risk was too great. She slipped upstairs and changed into clean clothes. She'd have to do a load of laundry soon. Flipping open her laptop, she checked her email; no word from anyone, which didn't surprise her. After a quick chatty email to Cecil, her sounding board and safe place to vent, she focused on recipes and new things she could do with the limited ingredients at her disposal.

"Ember, help!" Belinda's scream caught her by surprise, jerking her out of a recipe haze, and she flew down the stairs to see Sabrina standing in the door of Belinda's room, throwing silverware at her.

"Mom," Ember screeched, but Sabrina didn't even blink just kept throwing the silverware at Belinda.

"You stupid bitch, you and your Olympics. We changed everything for you. You should have died and I wouldn't be trapped here in this squalor. I'd still have my husband." She turned and glared at Ember. "Then you, Miss Special, 'look I can cook.' Bah, who cares? Richard was the important one. I wasted my time caring about either of you."

Even after all these months, the words still felt like oil burns on her heart. Ember let it go, glancing at Belinda to see a few red marks where stuff had hit here.

"Stop it." She didn't yell, but channeled every war movie drill instructor she had ever seen. Sabrina faltered, then anger flared up in her eyes again, and she grabbed another spoon out of the bunch clutched to her body.

Before she had time to think about it, Ember stepped in and slapped Sabrina hard across the face. Then she blocked the doorway to Belinda's room. "Enough. If you keep this up, I will call the police."

Silverware clanked to the floor as both of Sabrina's hands flew to her face. The bright red mark from Ember's hand stood out against her fair skin. Ember saw sanity return to her eyes, and her mom's lower lip began to tremble.

"Oh, dear god, what did I do?"

Sabrina stood there shaking like gelatin. Ember moved forward, and for the first time in way too long, hugged her mother. "It's okay. Go see Belinda. I'll get you another doctor's appointment."

Clutching Ember tight to her chest like a lifeline, it took

Sabrina a while to release her. When her arms started to stiffen, Ember moved away, letting Sabrina flee into the bedroom. She sank to the floor, gathering a weeping Belinda in her arms. "I'm so sorry, baby. I'm so sorry. I hate this, I hate being like this. Please baby, I'm so sorry."

Belinda sobbed, holding her tight. Ember watched both of them, waiting for the answering service to pick up. It clicked over, the sound foreboding, given her current mood. "Yes, I need an appointment for Sabrina Verre as soon as possible tomorrow. She had an episode and attacked her daughter." The doctor they had been referred to had seen her once and wanted to have some more time to research how this current personality change related to the anoxic brain damage before recommending anything. And it seemed to take forever to get all the medical records released between hospitals.

"I'll get the message to the doctor immediately. I know he is booked tomorrow, but he will fit you in. May I call you back at this number?"

"Yes." Her eyes never left Sabrina, fear having sunk its icy claws into her heart. When it had been her Sabrina attacked, she could handle it. But seeing Sabrina physically attack Belinda? That she couldn't handle, especially not with Belinda so fragile right now.

"Okay, I'll let him know."

She hung up and watched as her mom stood, walking towards her. "I'm sorry, dear. I can't stop. I hate what I've become, but I can't help my feelings when I'm in the throes of whatever I am."

The rambling made no sense, and Ember lurched forward, pulling her mother — she would always be her mother — into a tight hug. Her mother went stiff, and she knew Sabrina was back, and her mother was gone. She pulled back before she could be pushed away.

"Oh, please. I have a small, justifiable spurt of anger, and both of you act like the world is ending. Neither of you were hurt. Suck it up."

"You are going to the doctor tomorrow."

"Oh, yeah? Why? Because you say so?" The sneer in her mother's voice lashed against her, but this time the memory of Belinda, vulnerable and screaming, acted as armor and it didn't hurt. "Because otherwise I call the cops and press charges against you." She kept her voice flat and unyielding. She might have lost her mother; she wouldn't risk losing Belinda too.

Shock flashed across Sabrina's face, and then cold indifference reasserted itself. "Whatever. I needed to talk to him anyhow."

"Good. I'll let you know when we need to leave."

They stood there staring at each other, neither giving an inch. The ringing of Ember's phone startled both of them. She answered, her eyes still on her mother.

"Ember, its Doctor Lang. Are you both okay? Who did she attack?"

"Belinda."

There was a sharp intake of breath. "That is not good. Look, I'll squeeze you in as the last patient of the day. Do I need to commit her?"

"I don't know. But this has to change."

"I know. Can you wait until tomorrow?"

"I think so. I, I slapped her to get her to stop." She heard the guilt in her voice, even as she tried to justify it to herself.

"Ember, you were protecting Belinda. I think she will survive a slap. Get her here, we'll figure something out."

"Thanks. See you tomorrow."

Eyes cold and heart shattering, she turned to Sabrina. "We leave at three. Be ready."

"Fine." Sabrina turned and stalked into the bedroom, slamming the door behind her. Locking back tears behind her fractured heart, Ember didn't know why it didn't just shatter and quit hurting. Gathering her nerves together, she walked over to Belinda.

"You okay?"

"Yeah. I'm, I, I was scared. She's never been like that to me before." No, not to her favorite daughter, only to the one trying to save them all.

"I know. Tomorrow we'll get help."

"I hope so." Belinda wiped the tears from her face, and Ember helped her to bed. "Thanks."

"Always. I'm your sister."

Belinda flushed and ducked her head but didn't say anything more.

Ember climbed the attic stairs, feeling the weight of her responsibilities with each step. Sitting on the bed, she looked at her phone and played the voice mail one more time, facing the fact that she might never get that person back again.

The surprise treat in the bag was a ham and cheese roll laced with mustard and some other sort of seasoning. It was all baked together, letting the cheese and ham embed in the bread. David and he both agreed that with a piece of fruit to match it would have made an awesome lunch. But neither complained about it as their breakfast.

"One of these days I need to figure out what they do to make the coffee so awesome," David commented, holding his cup close to him as he inhaled the aroma.

"Yeah. I'd like to be making it like this at home."

Grinning, they started their day, ripping the carpet out of two rooms where some guests had decided to put their towels in the toilet. At least that part insurance would help cover. Once that was done, they would repair the toilets, but everything that was soaked had to go first. The rooms had been closed off so long, the smell was awful and they both wore respirators, worried about mold. Luckily, there didn't seem to be much, as someone had cracked a window and shut off the heat, letting the room stay dry.

When the day was done, he pulled David to the side.

"Look, we found more money issues and as of now, I don't know what is going to happen. I'll understand if you decide to get another job. But you've impressed the hell out of me, and if I can pull off a miracle, I'd like to keep you. Maybe even give you a crew to run if we can figure out how to do this. We have the idea, just not the money."

David looked at him for a long moment, features inscrutable, and then he nodded. "Yeah. Like working for you and this place. I'll give you some time to figure it out."

"Cool. I'll let you know how everything goes. Hopefully we will be meeting with the hotel management, and I want you in on it. I should have some idea of what will happen by then."

Ring finished the day at the hotel, double-checking that nothing he and David were working on would have to be redone once the remodel started; if the remodel started. The desire to stop and see Ember pulled at him like a lodestone. But he didn't have time to do more than say hi, and he wanted much more than that. Something else he didn't have the time or energy for right now.

At his mom's, he showered and pulled out the documents he had avoided the other day, not having the energy to deal with them. Sitting down at the table, he started to read and realized it was worse than he thought. It wasn't just that his dad had a second mortgage out on the property; he had a short-term balloon loan. And the entire amount plus interest was due in sixty days. Either he paid off the remaining fifty thousand plus three percent interest or he lost everything. For a minute, he wished it wasn't unmanly for men to cry, because bawling sounded like a good idea right now.

The doorbell grabbed his attention and he frowned. Mom would have said if she expected anyone. Which left Clay and Greyson. They must have flown to get down here this soon, or they cut some classes. Knowing those two, the latter would prove to be true. He opened the door to reveal the grins of his two best friends.

"Dude, I swear I thought you were never going to cry uncle and ask for help. There is such a thing as too much pride, ya know?" Clay clapped him on the shoulder as he walked in and dropped off his duffel bag at the base of the stairs.

"Ignore him. Clay is just upset I won the bet." Greyson tilted his lips in the slightest smile and winked at Ring. "He owes me a nice bottle of cognac now."

"How was I to know you were going to be all Mister I-Can-Do-It-All? I was sure you'd ask your two best friends, and the only moneybags you know, for help before now."

Ring just blinked at both of them as he shut the door. "How did you two know what was going on?"

"Me." Monica spoke from the door. Ring hadn't even realized she was home. "I knew you were going to play the martyr, and they kept calling and asking how it was going. So I told them. Not my fault you were keeping them in the dark. I had no such need."

He stood there trying to decide how he felt, and there was only relief. "So I'm an idiot. I'd like to point out, I'm your son too."

"True. Which means I gave you some rope to hang yourself. What do you know, you asked for help first." She smirked at all of them. "The house is open boys. Help yourselves. I've got an errand to run."

"Thanks, Mrs. J.," Clay and Greyson chimed as they pulled beer out of the fridge. They took some time dumping their stuff in the spare bedrooms, talking about Clay's new girl of the week, and the changes at school - none – before they sat back down at the table.

"So spill, dude. She just told us the high points, not the details. Cause apparently someone's been a little secretive about that also." Clay shot him a cheeky grin and dropped into a chair. It creaked as his weight hit it. Greyson rolled his eyes and sat down more decorously.

"Was not, at least not on purpose. I kinda wanted to ride to the rescue myself, if that makes any sense." Ring sighed, rubbing the back of his neck. So he wanted to prove to his dad he could do it all. Why? Looking back he couldn't figure out why doing it alone had been so important. Saving the hotel was the important part. Not him being, what did his mom call it? A martyr.

"Ah, the Prince Charming syndrome. Yes, you would want to play that part," Greyson mused, sipping on the beer.

"Oh, and what part would you cast the two of you in?" Ring retorted as he grabbed his own beer and the paperwork with all the damning details.

"Clay is obviously the Rogue. Handsome, whimsical, and his mouth gets him both into and out of trouble."

"I resemble that remark," Clay joked, grinning at them, his green eyes sparkling with humor.

"And you?" Ring didn't know if he should be amused or irritated, but he had missed these two.

"I'm the big bad wolf of course. Luring sweet young things to their doom and always escaping scot-free."

Clay and Ring glanced at each other and broke out laughing. "Please, you're no wolf. I'd say you're the black knight. Everyone thinks you're scary, but you're quietly rescuing damsels, giving money to orphans, then disappearing before anyone realizes it was you," Ring pointed out, laughing at the idea of Greyson treating anyone with anything except exquisite respect. He figured Greyson was still a virgin because he couldn't handle the idea of hurting anyone.

"Hmph. Shows what you two know." He hid a smile behind the bottle as Clay still snickered.

"I'm glad you two came. Want the whole sordid story?"

"That's what we're here for. Well, and to play Daddy Big Bucks to our poor frat brother."

Ring and Greyson rolled their eyes this time. None of them had any patience for the fraternity scene, which is how they ended up friends in the first place. Pulling out all the paperwork, Ring explained everything, all the debts, the issues with the hotel, and what his ideas were.

"Ouch, you did land in a money pit, didn't you?" Clay had toned down his act, looking over everything with sharp eyes.

"Pretty much. So what are your thoughts?"

Greyson leaned back, his finger tapping on the beer bottle as he spoke, measuring each word. "Clay and I discussed this on the ride down, and we've been talking with our parents since you dropped out. We both have accounts with about hundred-fifty thousand in them for experimental needs. Now, since we're still in school and under twenty-five, we required buy-in from our parents as the bank will throw up alerts once we take out more than ten percent."

Ring winced. No one in their right mind would help someone in his situation. And while he liked Clay and Greyson's families, they were rich because they weren't stupid.

Greyson continued. "They both agreed this would be an excellent learning experience, and a good chance for all of us to learn some of the pitfalls in trying to save a failing business, so we can liquidate up to fifty percent of what is in our accounts. And we are going to use this as our master's theses on how to revive a failing business. We talked to your advisor also, and if you do your own paper on this, you can use it as your thesis and just make up the class hours part time. You're a semester short given how much you'd already done."

"Yep. Dad thought it was a good idea for me to learn how to fail on the small scale before I get into the big times. And if I – well, we – pull it off, we'll learn what's involved in making a miracle happen. I'm pretty sure they investigated your situation thoroughly when you dropped out." Clay smirked sipping his beer. "Not that I intend to fail."

Ring just nodded in shock. Clay's father, Adam Hangdon, was a powerful businessman in Texas. The odds were he investigated Ring the first time Clay mentioned his name. But in some way, it made Ring feel better to know Adam cared enough about his son to want to vet his friends and, apparently, Ring had passed. That had to mean something, right?

"So let me get this straight. You are both going to contribute seventy-five thousand towards this, and treat it as a learning experience?" Two heads nodded. "What's the catch?"

Greyson shifted in his seat, focusing on the table. "Not a catch per se, just business. Both of our dads – conference calls with both of them on the line are evil, I tell you – pointed out that doing it as a friend and having it fail could destroy our friendship. And none of us want that." Clay nodded vigorously in agreement. "So in exchange for our contributions, you would sell us 15% of the business each. Leaving you with 60% and control. And in the contract, we would stipulate that you could buy us out down the road."

Ring glanced down, doing math in his head. His mom owned 10%, per the will, and he had no doubt she'd do the right thing every time. He could live with that division of the business. And if they pulled it off, all of them would make money. "I think I can live with that. Have to talk to my mother, though, as she's involved too, even if it was left to me. But that leaves us fifty thousand short on what we will need to pay off everything and pull off the remodel."

"No it doesn't."

Ring jerked his head around to see his mother leaning on the door jam. They had been so intent on their discussion, he hadn't realized she had returned.

"And for your information, I agree and support your plan, and will willingly sign over the 15% to each of you. And here is my contribution to saving my husband's dream." She dropped a check down on the table. Ring picked it up and blinked at the fifty thousand made out to him.

"Mom, where did you get this? I know there aren't any accounts where you had that much money."

"True, there aren't. I took a loan against my 401k. I have five years to pay it back or the money will be pulled out and I'll have to pay taxes on it. So, succeed. I'm not a fan of giving the government that much money." She winked at all of them and headed upstairs, leaving Ring speechless as he looked at the check.

"Have I mentioned your mom is cool? And I want to find someone just like her," Greyson remarked quietly, watching her head upstairs.

"Well, she is single you know." Greyson's hand lashed up and he hit Clay on the back of the head, hard, before Ring could even process the comment.

"Thanks, Greyson."

"My pleasure, Ring."

"Ow. You're just being uptight." He paled at the two glares he received and rolled his yes. "Okay fine, no more MILF comments."

"Ring, the semester is over in just under two weeks. It'll take a couple of days to get the house in order, and then we'll come down laden with tools and we'll help. That will give you free labor and help to get all of this stuff rolling. If you want, of course."

He looked at them and shook his head. What had he done to deserve such friends? "Hell, yes, I want. Thanks. I think we might be able to pull this off now. But I don't have a way to pay you back."

Greyson sighed at him. "This is what friends do. And besides, not like we are doing it for free. Both of us plan on making a decent amount of money, and proving to our dads we can do this."

"Hell, yes. I love it when I prove my dad wrong. Almost as much as he does," Clay crowed as they got down to the minutiae of figuring out how to save the business.

Chapter Fourteen

"Jimmy, I've got to leave early today. Medical stuff. Can you finish prepping? I've got it all laid out."

"Sure, sign off on my extra hours." Jimmy grinned as he wandered in back after they had closed and he'd cleaned the front area, putting it back together from the day's rather frenetic activities.

"Always. Thanks again. I know you don't want to be a baker. But you aren't awful."

"Oh I'm not awful, but I don't have the gift or the passion for it that you and my dad have. So, happy to help and get paid, but I'll follow my own dreams." His grin was cheerful as he started putting the prepped goods together.

"Good. I'll see you in the morning."

Jimmy just nodded, and he didn't ask where she was going or why, something else Ember appreciated. Today would not be a fun day.

Heading up the stairs, she hoped Sabrina would be ready to go, but she didn't hold her breath. When she entered the apartment, the living room was empty, though she hadn't expected Belinda. Today she had therapy at Children's and Ember thought she had seen the car that usually picked Belinda up heading out a while ago.

"Mom?"

Silence met her ears, and she muffled a groan. She headed up to her room to change her clothes first; makeup didn't matter in this case. She came down in clean ones, grabbed the car keys, and then knocked on Sabrina's door. "It's time. You ready?" She pushed open the door as she talked and repressed the sigh at the sight of Sabrina lying there still in her pj's, though she noticed her mom's hair had been washed and lightly styled. Good thing she had budgeted extra time, suspecting this might happen.

"Okay, if you want to see the doctor in that you can. Let's go."

"I'm not going, and you can't make me."

"Okay. I'll go call the police now, and tell them to come get you, as you are now a danger to your children."

Sabrina stiffened and whipped her head to look at Ember, lips thin and eyes tight. "You can't do that." Spittle flew with the words, and stress laced Ember's stomach at this proof her mother was getting worse.

"Yes I can. And I will. You will get help, or I will commit you. You aren't giving me much choice."

"Fine, get out. I'll be ready momentarily."

"Okay." Ember backed out of the room and found a discount Diet Coke in the fridge. Caffeine sounded like a good idea.

A few minutes later Sabrina came out, her armor clothes on, the ones that declared you were less than her. Ember had seen this armor so much, just the very presence of it hurt.

"Ready?"

"I don't seem to have a choice, do I?"

Ember shrugged and let them both out, locking the door behind her. The ride to the doctor's was silent. Sabrina refused to even look at her, instead staring out at the traffic.

She wanted to beg for her mom's attention. But she knew it would do no good. Ember checked them in at the desk and grabbed a magazine to keep her busy while they waited

"Sabrina Verre? The doctor would like to see both of you first," the nurse said.

"Well I don't want to share my doctor with her. She can find her own doctor. Besides, this is my business not hers."

The nurse nodded. "Normally that would be true, but she

still has medical power of attorney over you until you are declared fully recovered. As of yet, that has not occurred."

"Hmph. I know my own mind very well." Her voice came across as petulant and whiny. One more piece of evidence that her mom might be gone forever.

"Follow me, please."

Both of them went back to a room, and they sat in prickly silence until the doctor came in. He had a serious look, but he smiled anyhow.

"Ladies. Sabrina, I want to run you through a few tests. I've been looking over your previous tests from right after the accident, but I need to do some comparisons based on the research I've done. They will take some time, but they are ready for you. If you would go with the nurse, she'll get you through them as fast as possible."

Sabrina just sneered and followed the nurse out. Ember slumped, the relief from her being gone palpable.

"So tell me what happened?"

Ember replayed the entire scene for the doctor, who listened carefully and took notes.

"Have you noticed any other issues, or was this a one-time thing?"

"I think it is getting worse. She used to dote on Belinda and recently she has been getting snippier with her too. The attack was unexpected. If it had been me, I would have ignored it, but not with her attacking Belinda. And I think she is having more memory issues, but it is difficult to tell between her not remembering and 'forgetting' on purpose."

Doctor Lang sighed. "I wish I had met her before this. It is hard to get a read on how bad she is without a baseline. At this point, I don't know what else to do besides commit her for everyone's safety. She is your stepmother. You could walk away and let the state take this burden."

Everything in Ember rebelled at that moment. "She is my

mother, the only one I've ever known. My mother died in childbirth, and then Dad married Sabrina. She loved me through childhood illnesses, high school romance, and everything else. How could I walk away now, just because it is hard?" Ember didn't understand why people kept telling her to walk away. This was her mother. Blood had nothing to do with why she loved her. "I can let you hear the real Sabrina, if you want. The woman I love more than anything," Ember offered, even though the idea of sharing her talisman seemed to diminish it slightly.

"What do you mean?" The doctor glanced at her.

Pulling out her phone, she pulled up the voice mail and flipped it to speaker, then hit play.

Sabrina's voice came over the speaker, bright, cheery, and full of love. "Hi, honey. Excited to see you later tonight. We're going shopping, my treat. And don't make that face at me. I'm not about to let my oldest daughter, and future superstar chef, go to Paris in what you wear now. We'll have fun, promise, and I won't push anything on you that you don't love. You need a wardrobe worthy of France, and I'm just the woman to help you with that. We're headed to a party, so you'll get back to the house before we do, depending on how boring it is. Well, that's all. We've got to head out. Love you."

Belinda's voice piped in at the end, "Yay, shopping. See you tonight, sis. I need something awesome for all the parties once I make the team." The combined voices chimed in, "Loves, see you laters." And the recording ended.

"Oh." The doctor's voice rang in the air with pity and sudden understanding. "I didn't realize how drastic the difference was."

Ember forced a smile, though the corners of her lips quivered. "Underneath all of her anger and rage, she's still my mother. I can't let her fade away without doing everything in my power to save her. It hurts, but every time I look at her, the woman that left the voice mail is the one I see, and then she talks to me, and the illusion is destroyed."

The doctor took a deep breath. "Well then, that changes this slightly. So, no committing or placing in long-term care, except as a last resort."

"No. Though don't tell her that. The last few days that has been a very effective threat, and I may still need it."

Their laughter was short, and too bitter to be funny, but Ember enjoyed the momentary levity.

"Understood. I should have the tests back shortly, but I think it is going to be some new drugs and therapy. There is no miracle cure for this; she has to learn to control the impulses - the nasty comments that spring up. Hopefully, it should help, but again, don't expect a miracle."

"Oh, I'm going to hope for the miracle. Not sure I could survive if I didn't, but I won't count on it."

"Understood." The doctor's phone beeped. "Good, the test's completed, much faster than I expected. Let me pull it up on the computer." He walked over to the computer in the corner and after a minute pulled it up. "Okay, no bleeding, which is what I was really worried about. It is mostly chemical imbalances and healing areas. I think she can get better, but it will be a fight she has to choose to fight."

"And I can't convince her of that, so the therapist can, or will? I know she needs one, but I've been struggling to get through the system to get the right referral and then find someone nearby."

Dr. Lang smiled. "Yes. I'd advise a woman. I'll put in the request marked urgent, which should help cut through some of the red tape. If you're lucky they will get back to you this week. Here is the new drug. You can get it filled while I wait for them to bring her back and do some last-minute checks. It should help with the chemical imbalance and make the mother you remember easier to reach." The doctor tapped the keyboard. "I sent it over to the pharmacy; you can go pick it up."

Ember stood. "Thanks. Maybe I'll get my mom back."

"I hope so. For all of your sakes."

Thinking about everything, Ember walked to the pharmacy and saw her name on the board by the time she got there.

The pharmacy gave the medicine to her and rang it up. "Now that is a two-week supply. She needs to take them three times a day. Let's see, your portion is four hundred eighty dollars."

"What?" Her voice squeaked as the word exploded out of her. "Two weeks is that much?"

The pharmacist nodded. "Unfortunately, yes. And there is no generic. These sort of drugs to accelerate brain recovery are expensive because there isn't a large demand. Heck, the full price is 1100, but your insurance is covering part of it."

Her mind spun in a panic. Even with the little bit of new money coming in, she couldn't afford this for long. The safety net her savings had been giving them as she waited out all the legal and criminal stuff would disappear even faster. But it was her mother. If she had to, she'd start selling herself. A flash of humor at that idea made her snort. Like she'd make any money that way.

She handed over her credit card, wincing at the transaction. She had to get more money.

Sabrina was waiting for her when she got back, and she forced a smile. "I'll try. It's just so hard. Feels like two people live in me. And the angry one, that one wins most of the time."

"I know. That's what the therapist will help with. We will beat this. We will."

A shaking hand reached up and touched Embers cheek. "I love you. No matter what I say, that is the truth, in my heart."

Ember nodded, blinking, and walked with her mother to the car.

By the time they got back from the doctor, Ember's ability to deal had been destroyed. The extra money pressure sapped any joy she had in her. Belinda got back at the same time, and Ember helped her up the stairs, and with a tired half smile, Belinda headed for her room. Ember fled to her garret and flopped on the bed, her body tired, but her mind spinning in circles. Ideas and options came up and were discarded. She didn't see any way out, except to hold on and wait for the legal stuff to work out. She sat up and sent another email to her Aunt Seri, letting her know about the new disaster, and to the police asking for a status. She needed the accounts unfrozen.

Her phone dinged as she finished all of that with a text from Ring.

hungry, want dinner?

yes! she texted back and leapt from her bed. Ember debated on makeup, but decided he didn't care. No strings, remember? She threw on some mascara and brushed her hair out, then headed down stairs.

"And where do you think you're going?" The snipe came from her mother as she pulled a casserole out of the oven.

"I'm going to go out to dinner with a friend. I'll be back later tonight."

She saw her mom start to open her mouth then stop and just nod. At least Sabrina tried to not give voice to the bile.

"Beli, are you going to be okay if I leave for a while?"

Belinda took a deep breath, looking at her mom and then her cast. "I think so, but keep your phone on, so I can call if something happens."

"I will. I just, I need a break."

The smile from her sister was almost kind and her tone

light, so the words didn't hurt as much as they might have. "Like we don't? Believe me, I'd love to get a break from all of you."

"Goodnight." Ember didn't let herself address any of the undercurrents in the room. Instead, she walked out the door and tried to pretend none of it hurt.

where?

Standing, looking out at the beach, the cool air and the salt scent helped her to distance herself. To remember the mom who took her to the beach and spent the afternoon building sandcastles with her, making her laugh with delight as the evil tyrant Ocean came and swept them all away.

hotel restaurant, I get deal - 5 min?

15, am walking

k

The walk helped perk up her spirits, and Jordan sat on a bench in front of the restaurant waiting for her.

"I haven't eaten here before."

"I get a discount, it's Mexican. I've been getting their room services. It's just okay." He stood smiling at her. "Long day?"

"Aren't they all? But I'm starving."

He led her in and in moments they were seated, looking at the menu. "My treat. Want a drink?"

"Oh, you'd get sex for that offer." She flashed him a teasing smile but had to swallow as hungry eyes met hers and heat flared in her body. Part of her still couldn't believe she had fallen asleep the last time they had a chance to be together and kicked herself about it. "Oh, wow. Okay, point taken. Yes, I'd love a drink. A big lime margarita."

The heat level in his eyes dropped a bit, and he smiled. "The offer is always open."

She had to swallow to be able to speak. "So I see. Not tonight but always interested."

Jordan chuckled a bit. "Good, cause trust me, I'm still

dreaming of last time."

Ember shook her head and focused on the menu, sure she looked like a steamed tomato.

The waitress, looking totally bored, came by. "Whatcha want?"

Jordan blinked at her, a frown flashing across his face. "Two large margaritas, lime please."

"Kay," she muttered and walked away, ignoring the patron trying to get her attention.

"Wow, can you tell she loves her job?" Ember snarked, looking at the food options. The menu looked decent, and shrimp enchiladas sounded good.

"Yeah." He sounded preoccupied as he looked around, frowning.

"Something wrong?"

"Just..." He paused. "Not what I expected."

"You work for the people that own this place right?"

A half chuckle as he directed his attention back at her. "You could say that."

"Well, with attitudes like that, I'm surprised they have any patrons. Hell, I would have never kept the jobs I've had if I ever treated a customer like that."

He opened his mouth when she came back, tossing chips and salsa on the table. "Ready to order?" She didn't look at either of them, her eyes on the clock on the wall.

"Shrimp enchilada, please," Ember said, a bit bemused by the waitress' lack of desire to be here. Granted, at the moment, she delighted in having any job, but she had never taken a job she didn't like, so she didn't have a frame of reference. Maybe.

"Chicken enchilada," Jordan said, eyes narrow.

"Kay." And with that she was gone again.

Ember eyed the spilled salsa and sighed. "I hope she treats the margaritas with a bit more respect."

"Yep, cause alcohol abuse is a sad thing."

They both chuckled a bit at that, and Ember reached for the salsa. To her disappointment, it tasted like jar salsa not fresh.

"So work is going well?" He seemed to fumble, trying to figure out what to ask.

"Yes, it is. I'm learning so much. Makes me regret not making it to Paris even more."

"So what did you want to study?"

"Running my own restaurant. Granted that would be years in the future, but having that degree behind me would have helped immensely."

"Yeah. I had wanted to run my own business. But, I guess we take the hands we are dealt."

A busboy came out, smiled at both of them, and carefully placed the drinks in front of them. "*Disfrutar.*"

"*Gracias*," Jordan replied, and the boy smiled a blinding smile at them then disappeared.

"You speak Spanish? And can we have him for a waiter instead?"

"Not. I can say the basics, and that covers it. And I was thinking the same thing."

Ember shrugged and took a big drink of her margarita. Other people's staffing problems were not her worry. "Yum. At least that tastes good."

Jordan sipped it a bit, looking at the drink with a sharp look. "Maybe. Using the super cheap stuff." He frowned again.

"Not our problem."

"I guess." He shook his head. "So we're thinking on doing a Mediterranean remodel for this place. What do you think?"

He was the foreman, so she guessed his opinion would be asked. What did she know about construction? "Hmm." She looked around. "What colors?"

"I think, and mind you it hasn't all been decided yet, they

will be white and sea blue, with green accents. White wash all the walls, and add new terra cotta accents."

"Should be nice. Make it much brighter. This place would be dark as soon as the sun goes down."

Food came and interrupted their conversation. Ember glanced at the plate; it looked like typical enchiladas, nothing special either way. Her stomach grumbled and Jordan chuckled.

"Sounds like someone is hungry." She dared to look up at him, even though she mentally cussed at her stomach. His warm eyes held no condemnation. Instead, they were full of gentle humor.

"Told you. Long day." She took a bite and sighed, mediocre at best and the shrimp were rubbery.

"Yours too?"

His voice pulled her out of the contemplation of all the things she could fix about this dish, starting with not using freezer-burned shrimp.

"Mine too what?"

"Barely passable food."

"That might be an understatement. But I'm hungry, and I'm not paying." She flashed a smile at him that he returned.

"True. But this does explain a lot."

Ember caught the look of frustration on his face, and it made her curious. "What do you mean?"

He shook his head. "Never mind. Right now, let's forget about work – cause for me this is very rapidly straying into work – and enjoy the drinks and the company. We'll tolerate the food."

They both ate in silence, Ember turning over food in her head.

"This place is supposed to be a resort-style hotel right?"

"That is the general idea. Why?"

"Well, with food like this, you'd never draw the people

you need. People need to want to eat here. And honestly, if it wasn't free, I wouldn't bother. But you know, the Mediterranean diet is all the rage. Super heart healthy, good for diabetics, and meets most diets with little effort. Now if you had a world-class or at least a decent restaurant serving that sort of food, you would get some extra publicity as you could show all the healthy aspects." She grinned at him. "If you were the boss and could decide all that, at least."

"Well, you know that is a great-" He was cut off as the waitress came up.

"Look, I clock out in three minutes. Can I close you out now so I can get out of here?" She slapped the check down on the table, taking Ember back a bit.

"Uh, sure." Jordan looked hesitant, but glanced at the check then pulled out his wallet, putting enough cash to cover the check and give her a small tip. "Keep the change."

"Wow, big spender," she sneered as she flounced away.

Ember ducked her head and rubbed her eyebrow. "I really, really hope she's someone's relative. Cause otherwise the only way she has kept this job is she's sleeping with someone." She lifted her head to look at Jordan and forced a smile.

"Hey." He put up both hands. "It isn't me. Promise. I'm still trying to seduce you back into my bed."

That derailed her train of thought and she laughed. "I didn't think it was. Just saying." She finished off her drink and sighed. "I know it's early, but getting up at 4:00 AM hurts, and I need to do laundry if I'm to have anything clean to wear tomorrow. I gotta get going."

"Walk you home?"

"To the bakery sure. I'll find my way home from there."

"Ah, more secrets."

Ember shook her head. "No, more like the life that is tearing me apart. If you get too close, you'll get pulled in no matter what you do. And I need you separate for now."

He stood helping her out. "I understand. Come on, I want

to enjoy the walk."

Holding his hand and just walking to the bakery seemed like a dream. One she actually wanted, and not the nightmares she'd been having since all this happened.

They paused and she smiled at him. "And here is where I turn into a pumpkin."

"You don't look like a cinder girl."

"Flour?"

"Cinnamon and sugar." He leaned close and captured her mouth with lime-flavored lips, pulling her body close to him, holding her like he didn't want her to go.

She sank into the kiss, matching him. The knowledge they were standing in public prevented the pole climbing she wanted to do. Well, that, and how stupid she would look.

Wanting more, she pulled back, looking at him, knowing her eyes matched his, dilated and hungry.

"Go. I've got chores to do, then to bed, and you need the same thing. I'll see you in morning?"

"Always." One more fast kiss. This time he prevented it from turning into a long one, and he headed back up the hill. She watched him walk away, the embodiment of what she couldn't have, could only steal for moments at a time. Then she turned and headed around the building to her own personal hell.

Chapter Fifteen

Monica and Ring scheduled a meeting with all the staff managers for Friday morning. Ring had on his suit and looked forward to the meeting. They had secured financing. Help in the form of Greyson and Clay would be here soon, and his mom worked on getting the color designs and fabrics ordered. Leveraging her former partner's wholesale access, she saved them money on that front. But even with a meeting first thing, he would not give up receiving a smile from Ember. He pulled slightly on the suit he wore as he walked into the bakery. Jeans were so much more comfortable,

"Hey. Your usual?" Jimmy asked with a smile, already reaching for the cups.

"Not today, I'm afraid. I have a big meeting and I'm bringing treats. Can you get me a box with about two dozen things in it? Variety. And a large box of coffee."

"Sure coming right up. Ember, your boyfriend is here."

Ring froze at those words, and he saw that Ember, coming round from the back, froze also, both of them staring at the other.

"Just a friend, Jimmy. Not my boyfriend." Her voice was quiet, but carried in the quiet pre-rush bakery.

Jimmy snorted. "Then you're both either delusional or stupid. Either way, not my problem." Ring tried to convince himself the words didn't hurt. They were true, after all. They were just friends. Besides, having a clingy girlfriend right now was the last thing he needed.

Ember cast a glance over him. "You're all dressed up today." Her face asked the question her words didn't

"Yeah, big meeting rolling out the remodel plan and getting everyone on board."

"Ah. Hope it goes well."

"It should." God, she looked sexy, hair slipping out of her bun, and smiling at him. "So, ping me tonight? I might need some distraction depending on how the meeting goes."

The smile lit up her face and made her gray eyes sparkle. "Will do. Enjoy." She headed back into the depths of the bakery. And he hadn't had a chance to kiss her. Damn.

"Here you go." Jimmy handed him a huge box, and a carrier for the coffee container. "I threw in creamers, sweeteners, and stirrers."

"Thanks." Ring handed him the credit card and tried not to think about the balance currently on it.

"Enjoy. Some of her specials are in there." Jimmy handed him the receipt and card back. Ring cast one more lingering glance at the back, but she didn't reappear. With a disgruntled sigh, he headed up the hill to the conference room.

They'd scheduled the meeting for eight, but he knew his mother and David would both be there early. He entered, the box in one arm and the coffee in the other. Sure enough, his mother, David, and Serge, the hotel manager, were sitting there, all seeming to ignore each other. He rolled his eyes, not caring who saw him.

"What, are you all five? Mom, I expected better from you." He set down the box and cracked it open, the move bringing David up to him.

"You're a good boss, Ring. Her stuff. Yum." He grabbed something Ring didn't recognize and coffee and then headed back to the rear of the room, plainly hiding.

Monica moved up and shrugged while she looked at the selection. "It's the first time I've been back since he died. It feels"—she paused focused on the offerings—"odd."

"Ah, didn't think of that. You okay?"

"I'm fine. Has Ernie changed up his recipes? I don't remember these."

"Has a new girl working for him while his hip is getting replaced. She's rather creative with food."

"Hmm." His mom picked up one of the apple cheddar turnovers, and Ring didn't know if he wanted to try and steal it from her or watch her when she bit in. A new one grabbed his attention, looking like a cinnamon roll, but no cinnamon. He grabbed that and got his coffee.

"Serge, you ready for all this?"

"Stress seems to be a requirement in my life, so I might as well."

Ring looked around the room. The head chef, Julio Rameriz, walked in with Lee Thompson, the restaurant manager, followed by the head of housekeeping, Mary York. The last person to enter was the designer they had hired, Chris Thompson. He was a junior in his firm, but while Monica knew she could guide the colors, they needed someone to make the place pop, someone who would follow their lead for the vision of this remodel. Neither he nor his mom were good at taking a back seat.

"Everyone, please grab something to eat and some coffee, then we can get to work." He addressed the room, but he mostly wanted a few minutes to savor his breakfast. Various people came over to talk to him, and he never had a chance to bite in.

Once everyone found a seat, Ring accepted the inevitable and stood up to address the team he needed behind him to pull off this miracle. "Most of you know me, I'm Ring Jordan. I'm sure you're all aware that business has been less than stellar, even before Luke died, and we've come up with some ideas to change that. But it is going to require a lot of work from everyone. I'd like to introduce Chris Thompson, who has the mock ups of what we are trying to achieve."

Chris got up, set up his projector, and started going

through the presentation. Ring had seen it before, so he watched the people instead. Most everyone seemed interested. Well, David seemed bored but Ring knew he was itching to get some work done. Sitting and talking was not on his list of things to do, ever. Julio Rameriz, on the other hand, just looked at everything and sneered. What was his issue? With the poor quality of the food he currently served, sneering was not something he had a right to do at this moment.

He took a bite of the roll and almost lost track. Ginger and lemon exploded in his mouth, tart, spicy, tangy, yet still sweet enough to make you crave the next bite. Ember had a way with baked goods.

Chris finished his presentation; Ring quickly swallowed to clear his mouth and spoke up. "So now you see what we are going to try and do. We have six weeks to get all the cosmetic stuff completed, and David and I have the same amount of time to get all the major repairs done. So, help out as you can. We will be closing down various rooms as we update, and then entire floors as we replace carpets and paint. There may be some days we are sending people home early and others where we need people to work late. Talk to your staff and let them know. Find me the people that want to be here, and if we survive, I promise they will be rewarded."

The smiles made him feel better, but he caught the eye roll from Julio. The expression looked odd on the face of someone at least twice Ring's age.

"Any questions?"

There were a few, mostly involving logistics, so his answer consisted of "We don't know yet. When I know, you'll know." When they were done, he wrapped up.

"Thanks, everyone. Be prepared for dust and noise starting tomorrow. Julio, could you and Lee hang back? David, I'll catch up with you. Can you work on finishing up the plumbing for the new showers in the suites?"

"Yep." David snagged another baked good and more coffee as he headed out.

"So what's up, Ring?" Lee asked, a smile on his face as he sipped at his cup.

"I've got some concerns about the restaurant, and there are some changes we need to make." He sensed rather than saw his mother sit down next to him.

Julio bristled. "Concerns, what concerns? What changes do you need to make to my restaurant?" He slapped the table. "This is my restaurant. You don't get to tell me what changes need to be made. There is nothing wrong with *my* restaurant."

Ring sat back, looking at him, a mask dropping over his face. "There are quite a few things wrong." The polite careful method he had prepared disappeared, and instead he went with the bald, harsh facts. "Your food is mediocre at best. You have servers that are rude and ignore customers. You're using the cheapest alcohol and charging for Jose. Not to mention we need to completely change the menu. We are going with the Mediterranean theme wholeheartedly with food that matches. And given what happened to my father, we want heart healthy, diabetic friendly meals. Things you would get at a spa resort. Food that delights your tongue and is good for you, body and soul."

"Bah. Is a fad. My food is excellent. You came on a bad day and have no taste in food. What do you know?"

"That any kitchen that serves food to the public should never have a bad day. And if I think your food is poor, you have a major issue. I've been known to eat ramen for a week straight because the taste didn't matter, and right now you would have to pay me to go back and eat there. No restaurant can be attached to a vacation hotel if anyone thinks that about the food."

"You think you can do better? Fine, I quit. You can come cook." Julio threw the chair back against the wall, denting it, and stormed out.

"Lee, please take the cost of repairing that out of his salary when you write him his last check." Monica's voice resembled an icy wind as she turned dark eyes to watch Julio storm out.

"Oh, thank god." Lee sighed and sagged a bit. "Does that mean I can get rid of some of his 'family' and get real servers?"

"What?" His mom's voice overlapped with his as they turned to look at him. "What are you talking about?" Ring asked now, even more confused.

"It's been going downhill for a while now. In fact, I'm pretty sure he is - was stealing ingredients, but I couldn't prove it. I was starting to suspect he had something on your dad because no matter what evidence I brought, complaints, anything; your dad would just mutter about how Julio knew what he was doing." Lee sighed. "I was about to turn in my notice when Luke died."

"I see. Is there anything else we should know about?" Ring knew his voice was dry, but this just threw another knot in his plans. They had counted on a helpful staff, not this.

"Oh, about four people to let go, and then see what you want to do. The sous chef Karly should be fine to limp by, but honestly, she had no experience outside of school coming in when Julio hired her. She won't be able to pull this off. Don't get me wrong, she works hard, but I think he wanted to stare at her tits more than he cared if she could do the job."

Ring resisted the strong urge to beat his head on the table. "Can you get her to come down here?"

"Sure, give me a minute." Lee headed out and Ring turned to his mom.

"We are so screwed."

"Not necessarily. Look we want to shake things up, right?" He nodded in response to her comment. "Well, our goal is to get this place ready in six weeks. Let's have a contest. We know we need a new menu, business plan, etcetera? Have people submit all of it as their entry; menu, plan, costs, and sample recipes. Say three appetizers, three lunches, and four dinner recipes that have to be heart healthy, good for diabetics, and filling. The winner gets the job." She turned those sharp eyes to Lee, who had stepped back into the room. "What were we paying Julio?"

"Fifty-two thousand, plus ten percent of the net profits," Lee responded, his eyes narrow.

"So we offer forty-eight thousand, plus eight percent, raises to be agreed upon, and see what we get. Worse case we get nothing and have to find someone anyhow. But this gets us media attention, and maybe somebody hungry to prove something."

Ring turned the idea over and over in his mind and couldn't find any flaws. "Can you run that, Mom? Honestly, I've got my hands full with what I've got going on."

"Sure. I'll set it in motion. Besides, something like that will take someone a week or so to figure out anyhow." Monica smiled. "See, two problems solved with one solution."

"Maybe. But we have a lot of work ahead of us. I hope Clay and Greyson get here soon."

"Faith, child. We get what we earn. And you've earned this the hard way." She rose from the chair, heading to the door, and then paused. "By the way, that turnover was incredible. Feel free to bring some with you next time you come home."

Ring laughed and waited for Karly to tell her about the new development and see what help she needed.

Chapter Sixteen

Doctor Lang lived up to his word and sent Ember a few referrals for a psychiatrist. Ember settled on a Doctor Caulson. She specialized in anger management and traumatic incidents. Ember drove her mom down for the first meeting, but it sat right on the route for public transportation, so she hoped after the first few she might go by herself. It took a few days to get all the insurance issues settled and an opening for a new patient, but the urgent marking helped push the request through the system faster. Sabrina hid in her room most of the time, and even Belinda avoided her as they tried to get her the help she needed.

The office was calming, in shades of green and blue. She walked in, holding the door for Sabrina, and then sat down in the chair and pulled out her notebook. She tried to come up with some new recipe ideas and she played with money to see what stone she could squeeze blood from.

"What are you doing?" Sabrina's voice struck a shrill note as she stood in the middle of the waiting room.

"Waiting for you."

"So go check me in."

Ember didn't even look up. "You are capable of doing that for yourself. I'm just your chauffeur today."

She watched her mom through the corner of her eye, her hands trembling as she tried to adjust to the situation, and it took all the self-control she had to not jump up and make it right. After a moment, Sabrina walked up to the receptionist and checked in.

The proud look on her face told Ember it had been the right thing to do. Maybe not the easy thing, but the right thing.

"Sabrina Verre?"

A woman in her late fifties stood there and smiled at both of them. Ember let her mom go and tried not to hope.

Lost in stress and numbers that would not go down no matter what she did, she jumped when the same woman said her name an hour later.

"Ember Verre?"

"Um, yes?" Confused, Ember looked up at the woman.

"Would you mind coming in and talking to me for a few minutes?"

Not sure what was going on, Ember grabbed her stuff and walked into the office. The trickle of water from a fountain on the desk added a soothing sound to the room. A desk facing a wall and lots of light wood bookcases completed the room. Sabrina sat in a chaise lounge, her eyes red and her face puffy. Once again Ember had to resist going to her and making it all better.

"Please take a seat."

The doctor pointed to the chair next to the chaise lounge Sabrina sat on, while the doctor turned her desk chair around to face them.

"Ember, my name is Lori Caulson. I have a degree in psychology and my medical license. I've agreed to work with your mother at half rate until the legal issues have been worked out, then we'll go back to my normal rate." Ember though she might cry in sheer relief. This she could handle, though barely. "I've been talking to your mother, and we both agree she can't do this with just me and her prescriptions. I have your mother's permission to talk to you, so I'm not breaking any oaths. I need to explain some of what is happening to her, and how she is going to need your help.

"Okay." She knew her voice quavered a bit, but the idea of taking on anything more terrified her.

"Basically, when your mother woke up from the accident, her brain was damaged. She knew something was very wrong.

She knew her husband was dead, and she knew it was someone's fault. But she couldn't blame Richard. She knew it wasn't her fault, and she knew it wasn't Belinda's."

Ember caught her mother nodding at each "she knew" and realized the doctor was emphasizing this for some reason.

"So when she saw you, the first person she recognized, her brain imprinted, for lack of a better word, all the guilt on you, providing her mind a way out. Unfortunately, with the damage, it wasn't a short-term delusion, but something she has written into her personality. Hate and anger at you for everything that happened. Even though she knows you weren't at fault, she can't always separate out the knowledge from the feelings that are just as real and treat you appropriately."

"Oh, thank the gods." The words burst out, and the weight that evaporated from her made her very glad she was seated.

"Well, that was not the reaction I expected." The doctor looked confused. "Would you mind explaining?"

"It sounds stupid, but some of the things she said were so vicious, I had started to wonder if she had always hated and resented me; that my whole childhood had been a lie. I didn't believe it, not quite. But it was becoming harder and harder every time she pulled out how much she regretted getting stuck with me."

Sabrina reached up and wiped away a tear, shaking her head, and causing more disarray to her hair.

"Ah. The answer to that is no. The damage and transference allows her to lash out at you, when she knows the blame is on Richard and herself, but her mind can't accept that. We will be working on that a lot, and I have faith she will get better. But you need to understand she will never be the woman you remember. Both of you will need to create a new relationship almost from scratch if you want to have a chance at any sort of relationship that isn't adversarial. Sabrina has agreed to try, and the meds will help her think about what she says before she says it. Eventually, she'll create new memory paths in her brain. But it's going to be a long struggle."

"Okay, so how do I help? She's my mom. How could I walk away?"

The therapist paused and looked at Sabrina who nodded stiffly and got up to go stare out the window, her body tense.

"That might be part of the problem. You are the person she has focused all the blame on, and you are the one trying to help her. In many ways she is trying to reconcile two sets of memories and emotions. And the more recent one is winning. I hate to say it, but being with you is hurting her chances to recover."

The emotional punch hurt all the more for expecting it. Ember bowed her head, swallowing hard, trying to make sure her voice didn't shake when she spoke.

"So what do we do?"

"Is there anyone else she can live with? She is functional mostly, and someone without the baggage you bring might be best."

"No, she did this. She should pay." Ember jumped at the sharp words, but the therapist looked at Sabrina her face calm.

"Sabrina, we discussed this. You know this is not good for you. You are allowing the transferred guilt to drive your reactions."

Standing at the window, her mom hunched inward and then shrugged one shoulder, not turning around.

"Family? Anyone?"

"Not really. I have an aunt, her sister. But, I can't get a hold of her."

"Why not?" Lori frowned looking at both of them.

"Seri went on a backpack tour through Tibet and China. She was planning to be out of touch for about six months. I've sent emails, but I can't swear I'm even sending them to the right place. And until the police and lawyers are done with us, I don't have money to put her up anywhere else."

"Seri never liked to be predictable. She'll show up when she does." Sabrina sounded like she didn't care, but Ember heard the pain underneath the words.

"I see." Lori sighed and looked down. "It is going to make this more difficult, but we will try."

Ember wanted to cry. Even by doing everything she could, she was doing the wrong thing.

"I understand. What if I can get her away from me more often? We have a family friend, Cecil. I can ask him to take her out to dinner weekly, maybe even spend time with her? Mom. What do you want?"

Sabrina gave another indifferent shrug. "I don't seem to have much choice in the matter. So I guess I stay with the loser and suffer."

"Sabrina." The word from the doctor was a warning, and Sabrina nodded a bit.

"I like Cecil. He doesn't upset me." Her voice was muffled by the hand covering her mouth.

"I want her to come here twice a week, can you do that?"

She flinched internally at the cost, even at half her rate this was going to eat up money she didn't have. "As long as she wants to come. It is on the bus routes. She has a pass. But it is back in her court."

"Good." Lori shifted her attention to Sabrina. "You hear that? This is up to you. Which means if you quit coming, you are the one that failed. Not her."

If possible, Sabrina's back stiffened even more. "I'll do it. I won't let her beat me."

Lori cocked an eyebrow at Ember. "At this point, if the anger drives her to get help, I'll let it ride. Just don't let her words cut too deep. Underneath is the mother you remember. We just need to get her back in control."

Ember nodded, her throat too tight to speak. She stood up and headed to the door, pausing and waiting to hear Lori and

Sabrina saying their good-byes. She headed out the door, her ears tracking Sabrina behind her.

Once they got in the car and were buckled in, Ember spoke, not looking anywhere but straight ahead.

"I'll keep trying to find Seri, and see if there is anyplace else for you to live."

They drove in silence until there was a whisper from her mother that she had to struggle to hear above the road noise. "Thank you, for everything."

But when Ember glanced over, Sabrina stared out the window, ignoring her existence.

Work on the remodel started out full speed. With everyone on board, and more crew hired, David and Ring both ran their own crews. The laborers got off after eight hours, but Ring usually put in another four hours doing all the little things that he couldn't afford to waste experienced people on. He spent the extra time to pick up the area, order supplies, set the next day's schedule, and watch the budget with an eagle eye. The margins were too narrow for his comfort, but now, not only did his money ride on this, but that of his mother and his friends. Failure was not an option.

Mornings at the bakery were his major bright spot. Jimmy gave him a smile and Ember slipped out to wave or grin at him; those moments were precious. Most evenings they just texted, too exhausted to do much more.

A week before Clay and Greyson would be here, the day ended early. They were out of supplies for the next round of work, so Ring sent everyone home by three and collapsed in his bed, anticipating a nap.

He woke up around seven, his stomach growling. He ached

to see Ember.

busy? Want dinner and company?

you not too tired?

early day. Need some smiles

love to. Where?

bar? Long islands and food?

k, meet you in 20

Just the idea of getting to see her again rejuvenated him. A quick shower, decent clothes, and he walked down to the bar. The streets filled with people going about their day and taking early summer vacations, filling the air with life and noise. At the bottom of the hill, he stopped to look at the hotel.

The terra cotta would arrive next week, so they would be updating all the roofs with the tiles and the accent marks. That had been expensive, but Lincoln, California, still made the best terra cotta in the world, and they had gotten a deal on some accents from molds that hadn't been used in years. The supplier wanted to see how well they still worked. The white had been partially applied and the hotel almost gleamed in the late afternoon sun. When the blue and green accents were applied, it would glow and be inviting at the same time.

He couldn't wait. But right now, he wanted Ember more.

She stood in front of the door to the bar in a simple dress that hugged her generous curves, her hair up in the standard ponytail. It was the first time he had seen her in a dress since that night. The idea of slowly stripping it off of her sounded very good. Letting her know this right now, however, would make him seem worse than Clay.

"Hey, you look nice."

A blush spread across her cheeks as she glanced down. "Thanks. I've lost a bit of weight. A side benefit of heartrending stress, I guess."

The desire to ask her what was going on or how he could help slammed against the back of his teeth, but he didn't. "I understand that. I know my friends are going to spend the first week doing nothing but whine as they get back into the swing of things."

Ember arched an eyebrow as they headed inside, grabbing a booth. "Friends?"

Should he tell her? How did he avoid involving his dad, the sympathy, and everything else? He would tell the truth, the fun parts.

"Friends of mine are coming down to help on the remodel. Be nice to see them. I think you met Clay previously?"

"The one at the bar with you?"

"Yep. That's him."

"Summer work. Good for them." He squirmed a bit. Should he tell her everything? Or just let it be. With a sigh he decided to let it go. No reason to get his hopes up they might have a future when she might leave for Paris any minute. Just grab what he could, while he could.

"Yeah. We are trying to get everything done by the Fourth of July weekend for the grand reopening." They ordered drinks, and food. "So did you hear about the competition and the party?"

Her hands were tight around her glass, holding on to it firmly, like a lifeline. It sent a spasm of worry through him. But there wasn't anything he could do now.

"No. What about it?"

"Something the hotel is running. Remember how much the restaurant sucked?"

She snorted and rolled her eyes. "You could say that."

Ring snickered in response. "Well, when the chef was told about the changes, he threw a hissy fit and quit. Getting someone on board with this is going to take someone who wants it, so they decided to hold a contest."

"A contest? How do you find a chef with a contest?" There was a spark in her at this, something he had missed since that first, glorious night. It made him talk more, his own excitement rising.

"To enter, you have to provide a full menu for the new theme, healthy Med - like you suggested – a business plan on how to order the food and average costs, and a total of ten recipes for the chefs to create: three appetizer, three lunch, and four dinner recipes. All have to be high protein and low in bad carbs and sugar. So the hope is the person who wins will want this."

"I see." Her words were slow, brow furrowed as she sipped on her drink.

"Too bad you never got the chance to go to Cordon Bleu. I bet you would have been great once you got some experience. Cause I know the stuff you're making at the bakery rocks."

"I…" Ember paused and shook her head. "So how are they going to announce the winner?"

"Oh yeah. For the grand reopening, there is going to be a masquerade ball. And we'll announce the winner there. Since it is going to be a blind contest, where we only see the names after the winner is decided, the winner will claim the prize by coming up with their copy of what they submitted. Coming up with a name for the restaurant is part of the contest."

"A ball? Sounds kinda old fashioned."

"Maybe." Ring shrugged. "They were thinking Med style, so lots of masks and togas, etc. Should help get some publicity for the place. Say you'll come? You're the one I want to dance with. I'd go with you in a heartbeat, but I'm going to be working most of the time."

She smiled a bit at his words and he felt his heart leap again. "Why would their construction foreman be working?"

"Meh, just stuff. I'm more of the engineer in charge of this crazy train. But save me a dance." He avoided the question, but made sure the desire to dance with her came through clearly in his voice. Just the memory of the last dance they had could make him lose track of his thoughts.

"If I come, I will."

"I hope so." He wanted to see her smiling and laughing again. She worked too hard.

"Want to go for a walk?"

"Yes." She smiled and stood. "Back to your place. We started this deal with the hope of no-strings sex, and everything has been against us. I'd like to see how you do in a bed this time, and I promise not to fall asleep."

Ring fought for control. The smile made him want to start stripping that dress off her body now. "As you command." His voice dropped to a husky tone. He tossed money on the table for their bill and stood, offering her his hand.

The walk up to the hotel, while not at a run, was direct, and he kept her hand in his, mainly to prevent his hands from wandering a bit too much.

It took forever to get to the hotel room, and he pulled her to him the second the door opened, kissing her hard, his hands running over the body that had been haunting his dreams. Her passion matched his, and his heart radiated joy at the woman in his arms.

Ember pulled back and smiled at him. "Let me run to the bathroom first. I'll be right back." Her smile promised an enjoyable night and he let his eyes linger on her ass as she sashayed into the bathroom, leaving him no doubt she knew that he was watching.

The second the door closed, he sprang into action, pulling back the bed covers to make the bed look inviting and welcoming. He put condoms next to the alarm clock, in easy reach. He stripped down to his briefs, and then fidgeted, trying to figure out how to wait for her, torn between options. Finally, he sat down on the bed, watching the door, waiting for her to come out.

The door opened, and his eyes started at her feet and worked up to run into her dress. Confused, he lifted his eyes up to her face and sprang up as her look of frustration and upset registered.

"Ember, what's wrong? Is everything okay?"

She sighed and leaned back against the door jam, arms crossed, chewing on her lip a bit, and then raised her eyes. "My period started." Her voice was low and she wouldn't meet his eyes.

Disappointment washed through him, and he stood up and walked over to her. She sighed, pulling further into herself.

"Hey, no need for that." Knowing he looked ridiculous in his briefs while she remained fully dressed, he pulled her into his arms. "I take it you didn't know you would be starting?"

She sighed as she mumbled into his shoulder, "It's been stressful lately, and I was never that regular to begin with. I hadn't thought about it much. Too busy, too stressed."

"I take it you can't spend the night with me, so I can hold you?" He mentally crossed his fingers, but knew the answer.

"No supplies." She pulled her head up and looked at him. "You aren't mad?"

"Mad? Why would I be mad? It's part of being a woman. While I fully admit to the eww level of it"—he wrinkled his nose at her and she chuckled—"there is nothing to be mad about. Disappointed, oh hell yes. But never mad."

Ring tilted her head up and kissed her lips with gentle care. "May I walk you home?"

Stiffness he hadn't noticed leaked out of her. "Nah, I'll be good. But I do need to get going." She gave him a bitter twist of her lips. "It started with a vengeance."

He shook his head and kissed her one more time. "I like hanging with you, no matter what the outcome."

The smile she gave him stunned him in its brilliance. He fell asleep thinking about that smile.

Chapter Seventeen

The next day, the idea of her own restaurant kept playing thorough her head. Why hadn't she told Ring she had training: the last two years at the best college in the area for restaurant management, and the last three years as a sous chef in two different restaurants? Cordon Bleu was for the master's program, to raise her skill level so she could work in a world-class restaurant. The question twisted and turned in her head. Eventually she shrugged and let it go. She hadn't told him, so it was done. If it ever came up again, she could. Though she would never forgive her body for starting. It couldn't have waited one more day?

She forced her mind back to the competition. Winning would solve a large number of problems, but could she do this? Should she?

Ideas bounced in her head all day. She had enough attention to smile at Ring as he came in, then she went back to planning recipes, menus, and restaurant renovations in her head.

"Ember." Jimmy shook her shoulder, startling her. "You okay? I've called your name three times."

"Oh, sorry, just thinking about stuff."

"Hmm, well be careful. Being that distracted is dangerous. I'm heading out. See you tomorrow."

"Thanks. Enjoy."

The lights flipped off in the front, and she finished her work in back, still thinking. She gave in, and called Cecil while still standing in the kitchen.

"Hello, *Liebchen*. To what do I owe this honor?"

"Oh, please, you know I usually call to vent or whine."

"True, but you did that yesterday and you rarely repeat yourself."

"Humph. Know it all."

"Why, yes, I do. Your point?"

Ember laughed and told him about the contest. "So, do you think I should enter?"

"Darling, why wouldn't you enter? The most you will be out is the money to print all the stuff twice. Figure seventy-five dollars, worst case, that I can spot you if you need it. If you win, it solves a lot of problems, doesn't it?"

"Oh yeah. That it does. But…"

"But nothing. It is good practice for you, and it might just be the answer you were searching for. And if nothing else, you get to get dressed up and dance with Jordan. Sounds like a win-win to me."

The lascivious tone in his voice made her laugh. "Okay, okay I give. I'll work on it."

"Good girl. I'll come get Sabrina tomorrow. I'll take her and Belinda out the night of the ball if they don't have other plans."

"As always, Cecil, you are my lifesaver."

"Meh, if I have to be a fairy, I might as well be the fairy godfather. Now shoo, I have other things to do beside talk to women."

Ember rolled her eyes and hung up. Once everything was shut down, she headed upstairs to start working on the plan. She could use her laptop and save it to the cloud and print it once she had it done. As always, she checked email to see if Seri had responded, but at this point, she didn't expect it anymore. Ember wondered if she had been killed overseas and they would never learn, or if she had run away from them like most everyone else had.

The pounding on his door at 5:00 AM ripped Ring out of a wonderful dream involving Ember. Annoyed, he staggered to the door and yanked it open, ready to shout at whoever was at his doorstep this early in the morning.

The grinning faces of Clay and Greyson caused his prepared torrent of abuse to vaporize.

"Hey, what are you two doing here so soon?" he said, his voice cracking with sleep.

Clay glanced down at the tent in Ring's boxer shorts. "Happy to see us?" he said, with a smirk on his face.

"Morning, Ring. We finished classes, spent hours packing up everything, and headed on down." Greyson ignored the antics of Clay as he walked in past Ring.

"Yeah, we figured the sooner we got our asses down here to save yours, the sooner we could be making money off this place and proving our parents wrong." Clay grinned, while Greyson just shook his head.

Ring stepped back and let them in. He had moved to the penthouse a few days ago, as they never rented it because it needed upgrading. It had two rooms, one with a king, the other with two doubles, making it perfect for this pair of troublemaking lifesavers.

"So this means you two are ready to work?" His brain let go of the dreams and started to wake up.

"Wait, work?" Clay looked mock horrified. "I thought I was supposed to sit around and tell everyone what they were doing wrong. You mean you expect me to get sweaty and dirty? Maybe I need to rethink this."

Greyson boffed Clay upside the head, and then nodded to Ring. "Yes, we are. Parents shipped my tools to me, so they are in the U-haul. We should be able to do most of the tile work and update the pool area."

Ring once more thanked his lucky stars that not only were his friends rich, but their parents believed they needed to know how to work and made them work in their family businesses from the ground up.

"Well, you got me up about thirty minutes from when I would normally get up. You're crashing in there." He pointed to the bedroom. "Let me get a shower and get dressed, and I'll take you to the best food in the area."

"Coffee?"

"Good coffee. Give me a bit."

"Awesome. I so need caffeine. That drive was a killer."

Tuning out Clay's babble, he headed to the shower, wishing he had time to enjoy the fading effects of that dream. With a sigh, he did his normal morning routine, forgoing momentary pleasure. Ring headed into the seating area after he got dressed, his boots in hand.

"You two going to be able to handle working today?"

Greyson shrugged. "Mostly was going to get a storage unit, unload all our crap, and then get our heads wrapped around what we need to do and set a schedule. So probably no power tools until tomorrow, and an early night."

Clay nodded, a yawn preventing him from adding any color to the conversation.

Ring laughed. It felt so good to have these two back in his life. "Come on. She should just be opening by the time we get down there. We'll grab a table and get food and coffee."

"She?" Clay queried, a gleam in his eyes.

Damn, that was not good.

"The person running the shop. Come on."

With yawns and shivers at the early morning air, they hit the bakery just as Jimmy flipped on the "Open" sign.

"Hey. You're here early, and you've got company."

"Yep, more work for the hotel. They decided to wake me up a bit earlier than normal. I promised them coffee and good stuff."

Jimmy grinned. "We'll give the coffee about another minute or two. It's still brewing, but go take a look. She's got some new things out."

Ring headed up to the counter to look at what the offerings were, and his eyes locked on ham and mushroom mini quiche and a ginger lemon tart.

"These any good?" Greyson was looking at the cinnamon rolls.

"Very good. Trust me."

"Morning, you." Ember's voice pulled him out of his sugar fixation, and he glanced up to see a curious smile on her face. "Get woken up?" She nodded at Clay and Greyson, both who were focusing on the fresh-brewed coffee.

"Yeah. Calvary decided to show up before the crack of dawn."

"At least you have friends that support you. Must be nice." Her voice sounded wistful, and he couldn't help but ask.

"It is. I'm pretty lucky. Surely you have some friends?" He was curious; she never talked about anyone in her life, good or bad.

Ember shrugged. "Not really. I was always too busy with other stuff, and I had my m...," her voice trailed to a stop and she shook her head. "It doesn't matter. Go enjoy your day."

"Working all day and putting up with these two? You're right, it does sound fun." Ring grinned, then leaned closer and dropped his voice, "Going to miss you though."

"Me too. Enjoy, Jordan."

Someday he needed to ask her why she called him by his last name. He wanted to hear her moan his name.

"Jordan. You coming?"

Greyson stood there with the bag of pastries, at least twice what he normally got, and four coffees.

"Yeah. You get enough?" Ring arched his brow at the bag of pastries.

Greyson shrugged. "Smelled good. Long drive."

Clay stuffed his face with one of the cinnamon rolls, her special ones. His eyes were sharp, watching Ember head towards the back.

"She looks familiar. Where have I met her before?"

Ring brushed it off, not wanting to get either of them down that road. "Cause you've been with so many girls they all look familiar at this point?"

"No, it is more than that. That night at the bar. That was the girl you got with the last time we went out, before all this shit happened." Clay snapped his fingers and pointed at Ring.

Ring couldn't help but glance behind him and verify the door had shut, so there was no way Ember could have heard that.

"That's it. She's the plump one, the one you screwed."

Clay's voice had a teasing tone, but Ring saw red. He had Clay up against the wall of a nearby building, his hand around his throat, before either of his buddies had time to react. "Don't ever talk about her that way. She is one of the best things in my life, and if I ever hear something like that come out of your mouth again we are through and I will put you in the hospital."

"Whoa," Clay started to joke. He paused and looked at Ring with a seriousness that rarely graced his face. "You're in love with her. Shit, you're head over heels, forever in love with her."

"What?" Ring pulled away like he had been burned. "No. She's just a friend, someone I can talk to. Who said anything about love?" The idea roiled at the back of his mind. He avoided it and started walking quickly up to the hotel, trying to run from words that hung like glass dust in the air.

"Ring," Greyson's calm logical voice interrupted his

retreat. "You mentioned her. I thought she was headed to Paris. That's why you two didn't hook up again."

"Yeah. She was. Her life blew up like mine. But we don't talk about it. We just enjoy each other. She's smart, funny, sexy, and—" His voice caught as truth slammed into his hindbrain full force. "Oh god, I'm in love with her."

"Told you," Clay crowed, ducking as Greyson's hand swung towards his head, perhaps a bit harder than normal. "What? This isn't a bad thing, you know. So you got a girl. Be nice to have someone else to lean on. You tell your mom yet?"

"No." Ring whirled and faced both of them. "No one knows. It's just us, a safety valve. She doesn't know about Dad and Mom or any of it. She just thinks my life took a shit and I'm working here. You can't tell her. I can't put any extra stress on her. I think most days she is holding on by a thread with what is going on in her life. I'd help if I could, but she wants something that isn't part of it. And I'm going to honor that agreement. So drop it." He didn't recognize his own voice, the pain and need that laced it, and the love that he refused to face.

Both men looked at him, nodding, their faces serious. "Okay, Jordan. She's yours. I won't spill it. But doesn't she deserve to know you love her?" Clay asked, watching with that adult seriousness that reminded Ring of Clay's dad. He was irreverent, and his mouth ran away with him way too often, but moments like this reminded Ring why Clay was one of his best friends.

"Maybe someday. She acts like there is a light at the end of her tunnel. When she reaches it, I'll see if she can find room for me."

Greyson started to walk again. "Tell her before you lose her. You don't love easy, and you've never been one for the causal fling. Unlike Clay."

"What? I just like to have fun. Is that a sin?" Clay walked in silence for a moment and then mock whispered, "So,

Jordan, does she have any friends? I wouldn't mind finding a girl like her."

Ring groaned low and just kept walking. He had thought this was a good idea why?

Ember spent the next week researching recipes on her laptop and thought she had some good contenders, but she needed to cook them to see how to make them sparkle. That required extra money and might end up as inedible dinners.

Making every penny scream, she had brought home some salmon, zucchini, and the cheapest bacon she could find. Luckily, she had cleaned out their kitchen when they moved, taking every bit of seasoning, the cooking utensils, and the pantry supplies with them.

One night, she presented to Belinda and Sabrina her first dish, salmon sautéed in a balsamic and bacon reduction, served over flash-boiled julienned zucchini. Everything was topped with the reduction. Low fat, low sugar, high fiber, and with luck, high taste. Each of them got a two-ounce piece, and she had written down every step.

Setting it down in front of her mom and sister, she held her breath as both of them tried it. She hoped for truth, not ugliness.

She ate, eyes closed, analyzing the taste, texture, and scent of the meal. It tasted okay, but she felt like it lacked something, something to make it sparkle. Steeling herself, she opened her eyes and looked at the other two. It couldn't have been too bad; both of them had almost cleaned their plates.

Trying not to sound meek, she asked, "What did you think?"

"I liked it. Better than what we've been eating, that's for

sure." Belinda's eye roll made her snicker. She turned to look at Sabrina, biting her lip.

She watched her mother struggle to respond. The therapist had made a difference, and going out regularly with Cecil, who called her on her attitude every single time, also helped. Ember dared to hope.

"Better than that dog food you've been serving us. Though that isn't saying much." Sabrina's hand trembled as she reached for her water, and Ember saw her teeth sink into her bottom lip as she tried, tried so hard to not let out the anger seething inside.

"Thanks," Ember said, aching as she watched the struggle. "I'll clear."

Sabrina all but fled the table, and Belinda hobbled off, moving better every day. Ember needed to be exposed to more food, taste what other places were doing so she knew how to compete and beat them, but how?

A day or so later, Cecil had taken her mom out for dinner, and Belinda was at her therapist and trainer, keeping up her strength while her leg finished healing.

She stared at her menu and plan. The plan was solid, a repeat of the application that had won her the scholarship, but the menu had some major holes in it. Frustrated, she closed the laptop with a click. The lack of access to high-quality food ingredients was killing her. She could guess, and knew enough to get pretty close, but without cooking it, she couldn't figure out what to tweak to make it unique. Part of cooking for her was the smell, the sound of the food cooking, telling her what to do next.

Her phone chirped and, anxious for a distraction, she picked it up.

hey, you go plans? was the first text.

got plans? followed it up almost immediately.

Ember grinned, her mood lifting instantly.

nope. What up?

friends wanna get to know u. Want dinner?

Why did they want to get to know her? That idea sent ripples of concern and excitement through her.

where?

they're paying. Can afford trust me. Make them pay good

She snickered at that. It sounded like someone was a bit annoyed at his friends. But, he had mentioned they were well-off. Maybe they wouldn't mind the splurge. There was a place about twenty miles up the coast that did a Med/Italian mix. Maybe she could go there and talk them out of bites of their plates too.

Le Chantrelle?

good choice, and they can drive and buy the wine we can drink

pick me up at bakery?

yes - be there shortly

Her mood changed with that sentence and she sprung up, pulling on one of her few decent dresses and her Spanx. She took a minute to do her hair back in a French braid and put on some light makeup. At least she had shaved her legs this morning, so she just had to pull on sandals and she headed out the door.

She walked down the sidewalk and sat on the bench, realizing she had no idea what car they might be driving. She half shrugged; she'd figure it out, or they would.

A dark red SUV pulled up and Jordan jumped out of the back. Her smile widened, and she felt her heart speed up as she looked at him. The desire to just crawl into his arms and stay there forever pulled at her.

"Hi, ready?"

Fighting not to blurt out something overtly sexual, she stood and waved her hands at herself. "As ready as you're getting on this short notice."

Jordan helped her in and zipped around to climb in the other side.

"You realize you just cost me alcohol tonight?" Clay griped as he put the vehicle in motion.

"And how exactly did I cost you anything?" The man-boy amused her, all fun and games. There had to be more to him, if Jordan had him as a friend.

"I bet you wouldn't be ready and we'd have to wait for you. Greyson said you'd be waiting for us. How was I to know you weren't going to spend hours primping?"

Should she be hurt or not? Ember weighed both emotions, realizing she didn't care what people thought anymore. She had too much going on in her life to give a damn about the social niceties any more.

"Not my fault you're an arrogant boy. So, I'd say you should be driving, as obviously you aren't old enough to drink."

"Ouch." Ring laughed. "You so deserved that Clay. That's why I keep her around."

"Sure, rub it in, Jordan. Just cause you win the girl lottery. You found someone who's smart, pretty, and an excellent cook." Clay winked at her in the rearview mirror, letting her know he teased. "How come I can't get that lucky?"

Clay pouted, pointing to his pout. Ember rolled her eyes.

"I'm not a lottery ticket either. Believe me, money would solve a lot of problems."

"Such as?" Greyson spoke this time.

Ember shied away from that topic of conversation; she didn't want tonight tainted with reality. "Just life. You know sometimes it sucks. So do you know how to get there?"

"GPS for the win." Clay patted the screen in the vehicle that she now realized showed the directions. "So what made you want to try this place?"

Having her desire to compete revealed didn't sound wise, so she compromised.

"Jordan mentioned that they were going to do a new restaurant that had a Med flavor. Thought it might be nice to go to one so there's something to compare to."

She watched Clay's eyes in the rearview mirror and he frowned for an instant while she spoke.

"That sounds like a great idea. I have to admit, other than Kalamata olives, which I'm not that big of a fan of, I don't think of anything when I think Med food," Jordan replied with a thoughtful tone.

"See. Good company, hopefully good food, and someone else paying for it. What more can you ask for?" Ember said, a smile on her face, watching the boys.

"Women. I tell you, they're all alike," Clay joked.

Before he could continue, Ember finished for him, "The good ones won't have anything to do with you, and the bad ones just want to use you."

Greyson broke out in laughter. "I like her. She puts Clay in his place."

All of the men chuckled and the conversation drifted to the next part in the remodel, putting in the new mosaic floor in the entryway. Apparently, Greyson was in charge of that. He had some ideas about how to use smaller and cheaper tile to create a warm feeling as you walked in. He described it so eloquently she could see it in her mind and couldn't wait to see it in person.

"You guys are boring. You have a woman in the car, and all you talk about is work? Luckily we're here, so I can focus on the charming lady in our midst while you keep on with your boring talk."

"One, she is my lady if anything. And two, I'm pretty sure she'll make her own choices," Jordan protested as he smiled at her

The smile struck her as both hopeful and wary. Ember rolled her eyes. Clay had better lighten up the bullshit a bit, or she might snap and kill him before the entrees were served. At this point, she reserved her patience for family and work. Though, to be honest, Jordan had never required it before now.

With a smirk at Clay, Ember took Jordan's offered arm as they walked to the door. Greyson held it open, with a twitch of his lips. Delight filled her at their antics, and for the first time in oh so long, she felt like a person, someone people enjoyed being with, not the caretaker.

Ember mulled this over as they were seated. That was not true. Jordan never made her feel that way. Always, he focused on her, to the exclusion of all else. Having two other men do the same thing went to her head. And she loved it. Even Clay, who obviously was being a bit over the top, attempted to get her to laugh. She suspected the act hid a man who cared deeply about certain things but didn't want anyone to know.

Pulling her thoughts back to where they needed to be, here and now, she looked around the restaurant, taking in the color schemes and the way it was laid out. It struck her as dark and bland. The colors didn't bring to mind the light and ocean the way it should when you thought of Mediterranean. She pulled up the menu, letting the boys' conversation wash over her

The menu was… okay. Nothing that grabbed her, but there were a few entrées that might have promise. She knew she would need daily specials to match what was available locally. There were at least three things she wanted to try but how?

She leaned over towards Jordan a bit, lowering her voice, "Hey, there are a few things I want to try. I'm dying for some exotic flavors. You interested in any of these, and mind splitting a plate?"

Before he could respond, Greyson interrupted. "I have to admit there are three or four things I'd like to sample, too, but not sure I want a full meal of it. What if we all order something, and ask them to serve it family style so we can all take samples."

"Oh, could we please?" The idea thrilled her, and she

turned her smile on Greyson, whom she thought blushed.

"Sure, means none of us are stuck with something that we don't like."

"I'm game. So what wine would you like with dinner, Ember?" Clay asked, handing her the wine list.

Curious, she opened it and flinched at the prices. She hadn't thought about wine. She didn't know enough about wine to even start to create a wine list. Her heart quailed at the prices. Affording even one bottle would be out of the question. A wave of terror struck her and she had to lay down the menu before anyone could see her hand shaking. How could she do a plan well enough if she left out the wine menu? It would be another check mark against her and her entry.

"You order. I don't know enough about wines to say one way or another."

"I'm a beer man," Jordan said. "I'll drink wine, but Greyson here is the sommelier."

She caught the tolerant look on Greyson's face as he picked up the listing. "I'll order. I can educate you a bit if you're interested."

"Please?" It had been a class she'd been excited about taking in Paris, but for now she would take any information she could get. As she turned back, she caught a dark look on Jordan's face, and a thrill took her breath away. He was jealous. No one had ever been jealous over her before. The terror broke apart in the face of delight at someone wanting her that much.

She leaned close to him and whispered in his ear, "I like your friends. But you're the one I want to go home with."

His face lit up, and his eyes darkened looking at her, and she had to force herself to swallow, as suddenly food didn't sound that important.

"Okay, what did she whisper that made you look like you wanted to take her on the table? I'm jealous; I never get girls to whisper the good stuff to me."

Jordan just smiled at Clay. "That is for me to know, and you to never know," he said, his tone smug as his hand squeezed hers under the table.

Ember giggled at the pout on Clay's face. The sound surprised her. She couldn't remember the last time she'd giggled.

The waiter came back, and Greyson ordered two bottles of wine, both of which she recognized. She paled a bit at the idea of spending that much money on wine, but tonight she would enjoy.

They argued for a few more minutes about what dishes to order, and finally they settled on four, three of which were the ones that Ember was curious about. The waiter came back with the wine, and after presenting them, they explained their request. After a moment's conversation with the manager, it was arranged.

"Listen up, Philistines," Greyson commanded, and Ember fought a laugh again as both Jordan and Clay adopted "who, me?" expressions. "This is a Zinfandel from California." With that Greyson launched into an informed and hilarious discussion of the two wines he had ordered. Ember drank up every bit of it. She knew how much she didn't know.

Sipping her wine and searching for the hints of fruit Greyson had talked about, she watched them and envied their obvious friendship.

"So how long have you known each other?"

"Freshman year of college," Jordan answered promptly. "These two poor rich boys were looking for someone who wouldn't try to borrow money from them, and they found me."

"Yeah, he didn't borrow money. Just the car, laptop, stereo system, plane tickets to visit," Clay teased.

"Hey, you offered them." Jordan laughed. "Clay here is the son of an oilman who believes in working your way up. So

Clay was glad of any excuse to get out of some of the labor that holidays and summer breaks usually consisted of."

"Didn't work," Clay said, a disgusted look on his face. "No, Mr. I've-Never-Worked-On-an-Oil-Rig-Before thought it was a blast and worked all summer with me. I broke my finger because of him."

"What, did you pinch him on the ass?" The comment slipped out before she could stop it. Her eyes' widened and she set down the glass of wine. Being this giddy one glass in was not good.

Greyson laughed and winked at her. "Nah. But the summer he came and stayed with me, you should have heard Clay whining. My dad runs one of the biggest construction companies in Wyoming and has the same philosophy as Clay's dad. So we worked doing everything and learning almost every aspect of the labor part of the business."

Jordan smiled, his eyes on her. "We had fun. And as much as Clay likes to laugh it up, he works hard and is damn good. So, yeah. I'm lucky to have these two as friends. Heck, they gave up their summer to come help me."

"That is rather rare. Trust me, I know how precious friends who stay and help are." She sensed the curious looks and realized the other two would not abide by the agreement. Just then the waiter came with their food, rescuing her, much to her relief.

The servers laid the food out family style and Ember dropped out of the conversation to sample, taste, and think. When she refocused on the here and now, all three men were staring at her.

"What?" She used her napkin to wipe her mouth, looking at them confused.

"I don't believe I've ever seen a woman pay that much attention to food before." There was an odd note of reverence from Greyson. He watched her as he said this, making her shift in her chair.

"Does she pay that much attention to you in bed?" Clay's eyes were alight with something more than mischief and Ember felt her face heat.

Jordan just grinned and turned his attention back to his food.

Ember paid attention to the men for the rest of dinner, but kept her thoughts on what she had learned about the food in the back of her mind. She was determined to make her recipes better than what they served here.

When they dropped her off, Jordan got out too. "You sure we can't take you home?"

"I live right near here, so I'm fine."

He cast a glance around the near buildings, frowning at her, then he sighed and let it go. "Can't you trust me by now?" he said, a plaintive note in his voice.

Ember jerked her eyes up to his and touched his arm. "I do, trust you that is. But..." She trailed off and closed her eyes. "I can't let you see the ugliness in my life right now. It isn't a secret; I just don't want what we have to be tainted."

Jordan looked at her and smiled. "I understand, I do. But be warned, I'm going to kiss you, and I'm not going to stop until Clay makes a totally inappropriate remark to embarrass us."

"Oh, I think I can live with that." Her mouth curved in a smile, even as he pulled her close, wrapping strong arms tight around her.

Mint from the candy he had snagged walking out flavored the kiss, and she pulled him even closer. Her stress, worries, and memories disappeared, and all she felt were his hands on her body, his lips hot against hers, the feeling of his hair as she raked her fingers through it. One leg rose to wrap around his waist, to pull him even closer when the wolf whistle broke through her haze of desire.

"Yowza. Here on the street? I didn't realize you had such

an exhibitionist streak." Clay's voice broke the spell and they parted. Her heart raced and she saw the same reaction in Jordan, both of them wanting to continue.

"Night. I'll see you in the morning." Her voice was husky with need. He nodded, dropping a kiss on her forehead.

"Night." Jordan pulled at his jeans and moved stiffly to the car. The knowledge of how she affected him let her fall asleep, a smile on her passion-swollen lips.

Chapter Eighteen

Ring yawned. Twelve-hour workdays, with snatches of time talking to Ember, made for a boring life. Yet seeing the hotel revitalized in front of his eyes made it all worth it. The spring in his step wasn't caused by the work they had done on the hotel, however. He had a date with Ember that evening. Nothing major, walking down to the beach and talking. Ring had grabbed a bottle of wine, the same Zinfandel she had liked so much at the restaurant, and it waited in his room for them. Greyson and Clay were going down the coast to a club. They had invited him, and he had just smiled and shaken his head. Maybe luck would be with him, and this time they could end up in bed naked — together.

Walking into the shamble of ongoing construction that resembled his lobby, he zeroed in on Greyson fighting with the tile saw. They had rerouted the incoming guests – not that there were many – to the concierge area and were hoping to get the entire lobby retiled in three days.

"Hey. Problems?"

Greyson looked up, a snarl of frustration on his normally serene countenance. "Yes. Damn thing keeps choking. I've checked everything and the water isn't feeding correctly. It keeps cutting out and I don't know why."

"Do we need to get a new one?" Ring looked a bit worried. David was working on placing grout down for the whole pieces, but the entire design rested on the ability to cut the pieces to the sizes they needed.

"No. I just need to tear it apart and put it back together, making sure everything is cleared. Would you go unplug it for me, so I can tear it apart?"

"Sure." Ring walked the few feet from where Greyson was kneeling and glanced at the cord. "Greyson, did you know it was frayed here?" He bent to pick it up. The saw fired up, he heard tile explode, and a burn ripped into his stomach.

"What happened?" Ring spun and saw Greyson covered in tiny cuts as he flipped the saw off.

"Dammit. Apparently when you picked it up that made the connection. Damn thing fired off." Greyson snorted in disgust at the tiny wells of blood on his arms and reached up to his face, pulling off his safety glasses. He looked at the blood on his hands. "Damn, that could have been bad."

Both of them looked around, but they had walled the area off with tarp, and no one else had been touched. Ring sighed and pulled the cord from the wall outlet, wincing a bit at a sudden pain in his side. Maybe he had pulled something.

He brushed it off and walked back to Greyson, focused more on how to deal with this new issue. "Okay, go get a new one. We don't have time to repair the cord on this."

"We can rent. Cheaper. I'll drop this to get repaired." Greyson stood, then paused and looked at him funny. "You okay?"

"Yeah. Why?"

"You just look pale." Greyson's eyes flicked down to his jeans. "Did you get cut?"

"Don't think so." Ring shook his head glancing at his arms. He had dust, a few nicks on his arms, but no major cuts. "Why?"

"What is that on the top of your jeans? Near your left front pocket?" The worry on Greyson's face made him feel odd.

Ring glanced down and patted his dark navy T-shirt, and a bolt of pain sliced through him. Shocked, he pulled up his hand and looked at it. There was a smear of red across the middle of it. Confused he pulled up his shirt, revealing an embedded shard of tile about two inches wide sticking out of his abdomen. "Oh, I might be in trouble."

His voice sounded faint and far away. The world started to spin. He reached for the shard, intending to pull it out.

"Stop." The command had him freezing as he lifted heavy eyes to look at Greyson, who had paled and moved towards him, pulling a phone out as he did. "Sit down and don't touch it."

"Need pull out. Not 'posed to have things in you." Thinking was difficult and the world started to spin. Strong arms wrapped around him.

"Sit, Ring, I got you." Greyson lowered him to the ground as he talked on the phone.

"911? I need an ambulance at the Del Mar." He rattled off the hotel address. Ring heard him talking from a distance. "Construction accident, tile shard pierced abdomen. Need assistance immediately."

"No, can't go hospital. Have date." Ring struggled to sit up, but Greyson held him firm.

"I'll tell her. You're going to miss that date, Ring. I think you need to get to a hospital now."

"No." Ember was important. But he couldn't remember why, just the image of her face in his mind, and that everything was better near her.

Next thing he knew, someone tapped his face lightly. "Sir? Sir, can you hear me?"

"Yeah." At least he thought he said that.

"Can you tell me your name?"

"Hal Jordan, I'm the Green Lantern." He felt the grin on his face and couldn't figure out why he was so happy.

He recognized Greyson's voice. "His name is Ring Jordan. He's twenty-three. The Green Lantern thing is a joke between him and a friend, who always calls him Jordan, cause he's just as nice of a guy as Hal Jordan is. Even got him a ring to wear for fun."

"Okay, sir. We need to get him to the hospital. We don't know how big that shard is or how far it goes in. Good thing you didn't move it."

That sounded wrong to Ring. He knew that it needed to be removed and reached for it again.

"Shit. Strap him down. He pulls that out and it could make everything worse."

The last thing he remembered, the floor moved as he floated out the door.

The evening with the boys kept her smiling off and on days later. She couldn't wait to see him tonight and hoped that tonight maybe they could both get some adult exercise. She had to fight a grin, almost bouncing. The bakery had been busier than usual today, and it took a bit for Ember to register her phone ringing.

"Hey, Ernie, how are you doing?"

"Pretty good. And I have to say you are burning up the place. From the numbers I have in front of me now, you should get an extra eight hundred in this next check."

That amount would pay off the COBRA and keep her bank account stable for another month. She still wasn't sure what to do about a dress that would meet the requirements for the ball.

"That sounds great. So how is the recovery going?" The idea of extra money helped, and if something else would just break free, they might make it.

"Actually, that was what I wanted to talk to you about today." Her stomach and throat tightened up, and stress flared. "My recovery is going so well the doctors say I can go back to work in about three weeks. So I figured I'd start back up the Monday after the 4th of July. It would be just part time for about a month, but then I should be back to full time."

The gut punch had her grabbing the wall and leaning against it, trying to not break down and not pass out.

"I see. That's great." Her voice wavered a bit, as she tried to keep the bile down.

"Now I want you to know the apartment is yours as long as you want it. Just cover the utilities. It wasn't being used anyhow and what you've done to it will make it marketable when you don't need it anymore. And I'd like to buy a few of your recipes from you to use. I can see how popular they are. It's still three weeks away, but then you'll be free. Thank you so much for all the hard work you've done, Ember. You've been a complete lifesaver."

"No problem. Call me when it gets closer so I can start making arrangements."

"Will do. Thanks gain."

Ernie hung up and Ember leaned against the wall, her pulse throbbing in her temples and eyes burning. Three weeks. The party and award of the job took place the day before the Fourth, and she had to turn in her application in the next three days to make the deadline. Her mind whirled as she tried to think of anything else, but she was still trapped. The light she had seen at the end of the tunnel vanished like a will-o'-wisp in a swamp.

"Hey, Ember, you okay?"

She looked up to see Jimmy standing there looking at her, concern etched on his face. "Yeah. Just taking a breather. Your dad says he should be back part time in about three weeks."

"Ah. Okay. See, you know more than I do. Too bad. You're more fun to work with." Jimmy smiled at her and headed out to finish up the closing duties.

She gathered her composure the same way she pulled out ingredients, one strand at a time. She had a chance. Or, she would figure something else out. No other options but forward. The fractures in her heart that had started to heal cracked anew.

Forcing herself to redirect on work, she started getting ready for tomorrow's baking.

"Is Ember here?"

The familiar voice echoed into the back where she hid, and it pulled her out of her fretting. Not Jordan's voice, but one of his friends. She stuck her head out to see Greyson standing there, covered in dust and bits of dried blood.

"Hey, Greyson." His gray face and the lines at the corner of his mouth changed what she started to say. "Is everything okay?" She looked around, hoping for Jordan to stick his head in.

"There was an accident at the hotel. He's been hurt."

Oh god, not him too. She couldn't handle anymore, and the world started to spin. One more person she loved being taken from her one way or another. Love. She loved him. That knowledge struck the final blow, and her world went dark.

"Ember, Ember, you okay?"

She wrenched open eyes and looked up to see Greyson and Jimmy standing over her, worried looks on their faces. She nodded, unsure, and they helped her up from the floor and into a chair.

"Is he gonna die?" If he died, she was becoming a nun. This caring just hurt way too much.

Greyson blinked a surprised look on his face. "Not unless something goes wrong. He said you two had a date tonight. He isn't going to make it. I suspect they'll keep him overnight, but I'm guessing. He lost a lot of blood and was acting super weird, but I don't think it is life threatening." He swallowed and grabbed for a chair to sit on. "I hope not. Cause if it is, I'll have killed one of my best friends."

Ember and he just stared at each other. Jimmy broke the tableau by putting hot coffee, made just the way each of them took it, in their hands.

"Drink, it will help with the stress and shock. Can she go see him yet?"

Greyson sipped, and some color seeped back into his face. "I don't think so. They mentioned they were going to take him to surgery. I called his mom, and Clay went to get her. And I came here."

Ember had to concentrate to not crush the cup that held her coffee. A burn right now would add insult to injury.

"Okay. Do you think they'll let me see him tomorrow?" She looked up at Greyson, trying to deal with the knowledge that she loved Jordan and he was in the hospital. She hated hospitals. Something flickered in his eyes.

"I'll make sure of it. I'll call you tomorrow with the hospital information."

"Okay." Her voice sounded dull. All she wanted to do was curl into a ball.

"Ember?"

"Yes?" She felt mired in molasses and everything took more energy than she possessed.

"I need your number." His voice was sheepish. "His phone is with him, and I don't know how to get a hold of you. Warning though, Clay will grab it from my phone as soon as he knows I have it."

"Oh. That's fine. Give me your number and I'll text you."

He rattled it off, and she sent a text without thinking about it, her mind still swirling with the double punch.

"I've got to go. I swear if anything bad happens, I'll let you know. Call him tomorrow. He should be awake and be able to talk."

"Okay. Thanks, Greyson. And thanks for not sending Clay. If he made a joke, I might have done something inappropriate." She tried to smile at the jest.

A half smirk crossed his face. "Trust me, decking Clay is always appropriate. But he's loyal and will move the world for you once he decides he's your friend. Regardless of what you want."

Ember sensed a story in there, but now was not the time. "Thanks. I need to finish up here, but I'll go see him tomorrow." She couldn't stop herself, needing the reassurance, the knowledge of having fallen for him still shaking her up badly. "Are you sure he'll want to see me?"

Greyson smiled, a full warm smile that surprised her somehow. He was normally so serious. "I'm sure if you don't go see him, he'll crawl down here to see what is wrong with you."

"Oh." The knot of stress in her stomach slipped loose, and she started to plan something special to take with her for him.

"I'll see you later, Ember. I've got to get back to the hotel and get that damn tile cutter replaced."

Not sure what he was talking about, she just nodded. "Thanks again."

He left and she stared blankly at the floor, fixated on the dirt he had tracked in.

"Ember, go home."

"Huh?" She looked up into Jimmy's smiling face.

"You've had enough shocks today. I can finish. I might not enjoy it as much, but I can do it."

Gratitude filled her but she shook her head. "I need to work. It will keep me busy. If I go home I'm just going to stew and that won't be good right now. Thanks for everything."

Jimmy just ducked his head and finished cleaning up. She headed to the back, her mind whirling.

Chapter Nineteen

"Would someone shut that infernal beeping off?" Ring croaked out, then winced at how badly speaking hurt. A whimper slipped out when he swallowed. His throat felt as if he had breathed sandpaper for a week.

"Here, drink this, it will help." It was his mother's voice, and that made it less stressful to be here. Turning his head didn't hurt as much as swallowing did, though he hurt in places he didn't understand. His mother held out a glass with a straw in it. Sipping the water sent heaven cascading down his throat.

"Why throat hurt?" He still croaked, though not quite as raspy. "Remember bleeding from stomach or side?"

"They had to operate."

He quirked his eyebrow. The action was so much easier than talking.

"The tile shard pierced your stomach and went right in between your intestines. They had to go in and flush it out and verify you didn't nick or perforate your bowels. Docs said you were damn lucky." Her voice cracked a bit on those words.

Ring just pointed at his throat.

"Operation — they intubated you. It should fade in a day or so. The nurse said he'd be back to give you something for the pain in a bit."

"Home?"

"Tomorrow. As it is, just stitches. You'll be sore for a few days, but should be fine in a week or so. Light duty for the next week." She smiled, a grin that made Ring lean back against his bed in fear. "So you can help review all the business plans, menus, and recipes."

"Crap." It was worth the pain. He hated reviewing business plans, almost as much as he hated writing them.

"Don't give me that. You at least have experience doing this in college. Greyson and Clay informed me it was a regular class exercise to write and review other people's plans. And you know how to read a good plan versus a bad one. So suck it up."

And here he thought he had friends. Friends wouldn't do this to him. But the barely visible tremor in his mom's hand as she handed him the glass and the crack in her voice told him it hadn't been a minor surgery. He could suffer if it made her feel better.

"Kay." He took another grateful sip.

"So, on another topic." The smug tone brought his eyes up to her face, and he grew even more worried. That was matchmaker smug. "A very nice young lady named Ember called your phone. I answered, of course, concerned it was something about the hotel." She tried to smile, but he saw the quiver on the edge of her lips.

Ring rolled his eyes at his mom, who just smiled more, the quiver fading.

"She calls you Jordan, which I found odd, but didn't comment on. Mentioned Greyson telling her you were hurt and that she was checking to see if you were accepting visitors. I told her yes, in a few hours. But what I find most interesting is Greyson, having just delivered you to the hands of the paramedics, took the time to let her know you were injured. So exactly who is she?"

Ring just pointed at his throat and kinda shrugged. He knew it was a wasted effort, but he had to try anyhow.

"Nice try. Spill. Who is she and why do Clay and Greyson know her, and I don't?"

Maybe he would pass out now? He waited for rescue then

sighed when he remained lucid. There was never unconsciousness when you needed it.

"Met her at a club before Dad." He croaked it out, wincing at each word. The miracle of running into her again was still too fragile. And the knowledge that he had to figure out how to keep her ate at the back of his mind.

"And?"

"Won scholarship to Paris, was leaving." Talking hurt, and the pain increased the more he talked. He noticed her expression soften slightly, but knew he had to finish up, the barest essence at least. "Life blew up. Work at bakery. Makes new stuff."

"Ah ha. She is the one responsible for those delicious things you've been bringing in. I wondered when Ernie had decided to get creative." Monica fell silent and looked at him and he squirmed a bit, wanting to avoid whatever she was about to say.

"I'm glad she makes you happy. And it sounds like you're doing the same for her."

His jaw dropped, as she didn't pry and pull, and she started to laugh.

"Darling. You like, maybe even love her. And since you're way too similar to your father, in that he saw me and fell head over heels, I'm not going to do anything to damage this. If it works out, if she is the right one, you'll introduce us when you're ready. But I'll tell you this much. I like her already. You've been glowing lately. I thought it was the hotel, but it's her. She obviously knows that the way to a man's heart is via food, so she's smarter than I was. I used sex."

"Mom," Ring croaked in horror. The last thing he wanted was to hear about his parent's sex life.

The laughter that filled the room made it all worth it. She hadn't laughed like that in way too long. "We did make you, you know. And we even had sex more than once."

He cringed backwards and was rewarded with more

laughter. Cracking open his eyes, he saw that some of the stress on her had dropped off. If it made her feel better he'd listen to every gory detail. And then promptly get drunk enough to forget it all.

"Thank you, dear. I'll go. I told her to be here around four, as the doctors said you should be awake around two. I'll send the nurse in with some pain killers." She leaned over and kissed his cheek. "Be more careful. I've buried one of the men in my life. I don't want to bury the other."

She left in a brisk manner, and he watched, glad to see more life in her than he had seen in a while. The nurse slipped in and handed him some pills, which he took eagerly.

Ring laid back and waited for the pain to fade, too confused and tired to concentrate on much of anything.

The gentle squeeze on his hand pulled him back into the real world. He blinked, trying to focus, and Ember's face swam into view.

"Hey." It was still a croak, but it didn't hurt as much this time. And the half smile on her face made it worth it.

"You know, if you wanted me to bring you breakfast in bed, asking would have been much easier." Her tone teased, but he saw the lines of worry around her eyes.

"I'll remember that next time." He bit back things he wanted to say, his eyes roving over her face and wishing he could find out all her secrets and save her. Clay's accuracy about his Prince Charming complex tended to be disturbing.

"I brought you something. Do you know if you can eat?" Her voice was soft as her pale eyes watched him, and what he wanted to do involved curling up with her for the next week, or year.

It took him a minute to process the words. "I think so. They asked me what I wanted for lunch. I think I'm getting a sandwich."

Ember wrinkled her nose. "With your luck it would be

icky white bread and processed meat. I made food today with you in mind." She reached down on the floor and brought out two things wrapped in wax paper.

"This one is a remake of the apple cheddar one. I added some more savory spices, and added asiago to the dough." She pointed to the other one. "This one is a new mix, egg bread with spinach, cheese, and minced ham to give it protein."

Just unwrapping the paper released scents that made his mouth water. He looked at her and wondered how you asked someone to be with you for the rest of your life when you didn't even know her last name. That thought made him flinch and swallow hard. The resulting pain pushed the thought away.

"Smells awesome. So you are going to the party right?" He tried to keep the hope out of his voice, but it cracked on the last word; he figured his need would be obvious.

"I'm going to try. Have some things going on causing complications." She flashed him a smile. "And you getting hurt was one more I didn't need."

"I'll be fine. And I'm getting dressed up." Anything to get her to come see him.

"I see. I'm trying, I promise." She glanced at her watch. "I have to go. Come see me as soon as you get out okay? Or call if you're going to stay and I'll come see you again. And rescue you from hospital food."

"Okay." She leaned over, kissed him on the cheek, and headed out. His eyes never left her form, and the room seemed darker when the door closed behind her.

He wanted that woman, forever, and this time the knowledge seemed right.

Even with the distraction of Jordan getting hurt, she finished her entry, the menu polished and the recipes tested as much as she could. She was pretty sure they were better than what had been served at the restaurant, and were good for you and cost effective. The wine she faked, adding a note about local vineyards and setting up purchases for Californian wines. Now she needed to print, submit, and get a dress. That was the sticking point. Cecil had gifted her money to get it all professionally printed, but it was a masquerade ball. What was she supposed to wear?

The problem ate at her all day as she tried to figure out a way out. Not to mention the fact that this was a shot in the dark. She was an unknown, with no credentials behind her name. The odds of them selecting her were astronomical. She needed to keep working on other options, find other ways out.

An invisible clock ticked in her mind, counting down so many things. Time until Belinda needed to be training full time to prepare for competition. Time until her job would disappear. Time until she couldn't juggle all of this anymore. Time until she lost Jordan.

The clocks created havoc in her mind and she had to fight to keep it together. She had to try this because at this point she didn't know what else to do. Checking the email one more time, hoping for something from her aunt, the lawyers, something to give her a path out, the answer didn't change. Nothing. Swallowing, she headed down to the bakery and prepared to give up part of herself again.

Prep and getting the morning going was automatic, as she mentally prepped for her talk to Jimmy.

The click of the lock and the ring of the bell told her he was here. It was now or never.

"Hey, Jimmy. You got a minute?" she asked as she walked out into the main area.

"Always? How goes it? How's Jordan?"

"Okay. He said he'd be back to work next week, but just supervising for the first few days." She cleared her throat and forced herself to look him in the eye. "I don't know what your dad told you about my situation, but I'm in a bit of a bind."

Jimmy sat down and looked at her, his normally amused-at-life look absent. "He said you'd had a bit of bad luck and were taking care of your mom and sister that were hurt in an accident. And since you needed a place to stay you were trading it for salary and the old apartment."

Ember shrugged and sat down. "Mostly correct. Because of the accident and the police saying my dad was drunk driving and killed someone, everything is locked up. We can't get to any accounts that had his name associated with it, due to the lawsuit the other driver filed. My parents had just sold the house and the new buyers were moving in, so we had to leave. I had some savings, but he had the health insurance. With the accident, I couldn't afford to not keep paying the premiums, which for three people is a lot of money. Like over a thousand a month. "

He whistled. "Ouch. But even so, with what Dad is paying you, you should be doing okay."

"Um. No. He is paying me five hundred a month. I worked out a deal with him to get some of the extra money from the new things I've been making, so it's almost up to 1k a month. But still not enough to pay for food, doctors' visits, etc." She shrugged and was about to start talking again when the funny look on Jimmy's face caught her attention. "What?"

"Ember, I love my dad. He is a good guy and will help anyone who asks. But to say he is a cheapskate is an understatement. He hired me because I'm his child and he pays my insurance for me because I am a student. He doesn't have to pay workers comp or insurance for me. And since you are a contractor that is being paid per the profits, he saves money there. I know he is clearing over two thousand a week on this place. And he owns all of it. Most of the other people he approached were demanding on average six thousand a month. Which would have been close to half of his profits. With your new stuff, he's now clearing over three thousand a week. After everything is taken out. He's totally taking advantage of you."

The numbers were a slap and her mind spun as she thought back to the original conversation. She had been so grateful for the place to live and any money, she never thought about making a counteroffer. She'd been desperate to just find a place to go and some time to find her balance.

"Oh. I didn't know." She felt flat, rolled out.

"Obviously. So if you weren't asking about that, what were you going to ask?"

She stuttered, trying to wrap her mind around everything that she had just learned. "I'm going to compete in the contest up at the hotel for the new chef. I've got the entry ready and a friend gave the money to get it printed up and sent off. But, I need a dress for the masquerade ball, as that is where they will be announcing the winner." She shifted almost backing out, but plowed ahead. "I was wondering if I could have the tip money for a day or so, so I could try to get a dress that might be passable for the ball."

Jimmy laughed. "Ember, you have to be the nicest person I've ever met. Yes, you can have the tip money. And after my classes tonight, I'm going home and ripping my dad up one side and down the other and bringing my mom in on it. I can't guarantee you will start getting paid more, but I'm going to try my best." He stood up shaking his head. "Your baking is incredible, better than Dad's, and I hope you win. Cause I know I'd be eating there if you were the chef."

The support just about overwhelmed her, and she started to think that maybe she could have the sort of support system Jordan seemed to have. Just because her family had poor taste in friends previously, didn't mean everyone was like that. And that maybe it was time to give the lawyers and the cops another kick in the pants. Maybe. The next three weeks would give her enough time to figure things out.

"Thanks, Jimmy. You can't know what this means."

"I have an idea. Now let's get this day going."

Both of them jumped to their own jobs, and with her mind in a whirl, the day sped by. She missed her morning visit from Jordan and resolved to call him that evening.

Chapter Twenty

The hospital released him the next afternoon, instructing him to take it easy, but Ring was determined to be back to work in a few days.

"I'll be fine once I get moving," he assured his mother.

Monica laughed at him.

"What? I will," Ring protested, sure that he could overcome the tenderness in his stomach; after all, he'd been hurt before and worked through it.

She bit down another laugh and just nodded her head. "Okay. I'll check in on you before I leave for some errands for the hotel. About nine okay?"

"Yeah, might be good to sleep in a bit."

"Sure. I'll bring you some soup. Why don't you go to bed?"

The exhaustion he had been trying to ignore threatened to swamp him when she mentioned bed. "I think I might. Thanks, Mom."

He climbed up to his bedroom, wincing at each step. The pain pills he clutched were starting to look more and more attractive.

Stripping off his clothes and pulling on a fresh pair of boxers, then climbing into bed left him white with agony. How could a little hole, not even two inches wide, cause so much pain?

A knock on the doorframe had him glancing up to see his mom, a cup of soup in one hand and a bottle in the other.

"I brought you a sports drink. Figured you needed the vitamins and calories. Soup. And where are your pain pills?"

Ring groaned as he realized they were in the pocket of his

jeans. On the floor.

She followed his eyes and snickered. "I got them." Pulling them out, she dug two out of the bag and handed them to him with the drink.

"You have the prescription. You want me to go get it filled?"

Ring started to say no, and the twinge changed his mind. "Might be a good idea, just in case."

"Okay." He could see her fighting not to smile and tried to glare. But it took too much energy.

"Eat. Leave the bowl on your nightstand. I'll get it later." Monica moved to the bed and kissed his forehead, a move she hadn't done in years. "Get some sleep, love."

"Thanks, Mom."

Ring managed to finish off the soup and half of the drink before sleep pulled him down.

"You awake?"

His mother's voice encouraged him to gain consciousness, but it was a struggle. He forced his eyes open to see her looking at him.

"You wanted me to wake you up remember?"

"Yeah. Thanks. I'll get up." If nothing else, his bladder was encouraging that choice. He sat up and almost passed back out. He didn't scream, quite, but it was a close call. His stomach felt like it had been set on fire, and a whimper slipped out.

"I see." Her voice carried tones of amusement and worry. "Want me to help you up and get you some pills?"

"Please?" His voice squeaked as he said the word, and he fought between not wetting the bed and breathing through the pain. With her help, he managed to get leveraged up and stagger, as quickly as he could, to the bathroom. Never had he been so glad he didn't have to sit down to urinate. He came back out a few minutes later to see his mom, the corners of her mouth twitching slightly.

"So I take it you're staying home today."

He nodded, careful not to move his body too much. "Yes, I believe so." He summoned up the courage for a mock glare. "Why do you find this so amusing?"

Monica bit her lip, trying very hard not to laugh. "I had you via Cesarean, so I find the idea of you just waving off a stomach injury rather amusing. Everything hurts. And it hurts for a very long time. So, sorry?" She didn't sound very sorry and her mouth kept twitching.

"Oh." The information was obvious, now that he thought about it, and meant he might not being going back to work in a few days. "So, I should not push it?"

"Hmm, that might be smart. I left food in the fridge. Take it easy, and use the railing going downstairs." With a wave she headed downstairs. He stood there staring at nothing, trying to decide what he wanted to do.

"Clothes, then food. Shower too much effort." The sound of his voice shocked him out of the pain haze, and he hobbled over to the dresser to pop the pills she had left for him. Then he began the arduous process of finding some pants and getting dressed. The shirt wasn't happening. The idea of stretching his arms up to pull on a shirt made him wince.

It took way longer than he could have ever believed, but the pills had started to work by the time he made his way downstairs and found the frittata his mother had left for him. And more sports drink.

By the time he was done eating, he was ready for a nap. Forcing himself to clean up the dishes, he flopped into the lounger by the couch and spent the next five minutes promising himself to not do that again until fully healed.

Daytime TV managed to entertain him for about an hour, but gradually boredom overtook him. He levered himself up and headed to his dad's desk. The journal he had picked up from the PO Box caught his eye. He never had gone through it, getting caught up with the remodel. He picked it up and made his way back to the table. Sitting up straight hurt much less than trying to recline, and he knew he would be ready for another pill soon. And then maybe that nap he'd been avoiding.

He paged through the journal. It seemed to go back at least two years. Near the beginning there were logical notes – vendors coming out, times, payment notes – but as he went into the journal, things began to slowly change. At one point, there were notes about paying the same vendor twice or conflicts about what account money was supposed to come out of. By itself it didn't seem that big of a deal, but it started being repeated over and over. He found another account they hadn't known about, with login information all written in the journal.

That made him pause and get up to go to the computer. Logging in he found the account. It held a bit over twenty thousand dollars, not enough to take care of everything, but enough they could spend that extra on the restaurant and make it pop. Frustrated this hadn't been part of the financial stuff, he noted it down for his mom and kept reading.

About four months before Luke died, he noted a new doctor's appointment for a doctor he didn't recognize. Sighing and bracing for the pain he got up and went back to the desk, finding the list of the doctors. Heart, adult med, but this Lee Samson wasn't on the list. A number was listed next to the appointment time. Curious and wondering if it would give some insight to his dad's odd behavior, and given that he didn't have anything else to do at the moment, he called.

"Doctor Samson's office," a perky voice answered.

"Yes, I'd like to speak to Doctor Samson please."

"What is this regarding?"

How do you say my dead father, and not be crass? "Luke Jordan. A patient of his, I believe."

"One moment sir, let me see if she is available."

A click, then staticky Muzak came on the line. Maybe they played that awful stuff to encourage people to hang up. Shifting, trying to find a comfortable position while he waited, Ring kept flipping through the book.

Things got more disjointed, and at one point he found a check meant to pay a vendor, one he had already paid off, clipped in there, as well as five hundred in hundred dollar bills. None of this made any sense. As a teenager, his dad had taught him how to keep a checkbook and log everything. The journal was nothing like the ledger he remembered Luke using. A ledger lay on the desk with everything listed out in his father's increasingly messy handwriting.

"Sir, the doctor would like to speak to you. One moment please." The receptionist put him on hold so fast he barely managed to pull himself from his musing, having tuned out the hold music, if you called that music.

"Hello, this is Lee Samson. To whom am I speaking?" A rich feminine voice came over the line, jolting him slightly.

"Hi. This may sound weird, but I'm Ring Jordan. Luke was my dad."

"Was? I take it something has happened?" Her tone was soft, and the lack of surprise bugged him.

"Yes, he died about three months ago."

"Ah. I had wondered why he missed his appointments and didn't return the calls. So how can I help you?"

"Can you tell me why he was visiting you? I know about his other doctors, but you weren't listed in any of the other paperwork."

He could hear the clack of keys on her side, then her voice, a soft smile clear in it. "He listed you and a Monica Jordan as emergency contacts, with full access, so yes. What do you know about your dad's NFL career?"

That blindsided him, and Ring shrugged. "Just that he played. I mean I know what team he was on, and that he played the left tackle position. He wasn't a star or anything, but he played for about six years before a knee injury took him out." Embarrassment made his throat itch. Why did he know so little about his dad? Granted, he hadn't even come along until his Dad had been retired for at least a year or more.

"Well in the course of those six years, the team docs recorded at least twenty concussions. He came to me because he started having trouble tracking stuff. I take it he never told your mother about the confusion or inability to remember things?"

Ring felt like someone had just tackled him and threw him to the ground.

"What? No."

"Yes, he had been concerned and requested a referral to me as I have experience working with concussions, and more and more athletes are starting to seek treatment for them. Some of the long-term side effects the medical community is discovering are problems with tracking and memory as the patient gets older."

"Why didn't he tell us? Or at least Mom?"

He could almost visualize the shrug from the doctor. "I don't know. I encouraged him to, because he admitted he was having a harder and harder time tracking things with his business. But I couldn't make him. When he never came back, I wasn't sure what to think. But the contact number he provided was his cell."

"And that fell into water when he had his heart attack. So we never could get anything from it." Luke had been kneeling to put chemicals into the hotel pool when the heart attack had happened. The phone had fallen out of his shirt pocket into the pool, and it had been the last thing anyone had worried about until way too late.

"I am sorry to hear that. I wish he had shared with his family. There were some things that could have been done to help reduce some of the side effects, though at this point, much of it is still experimental."

Ring felt like a weight that had been tied to him was gone. This didn't make it all better, but just knowing that his dad hadn't been trying to be secretive but had been dealing with something that sounded scary, helped.

"Thanks, Dr. Samson. Just knowing helps to explain some of the stuff that made no sense."

He hung up and spent the rest of the day going over the journal, and making sure there was nothing else they had missed. When his mom got home, he knew he had to tell her.

"Mom, get a glass of wine and sit down."

Her eyes darted to him then darkened. She said nothing but left the room. Fifteen minutes later, dressed in her casual home clothes, a large glass of wine in her hand, she sat down and carefully placed it on the side table next to her.

"Okay, I'm ready. Go."

Ring explained everything: the journal, what the doctor had said, and the cash he had found. Monica listened to all of it, then with a trembling hand reached out and took a large gulp of wine.

"Thank you. I swear I'm going to beat that man when I meet him again. Did he think I would leave him? Or hate him? I went to all those games. I was terrified every time he got pulled off the field after an impact." She took a deep breath and let it out shakily. She wiped at the tears leaking from her eyes with a sharp impatient gesture.

"I think I'm going to go get quietly drunk and have a long conversation with him in my memories." She swallowed and stood, a bit pale. "Then I'm going to forgive him and let him go."

Ring pulled himself up and hugged her tightly, ignoring the stabbing pain in his side, before she left the room. Tears still trickled from her eyes.

Ember couldn't get it out of her head how much money Ernie made off the place. But she, while frustrated, couldn't blame him for wanting to make a profit. And for all she knew, Jimmy's information wasn't accurate. But it still hurt to know how close to the edge they were. She budgeted expenses down to every penny. Groceries and gas were the two biggest variables, and shopping for food induced stress like crazy. The extra bread from the bakery ended up being the basis for meals all too often. She knew it didn't help Belinda, who needed lean protein and vegetables to get her shape back, but she didn't have any other options. She needed to start job hunting, getting her resume up. If she could manage another few weeks, she would have time to find another job. Not the race of stress finding this one with a place to live had been. The knowledge she had to start interviewing caused her stomach to clench and she felt sick.

Trying not to focus on money, she cleaned up the kitchen after a busy day. When Jimmy came into the back, a wad of money in his hand, Ember frowned, but he spoke before she could ask any questions.

"I know how important this is, so I might have spun a bit of a sob story, fairy tale princess needing a dress for the ball. But I got you some tips. I don't know much about dresses, but I don't think it is enough. But maybe it will help?" He thrust his fistful of money towards her and she took it, trying not to fumble. "It should be about sixty dollars, so…" He shrugged and shuffled his feet. "Maybe you can do something with it."

Ember stood there with her mouth open, no idea what to say. Her throat was so tight she could only look at him and then the money in wonder. This made three good things to happen so far this summer, along with Cecil and Jordan.

"Thank you." Her voice broke, but there weren't any other words. She knew the odds of her winning were remote, but everything else she had tried had petered out. At this point, she needed a miracle.

"You're worth it. Heck, if Jordan wasn't so obviously head over heels for you, I'd think about asking you out myself. You're pretty awesome." He grinned at her. "Now get out of here and find something great. I'll finish up front. Let me know if you need any help back here. Might as well learn more. Figure dad's going to need help when he loses you. Regardless of what he thinks."

With that comment, he disappeared to the front, leaving her standing there, blushing and feeling like – just maybe – things might work out.

She finished up for the day and rushed upstairs, grabbing a USB jump drive and putting her entry on it. The nearby strip mall held a Kinko's, and there were two thrift shops nearby. With any amount of luck, she might find something she could alter a bit to make it work.

Trotting down stairs, she saw Belinda doing stretches and strength exercises with her weights, one of the things Ember had made sure she packed.

"You look like you're doing better."

Belinda shrugged, a sullen look on her face. "Yep. The doctor said I should be able to get my cast off in a week or so. And Rosemary finally came back from her boarding school. Is it okay if she comes to get me and we go to lunch tomorrow? And maybe dinner and shopping the night of your party?"

She was relieved that some of Belinda's friends would take the time to come down here. With luck, it might improve Belinda's mood. "Of course. Just make sure you have her help you up and down the stairs." Ember hesitated and then spoke, treating each word as if it was a soufflé that might collapse. "But I don't have any money to give you to spend."

Her sister shrugged, and Ember saw her try to pretend it didn't matter. "It's okay. Rosemary owes me a birthday present anyhow. I'll make her buy for me." A smile almost appeared on her sister's face.

She fought back a chuckle. "Okay, I've got to run an errand. I'll be back in a while." The apartment's emptiness registered. "Where's Mom?"

"Cecil came to get her. Said he needed to get his nails done, and so did she."

"Good." Cecil had become Sabrina's main social outlet, and Ember would never be able to repay him for his kindness.

"I've got dinner in the Dutch oven, so it might be done by the time you get back."

Ever since the showdown at the hospital, she had tried to be a bit better, but Ember still worried Belinda had never really grieved for their dad. Ember didn't know how to help with that. Shaking her head, acknowledging all the many things she couldn't fix or change, she headed out, hope shining inside. Between the money Cecil had gifted her and what Jimmy had provided, she thought she could pull it off.

Approaching a stop sign, she stepped on the brakes, her mind elsewhere as she went over money options, trying to figure out how to get the most value for what she had. Her mind registered the fact her car continued to move, and Ember stepped on the brakes again. Nothing. Fully in the moment, she stood on the brake pedal, and the car barely slowed. She glanced at the intersection and saw cars crossing, and terror gripped her body. She laid on the horn over and over again while pumping the brakes in a frantic rhythm and coasted through the stop. Other cars paused to let her go through, though with a lot of horn blowing and fingers stuck outside window. On the other side of the intersection the brakes kicked in, causing her to jerk to a stop.

She pulled over to the side and sat there shaking as adrenaline pumped through her. Images of dying in a car accident, leaving her mom and sister behind, caused her to shake worse than the chemicals fading from her body. Checking her phone, she verified the existence of a repair shop two blocks over. Flipping on her hazards and keeping the speed down to a minimum, regardless of the angry honking and people whizzing around her, she managed to get to the shop and pull in. Ten minutes later, she managed to pull herself together enough to climb out of the car and go in.

The employee listened to what had happened, and nodded. "I'll get it in for a quick inspection. That's free, and we'll see what is wrong. Why don't you take a seat in the waiting room. There's free coffee, if you want some. I'm sure you must be shook up."

She nodded and all but collapsed into the chair, trying to get her emotional balance back. Her body finished shaking about the time the technician walked back into the waiting room.

"Miss? We found the problem. It looks like your brake line sprung a leak. We can fix it today if you want."

Ember looked at him, and somehow found the strength to speak. "How much?"

"We need to replace the lines and refill the fluid. So ninety five for credit, or we've got a special going today, eighty-five if you pay cash."

Her cards were maxed. She was paying as much as she could, but the prescriptions had hurt. She thought of the money in her purse for the entry and the dress and nodded. The jerky movement felt unnatural, but the attendant didn't seem to notice.

"Cash." Her voice croaked as she responded. Feeling mired in molasses, she forced herself to stand and went to pay, fighting her dreams as she pulled the cash out of her purse.

"Thanks, we should be done in about forty-five minutes." The cheerful voice felt like lemon juice on a cut, and she flinched backwards.

"Okay." Her voice was so faint she couldn't hear it herself. In a daze, she went to the bathroom and locked the door. With shaking hands she counted out the money she had left. Twenty-five dollars. She didn't know if she could even get the entry printed for that amount. It just became too much. Sitting on the toilet in an auto repair shop, Ember gave into the stress and cried.

She didn't know how long she sat there, but eventually the pain faded, leaving numbness. Not knowing what else to do, she let it all go. Sitting in the waiting room, she didn't think, didn't feel, just existed.

When they called her name, she got her car and drove to Office Depot. She had no idea what she could do. Walking in, she found an employee and pulled out her jump drive.

"Welcome to Office Depot. I'm Kelly. How may I help you today?" The girls' perky voice hurt, but Ember tried not to let it show.

"I need to print two copies of these, at least one needs to be professional looking." Her voice remained flat and uninflected, and she knew her eyes were still red and swollen.

The girl looked at the documents on the drive for a while and then nodded. "Sure, I can do that. Getting everything printed, looks like one tri-fold on glossy, and five pages single-side photo quality, then three pages of normal." She typed on the calculator a bit. "For two of everything, it will be forty-five dollars."

At this point Ember couldn't even feel pain anymore. "I have twenty-five, and I need at least two dollars to mail it. It is an entry to a competition and one proof copy for me." She didn't beg, didn't plead; she figured she had already lost.

Kelly looked at her, eyes solemn, and then tilted her head to the side. "Tell you what. I've got some sheets that are part of a discontinued brand that I can give you at a discount, and rather than printing your copy on the same paper, I can do yours on basic paper, and throw in the envelope to mail it in, for…" She typed on the computer and then smiled. "How about twenty?"

If Ember had any tears left she might have cried again, but instead she just nodded, her head too heavy to hold up. "Thank you." Her voice cracked and the girl patted her hand.

"Have faith. If your recipes are anything to go by, you'll do good. Give me a bit."

A while later, Ember walked out, her copy in her purse and an envelope in hand, neatly stamped, addressed, and sealed. She dropped it in the mailbox. It was done. At this point it had been removed from her control. Exhausted, she headed home and climbed the stairs. The smell of food made her sick, and with a weak smile to Belinda, she headed up to her attic room and collapsed on the bed.

No money, no dress, and no chance. Her eyes burned as her mind spun, trying to think of something. Toga floated through her head.

Jerking upright in bed, she headed downstairs to the small closet they used for linens, and yes, at the bottom, still in a bag since there wasn't a king bed in the apartment, 1500 thread count pure white sheets. She had kept her small sewing machine. She wasn't very good with it, but she used it to hem skirts and repair small tears. It wouldn't be high fashion, but it might just pass.

With a small smile on her face at something she could control, she hit the web looking for a simple toga pattern, and found something she could do with a minimum of sewing. With a half smile and a mental note to not let her mother find out what she used her expensive sheets for, Ember got to work. This would take her a few nights.

Chapter Twenty-One

After being at home for two days, Ring's boredom had him climbing the walls. He needed to see Ember, even knowing she wouldn't have time to talk to him. Monday morning he drove to the hotel and parked and then walked down to the bakery. The doctor said walking would be good for him. Mom wouldn't need him until Wednesday, and to be honest he didn't know if he'd get through a full session right now, but seeing Ember mattered more.

Jimmy greeted him with a smile that dropped into a frown. "Man, I'm pretty sure you aren't supposed to be up and moving around yet. You're gray. Go sit, I'll bring you something to eat and drink."

Ring nodded in relief. The walk had wiped him out, and all he wanted to do was collapse. The outside seating area was relatively full, but a table opened up, and he sat down gratefully, chafing at the weakness of his own body.

"Here you go." Jimmy set a tall iced coffee in front of him, and something that just looked delicious. "I'll add it onto your check next time you come in. Get better man. She didn't react well to you getting hurt."

There was no doubt who the "she" was, and part of him smiled at knowing she cared. Another part frowned at causing her any more stress.

"Thanks."

"No prob." With that Jimmy was gone, and Ring sipped on the iced coffee, trying to get his strength back.

"You mind if I sit here?"

Ring lifted his eyes to see a stunning blond, about

seventeen, with a walking stick, and her leg in a cast, looking at him. There was something familiar about her, but he couldn't place her.

"Sure."

The girl awkwardly sat down, and she looked as tired as he did.

"What'd you do to your leg?"

She scowled down at her leg, which reduced her beauty quite a bit. "Broke it. Three places."

"Wow. How'd you manage to do that?" Given the full cast, he figured the femur had been broken. That bone was tough, and breaking it wasn't easy.

The scowl stayed. "Dad drank and drove. Got killed." Her voice was flat, and it just set off all sorts of warning bells in Ring's head. She obviously had not dealt with the incident.

"That sucks. Sorry."

"Would have been okay but for my stupid sister. All her fault."

"How could your dad drinking and driving be your sister's fault?" He wasn't tracking; maybe he needed to cut down on the pills. The twinge of pain in his side reminded him why he was still taking the painkillers.

"All this money stuff. She made us move down here. Won't let me do anything fun or go anywhere. Says we can't afford it. All I get to do is training and therapy. I'm bored and wanted to go buy new clothes and get back to swimming."

Ring blinked listening to this. "And what is your sister doing?"

"Working. That's all she does. Works all day, then comes home and drives my mom to her appointments, or disappears to do something. She is fine being fat and ugly and wearing awful clothes. But I need to wear things that look nice." The petulance came through clearly, and it added a large grain of salt to what she said.

"Why can't your mom drive?"

Her face shifted now, a bit of concern flashing across her face, a much more attractive look than the scowl. "She was hurt in the accident too. Brain damage. She's different now. Most of the time she is just mean to my sister, who deserves it. But she's started being mean to other people too." There was an odd pause and her voice dropped a bit, "Even me."

"How does your sister deserve it?" None of this made any sense. It sounded like the sister was killing herself to take care of her family who didn't appreciate it at all.

"If she had gone with us that day, Dad wouldn't have driven. Or if she could have gotten the lawyers and police to let us into our accounts, we could have stayed at our home. But no, she said she couldn't until the criminal and civil cases had been settled. All she talks about is how tight money is, and that we need to be careful until everything is worked out. I could have stayed with my friends. They would have taken me in, and then I wouldn't be here. But she said no one could at this time, and that her savings weren't large enough to pay the health insurance and rent someplace near home." She sneered at the area around here.

Somehow he doubted that. In fact, he would bet that sister had tried everything.

"I bet she is the reason why my dad crashed too." The petulance came back, and he had to resist the urge to slap her.

"Oh really?" At this point Ring guessed that everything coming out of her mouth was twisted and distorted so far it had little to do with reality.

"She was going to leave. She probably did it for the life insurance. At least my mom said that."

"The same mom who is mean to her because she 'deserved' that treatment."

The smile was blinding, and her beauty lit up the area, and all he could see was the ugliness of everything she had said.

"Yes. See you do understand. It is so not fair."

Ring took another sip of his coffee, thinking how incredible having someone who would give up everything for you would be.

"You're right, it isn't fair." The blond smiled again, and all he felt was sad. Sad for her and whomever her sister was. "It isn't fair your sister has such an ungrateful and ugly family."

Her head jerked up in shock. She expected pity and sympathy and he had none to give her. Losing your dad, and then having your family turn on you. He couldn't imagine the level of her sister's strength and patience.

"She's given up everything for you. Spent all her own money from what you said, and is devoting her life to you while you are both hurt. She sounds pretty awesome to me. Too bad she has such an ungrateful, selfish sister."

He stood, finishing off the drink. Any desire to stay had fled. "She sounds like someone pretty wonderful. And you don't deserve her."

His final comment left the girl with her mouth open and a shocked look as he walked away. Moving slow, he thought longingly of more pain pills and the sudden desire to give Ember a hug. He wanted to stay and talk to her, but he knew he had overdone it. She had to work, and right now his room and pain relief called to him. They could text later.

Tuesday night, with her hopes in the mail, and the timer clicking down, Ember started looking and planning. But that meant talking to her mom and praying that the prescription and therapy helped to the point that she could interact, not attack.

Walking in the door, Ember blinked at the sight of her sister picking up the living room.

"Hi." She couldn't help the wariness in her voice, but Belinda had rarely been helpful the last few months.

"Hey." Belinda glanced around and shrugged. "Therapist said I needed to move more, or I was going to lose what tone I had. So figured I'd clean up. Dinner is going too."

"Thanks. Mom here?"

"Yeah, in her room. Said she had some therapy homework to do." Belinda wrinkled her nose. "Not sure what that is all about."

"Mood?" Ember hated how cautious she sounded, but she needed a helpful Sabrina, not one that lashed out at her.

"Pretty good. She smiled and said thanks when I brought her some tea."

"I'll take that as a win." Girding herself for the battlefield she was walking onto, Ember knocked on the door. "Mom, you have time to talk?"

Her answer was the door opening and Sabrina stepping out, a half smile on her face. The lack of stiffness in her body let Ember feel a bit more relieved. Maybe this wouldn't be so bad.

"Belinda, you want to come too? This affects all of us."

The two women sat down on at the kitchen table, and Ember sank into a seat, keeping her defenses high as she tried to figure out how to break the news that she had failed to solve everything.

"I talked to Ernie - the guy that owns the bakery. His recovery is going well, and he expects to be back to work after the Fourth."

There was a sharp gasp from Belinda, but Sabrina didn't say anything, just watched Ember with a steady gaze.

"I've got a few things I'm trying, and I'm hoping one will come through, but nothing is guaranteed. He promised we could keep the apartment for a few months after he is back full time. But we can't stay here forever. I'm trying a Hail Mary idea, but most likely I'm going to have to start job hunting. So,

I'm working my resume and I'll start checking the want ads."

Much to her surprise, Belinda reached out and touched her hand. "We'll figure it out. We haven't been much of a family to you, but this time at least I can be."

Warmed by seeing a hint of her sister back, the voice of her mother doused her with ice water.

"And I can't."

Ember and Belinda both snapped their attention to her. Her face was remote, but she kept speaking. "I can't separate out the child I love and the woman I hate and blame. Me staying here will hurt both of us."

She wanted to protest, to swear she could help, to say she could make it all better. But she couldn't and in some way, she knew she never could have.

"I don't know where you can go."

"Neither do I. But rather than focusing on a place for all of us, we need to find a place for Belinda and you. Where she can get the training she needs and go back to school in the fall."

"Okay. I have a party to go to at the end of next week. It is one of my hopes. But Mom, I'll keep trying to get a hold of Seri, or something. And I'll call the cops again and see if anything has broken loose."

"Good. And if we don't hear from Seri by the time your boss comes back, I'll find a residential treatment center and turn custody of Belinda over to you. I'm trying but I can't be here for you right now, not if I want the chance to be your mother again. And unfortunately, there is a large part of me that doesn't." Ember forced herself not to react to that remark, repeating everything the therapist had said in her head. "But the part of me that loves you is fighting, and me not seeing you every day will make that fight a bit easier."

Sabrina reached out and touched Ember's hand for the briefest moment. "I'll make sure I have plans the night of the party. To help prevent me sabotaging you." With that she stood up and walked away, the tension in her back giving away her stress.

"I'm sorry." Belinda's voice was a whisper and Ember gladly turned to her, willing to focus on anything besides her mom.

"For?"

"Being a bitch so much, enjoying seeing you hurt. I was mad, and you were the only person I could punish."

Her throat tight, Ember just nodded.

"I talked to this guy the other day, and he kinda slapped me." Ember started, rage climbing inside her. "Verbally, I mean. And pointed out everything you'd done. When you could have just said, 'not my problem' and left. So thank you. And I'll try to help more."

Her sister was back. Ember reached out and pulled her into a tight hug, and for the first time in a long time, she didn't feel like she was trying to fight the world alone.

"So, sis, wanna help me get my dress ready for the ball?"

Belinda's face lit up. Her fashion sense was so much better than Ember's. "That sounds like fun. Is that the buzzing I've been hearing? You have a sewing machine up there?"

"Yep. Trying to make something that looks like it has Mediterranean roots."

"Oh, that sounds fun. And I bet we can scavenge some stuff from my old stuff. I brought a bunch of my fancy gowns just to be a pain." She looked away shamefaced. "Just to make you bring it up here."

"I know. But I love you so I did it anyhow."

Belinda just shook her head. "I don't know what I did to deserve a sister like you." Ember hugged her again and headed upstairs to get her dress stuff. She left a message for the cops, asking for a status. She sent another email to Seri, asking once again for help, or the name of someone else that might help. Ember sent another email to Cecil to share the fact that

Belinda had started to come around and information about the party. She let him know that Belinda had other plans, but she didn't know about Sabrina yet.

Then with her heart still torn in two, she headed back down. At least now half of it was starting to heal.

Chapter Twenty-Two

Wednesday, after relocating back to the hotel for the duration, Ring met his mom, Karly the sous chef, and Lee the restaurant manager in one of the conference rooms. They had a stack of manila envelopes piled up on the table. There had to be two or three hundred. The hair on the back of his neck stood up as he took the scene in. This was not going to be good.

His mom looked up as he walked in and gingerly sat himself down. He had never realized how much you used your stomach when you moved. While he had figured sit-ups were out, he hadn't realized how much everything else would hurt.

"Ring. I'm glad you're here. Since working on the hotel is not advisable, you get to help us with reviewing the entries." She paused for a minute, sharp eyes taking in his still stiff movement. "As I said, Clay and Greyson mentioned you are rather good at it and had to do it often for class."

He groaned, and only the knowledge of how much it would hurt his stomach prevented him from head thumping on the table. "I have traitors for friends. Traitors! Did they also mention how much I despised it?"

Monica's mouth twitched. "They might have said something about that. They also mentioned you were rather good at seeing possible problems or faulty logic also."

"Apparently not. I seemed to have trusted my so-called friends, and look how they just threw me under the bus," Ring muttered, looking at the stacks without any enthusiasm.

"Oh well. You'll live. Besides, while I can look at the ascetics of their stuff, and Karly will have an idea of how the recipes might taste, neither of us have any idea how to analyze the growth nor marketing ideas. That will be all you."

"Fine, fine. I want this to succeed, so I guess I'll live. But I want it pointed out that being operated on was more appealing."

Monica arched an eyebrow at her son.

"You'll find out, trust me." Looking around, he grabbed three different colors of Post-its. "Grab a color, then grab a packet and appraise it based on your skills. Mom, as you said, do the ascetics. Karly and Lee, your job is the food - does it sound edible and meet the criteria of heart healthy and good for diabetics? Remember, salt is bad. Then I'll go over the plan. If you grab it and it isn't worth your color Post-it, put it at the end of the table, and the other two won't bother even looking at it."

"See. You are good at this." His mom beamed at him.

"Self-preservation only, you'll see soon enough."

Monica looked at the pile. "I removed all the names of the submitters, just writing the number on the packet, and I have the master list matching up the number to their contact information. So we can do this with no idea as to gender, name, or anything."

"That works. We did something similar with class assignments so you didn't know who you were reviewing."

With a sigh Ring didn't bother to hide, he pulled out the closest one and cracked it open. Ignoring everything except the business aspect — after all, he thought plaid and stripes went fine together — he flipped to the first one and sighed and tossed it to the end.

"What, already?" His mom looked up surprised.

"They thought they would need a food operating budget of a thousand dollars for a month," he said, his voice dry.

Lee goggled. "A month? We go through that every few days."

"Which is why it's in the discard pile."

Looking much more apprehensive, the three of them started on the ones nearest to them.

"Good lord, this person thinks fuchsia and neon orange are good colors for a Med restaurant?"

"Cook the salmon for thirty minutes? What are we making, jerky?"

"Pay all the cooks minimum wage. Hah. They'd quit the second they saw that. And anyone you hired would be worse than a fry cook," Lee muttered as he and Karly worked on one.

"I resent that. I started as a fry cook," Karly pointed out.

"Would you have accepted minimum wage?"

"Hell, no."

"My point stands," Lee said and put that packet aside.

"Mashed potatoes in heavy cream and butter are low carb and heart healthy? Did they even read the contest guidelines?" Karly wondered as she looked at the recipes.

"Plaid togas for all the waitstaff?" Monica muttered, looking at a packet.

Both Karly and Ring stopped to snicker at that one. They all kept plowing through. After four hours, they were exhausted, but all of the submissions had been reviewed at a high level and they were left with twenty that had possibilities.

"Now what?" His mom sounded exhausted, and he wanted nothing but some pain pills and a nap.

"Now we walk away. We come back tomorrow and review them all collectively. See you here at eight tomorrow morning?"

Everyone nodded, and he painfully made his way upstairs, absently patting for his phone as he went. It wasn't there. Growling under his breath, he headed towards his bed and there it was sitting next to the bed: A text message flashed on it.

how you doing? Free tonight?

He wanted to, but that had been a long time to be sitting

and even food didn't sound good, though her in his arms did.

can't, hurt, taking pills, see u in morning? Make box for me?

ah, so now you're the delivery boy. Nice I always had weakness for cute young men

Ring grinned, just talking to her helped.

I take tips in kisses

I'll remember that. Night

He popped his pills and lay down. He set the alarm and lay back on the bed, closing his eyes.

The alarm pulled him up the next morning. The idea of her waiting for him, maybe with a kiss, got his ass out of bed and moving. Standing in a shower, the heat pounding on his aching body, helped make him feel almost human.

"You heading out early?" Greyson asked, walking out into the common area, his work boots in his hands.

"I don't talk to traitors, and I don't let them know I'm going to see Ember and getting a box of goodies to sustain Mom, Karly, Lee, and I." Ring mock glared at him, though he knew he would have been offended if the winner had been chosen without his input.

"Bakery? I'll be at the conference room shortly. I'm not missing out on that stuff." Clay walked out naked, toweling his hair.

"Man, put some clothes on. I so don't need to be seeing your junk this early in the morning."

"What? Jealous?" Clay puffed up his chest and thrust out his groin.

"No, nauseous. I hurl and I'm aiming for you," Ring warned as he saw Greyson trying to hide a smirk.

"The ladies love this. It is a work of art," Clay protested as he wrapped the towel around his waist.

"Yeah, trashed art. I'll see you later. If I'm lucky I'll be back to working by next Monday."

"Good. Lobby should be finished today. Mostly trim to put back on, then that leaves this suite and the other to remodel from top to bottom."

"Kay. I'll figure out where to move us, but do the other one first. Probably be at Mom's for the rest of the time." He paused heading out the door. "Thanks, guys. For everything."

Clay waved him off. "Pfft. Sweat equity, and besides, now I own a piece of this place. I don't like losing money, so we need to make money."

"It's actually been fun." Greyson shrugged.

"Yeah, it has, hasn't it?"

With that thought running through his mind, Ring headed downstairs and walked towards the bakery. The early morning air was cool, and his stomach felt much better.

The door jangled as he walked in and Jimmy looked up. "Ember, boytoy is here."

Ring choked a bit on that name, but the idea of being her boytoy sounded extremely appealing.

"Jimmy." Her voice cracked as she looked at both of them with horror. Jimmy just snickered and rung up the charge on the register.

"Here's the total, and I added in the coffee and stuff from last time."

"Thanks." Ring absently handed him the credit card while he looked at Ember. Her face was bright red from Jimmy's comment, and she had a box in her hands. She looked gorgeous.

"How was your evening? Sorry I wasn't available."

She shrugged. "Nothing too drama filled. So happy with that."

One of these days he had to break his promise and find out what happened, but not today.

"Those for me?"

"Yeah. A few of your favorites and some new things I'm trying. Let me know."

"Will do." Jimmy handed him back his card and receipt with a smirk. "So..." He paused, looking at her. "Do I get a tip?"

Her blush, which had faded, flared back up, but she smiled. "Oh, I think I can spare one for my favorite delivery boy."

"Boytoy, I tell you. Way more fun," Jimmy commented as he went to deal with refilling the coffee.

She wrinkled her nose at Jimmy, turning back to Ring. He didn't think, just set down the box and pulled her into his arms. She smelled of nutmeg, sugar, and cinnamon. She tasted of ginger and lemon, and he knew what was in the box. His mouth slid over hers, kissing her deeply as he held her lush body to his.

"Okay you two, get a room." The teasing brought him back to the here and now, and he wished he could take her back to his room, strip off her clothes, and taste every inch of her body.

"See you tonight?" his voice was husky, and his jeans too tight.

She nodded and swallowed. "Yeah."

One more quick kiss on the nose and he grabbed the box heading out the door, ignoring the amused smiles of the early morning customers. The kiss had been worth it.

Lost in a haze of memory, he made it to the boardroom unaware of much of anything. Only Clay and Greyson, both sitting at the table chatting with his mom, snapped him back into reality.

"Finally. I thought we were going to starve to death. Gimmee." Clay stood, reaching for the box.

"Excuse me. Ladies first." Ring mock glared at Clay who slumped back into his chair, looking like a pouting six-year-old.

"Why, thank you." Monica grinned at him and took

something out. Ring held the box out to Karly, and she grabbed one also. He then turned to Lee.

"Grab one before they get their grubby mitts on them."

Lee arched an eyebrow but took one. "Thanks."

"Now you ingrates can help yourselves," he said as he set the box down, but not before grabbing his normal ginger lemon twist.

Monica had flipped to the first packet as she took a bite and froze. "Oh my. This is delicious."

"Which one did you get?"

"I've got peaches and plums wrapped in sourdough. The zing of the sourdough makes the sweetness of the fruit explode."

"Oh yeah, that one is great." Ring glanced at Karly who chewed on her pastry with her eyes closed.

"What about you Karly?"

She opened her eyes with effort. "I didn't realize you could mix apples, cheese, and caramel like that."

"Actually it's quince."

Karly shot him a quick look. "How do you know that?"

"I asked her. Ember — she's great." He tried to control the dopey tone, but from the smirks of his friends and sharp look from his mother, he doubted he succeeded. "She told me she uses quince, as it stays crunchy after you cook it."

She took another bite, eyes closed. "I wish I had thought of this. It is wonderful."

"Now you know why the bottomless pits over there were willing to wait for the box."

"I had wondered," his mom commented as she finished her treat. "Now I understand. But now it is time for them to get to work, and for us to get back to evaluating." She looked mournfully at the pile left. "I will never tease you about dreading this again."

Greyson and Clay both grabbed one pastry and headed out as Ring shifted to a more comfortable position.

"This next part isn't so bad. So they all have Post-it's on them. Go through them again with your interests and give each one a score of one to a hundred. Anything with fewer than fifty, automatically put to the side. Then we'll see where we are."

Lee stood up. "I'm going to let Karly run with this. I've got orders coming in this morning for the restaurant and some new people starting to replace ones we released. We talked it over and she has a good idea of what we need."

Karly nodded. "I know the basics, but the running of the restaurant stuff still escapes me. And I'm a recipe cook." At Ring's confused look she explained. "I don't have the spark that lets me twist things. Technically, I've got the basics, but that knowing how to make the food explode like that?" She pointed to the box from the bakery. "I've never managed to figure out. But I can weed out anyone else that can't at least get past my basic knowledge."

Ring shrugged. "Works for me. Have a good day, Lee."

Lee chuckled and headed out the door. The two women glanced at each other and shrugged, then reached for a pile. Ring did the same, pulling out his phone and pulling up the calculator to do some more math on the feasibility of what each plan said.

By lunchtime, the pile was down to ten.

"And at this point I'm out. Most of the business plans are workable. Some will need to be enhanced, but once they are given the real information they'll be more accurate. But for the most part, any of those ten have the know-how to do what we need."

Karly grinned. "Now it's my turn. All the recipes sound good, but tasting good is a totally different story. Give me a weekend and I'll cut this list down. They have to cook fast, share ingredients, and still be things people will eat. If I can't follow the recipe and make it work, it's too complicated."

"Good. I'm going to take a nap and then punch-list the other suite so we can start the upgrades there."

"Okay, dear. And thank you for all the work. It was less fun than I thought."

"It always is." Ring grinned and headed upstairs for a nap.

Chapter Twenty-Three

The day of the ball, Ember tried not to think about the contest. She forced herself to focus on her baking and ignore the timers clicking down in her head.

"Hey, Ember, this place smells great."

Ernie's voice pulled her attention away from the recipe in front of her: a pineapple fritter, with ginger to give it zing. Her heart quailed a bit; what if he was here to tell her today was the last day?

She forced a smile. "Hi, Ernie. You look good." She watched him walk towards her. Slow, with a slight hitch in his gait, but overall he looked pretty good. He even had a tan.

"Thanks. Tired already, so no worries about me taking over quite yet. But I wanted to come down and talk to you." He sank down on to a stool, and a sigh of relief filled the room. "I thought I was ready for a day out given all my therapy. Shows you what happens when I think." He shook his head and focused on her, his eyes the mirror of Jimmy's.

"So Jimmy came to see me. And brought his mother in on the conversation."

Ember knew she was going to be sick; she was going to lose everything. Desperate, she shoved a piece of raw ginger in her mouth, the burn helping to keep her mind off her roiling stomach.

"Those two chewed me out, up one side and down another for about an hour on how I was abusing you. And taking advantage of your situation." She braced herself, mind racing, trying to figure out where they could go, how she could get someone here to get their stuff.

"And they were right."

What? She froze looking at him, mouth open in shock.

Ernie half smiled. "You've been great, and I'm a cheapskate. Your recipes alone have doubled what I was making, and overall business has increased. And I wasn't giving you enough credit. So starting with your next paycheck, you'll be making fifteen hundred before taxes, rent is still included for free, and you get everything above baseline income. Period. You're working too hard, and I'm giving Jimmy a raise. He deserved it just for standing up to me for someone else. That alone is nice. He's always been a bit self-centered."

Her head spun and her knees threatened to buckle. She could get a bill or two paid off. Even if the pay didn't last long, it was something. Belinda could get the in-depth therapy time she needed to get back in shape. And her bank account, which had about thousand left, might stop hemorrhaging.

"Thank you. Oh, thank you so much. You don't know what this means." Ember babbled at him, trying not to act even more insane. After the stress of the last few days, this might kill her from sheer relief.

"Oh, I have an idea. You've taken on a lot, and Jimmy looks up to you. I expected to lose money, not make it. So thank you."

The burn in her mouth tasted of hope, so sweet, and so likely to burn her.

"So on that note. Go home."

"What?" Ember felt like she couldn't track the conversation changes.

Ernie smiled. "Jimmy told me about the ball, and that you submitted an entry. I hope you win. You're damn good, and wasted on this place. So go home early, get all gussied up and go see if your dreams are going to come true. You've earned it. Jimmy and I'll finish the prep work today."

She had time to get dressed up, to relax before seeing

Jordan. They had both been so busy this last week that even the text messages tended to end with one of them falling asleep on the other.

"Thank you." She pulled off her apron, and pointed to the recipe. "I was making that if you want to finish."

He heaved himself off the stool and went to look. "Oh yeah, that looks delicious. Sure will. Good luck tonight."

Her smile so wide it hurt, she darted upstairs the back way, bursting in and almost hitting Belinda.

"What're you doing home so early?" Belinda asked, surprise in her voice.

"Ernie came in to cover to give me time to get ready for the party." She glanced at the wall. Two o'clock. The ball started at six, and she wanted to make sure she didn't have to walk fast to get up the hill.

"I think I'm going to take a quick nap. It might be a long night." She looked around, listening. "Mom?"

"She left about an hour ago. She said she'd go see a movie then attend a group therapy event her doctor wanted her to try. So she won't be back until later as they were supposed to go to dinner as part of the therapy. She took a twenty from the emergency funds." Belinda looked a bit worried at that, but for once that gave Ember no extra stress.

"That is fine. Ernie is giving me a big raise. Maybe we can get caught up on bills. And get some better food."

"Awesome. Go sleep. I'll get your dress ready."

"Thanks, dear." Ember gave Belinda a quick hug and headed up to her garret. She stripped down to her underwear and dropped on the bed, thoughts of tonight whipping through her mind. Taking a minute to set her alarm, she lay down and let hope pull her into sleep.

The beep of the alarm had her springing upright in bed, just narrowly missing hitting her head on a beam, her heart racing as everything clicked into place.

She grabbed her stuff and ran downstairs and jumped in the shower. She took her time, shaving her legs, and imagining Jordan running his hands over them. The bubble of joy lasted until she stepped out of the bathroom, in only a robe, to let the steam fade before she tried to do something with her hair.

"Ember, could you come here please?" Belinda's voice quavered on each word, and Ember changed directions to go see if something was wrong. Maybe she'd hurt her leg again. Concern drove her into the living room, where Belinda stood rigid, face pale, and tears starting to leak out of her eyes.

"What's wrong? Are you okay?"

Her eyes ran over her, looking for a wound, but she didn't see anything.

"I'm sorry. I wanted to help, so I thought I'd iron the dress for you. I got distracted and left the iron on it too long, and it burned. I'm so sorry, Ember. I swear I was trying to help." Guilt laced each word as Ember turned to see her dress, the one they had worked to make into something that would at least not look awful, with a burned spot right in the center of the front.

A scream welled up at the back of her throat. She sealed it down and forced out the words, "It's okay." Belinda broke down in sobs, and it took everything Ember had to walk over and pull her into a hug. "It is. I know you were trying to help."

Her sister looked up, grief in her eyes. "I was." The sheer panic on her face, and the next words, convinced Ember she told the truth. "You can take my iPod and pawn it. You can get at least a hundred for it. It is last year's model. Take it." Belinda fumbled for the always-present device in her pocket.

"No. It'll be okay. Somehow." Ember wished she could believe it herself. "Let me head upstairs for a bit and figure it out, okay?"

Belinda nodded, looking miserable as Ember pulled away. She made it up to her room and shut the door before she picked up the pillow and screamed into it over and over, the muffled sound carrying the stress and anger. No matter what she did, she couldn't succeed.

She let herself scream out all the stress from the last two months, the worry about her family and the money stress. She had trailed off, fighting choking sobs, when her phone rang. Cecil. Swallowing the last of the sobs, she answered the phone.

"Hey, Cecil."

"*Liebchen*, I called to see if your mother required a dinner date tonight."

"Um, no she went out to dinner with her therapy group and to the movies." She knew her voice sounded thick, and she tried to sniff her nose clear. And instead snorted so loudly it echoed in the small garret.

"Ah, that is right. You told me that in an email. Ember. Why do you sound like you've been crying? What happened?"

The caring tone in his voice kicked it all off again, and she spilled the entire story. Emphasizing how hard Belinda had been trying lately.

"Hmm, well good to know the child has decided to grow up a bit. Her petulance had become wearing. I, your fairy godfather, have a solution though." Smugness filled his voice.

"How? I'm still broke, and finding something for a Mediterranean ball is going to be impossible."

"Ach, I told you. Trust me. Get dressed in your nicest foundation garments and take a cab here. I'll pay. Trust me, I have something up my sleeve."

Ember sat on the bed looking at the phone in disbelief, then shrugged. What did she have to lose? "Okay, I'll be there soon."

She grabbed a bag, put in her shoes and makeup, and threw on some clothes, her hair still damp from the shower.

"Belinda," she said when she got down there. "I'm heading over to Cecil's. He said he has a fix. You going to be okay?"

The girl nodded, her eyes still red. "Yeah. Rosemary wanted me to go out to dinner with her tonight. I should be back about 8:30 or 9. Is that okay?"

The knowledge that Rosemary still cared and still thought of Belinda as a friend helped Ember feel better. "Sure. Go enjoy."

"Thanks, and I hope Cecil comes up with something wonderful."

"So do I, dear. So do I."

Ember fretted the entire taxi ride over, trying to figure out what miracle he could pull off. At least it would be something; which was more than the nothing she had now.

Cecil was standing outside with a smile in his normal impeccably tailored slacks and a lavender oxford shirt. She looked at his outfit and realized how much of a poor relation she looked, dressed in jeans and a T-shirt with slip-on shoes. She sighed as she got out of the cab; one more thing to owe someone.

"Stop it right now, *Liebchen*," Cecil commanded as he paid the taxi driver, then ushered her up the stairs. "You're my great goddaughter and you don't owe me a thing."

Ember blinked at him in surprise. "How did you know I was thinking that?"

"Simple. You had the same look your father would get whenever he needed to borrow something or ask for help. He hated owing people. A bad habit you seemed to have picked up. But you owe me nothing. Is that clear?"

His manner was so imperious, she couldn't help but agree.

"Good. Now I importuned Simon to come over and help. He is a wizard with makeup and hair, so trust me, you won't recognize yourself when he is done with you."

Bewilderment allowed her to just nod and follow along as a thin young man with wild hair grinned and winked at her. "No worries. I'll have her looking like a princess. You just find me the outfit, Cec."

Her brain locked on to that word. "Yes, outfit. Cecil, how can you help? I love you, but you're a..." She paused and changed her word, not wanting to offend. "A confirmed bachelor, who's never had many women around. It isn't like you have some dress an ex-lover left that would fit me."

Cecil started to laugh, a tinkle of deep bell tones. "Confirmed bachelor. Please, let's call a spade a spade, *Liebchen*. I'm an old fairy, who has had many lovers, some of which did leave dresses. And while I don't have sex with women, I have many women who are dear friends. I'm gay, not misogynistic." He led her into his spare bedroom while he talked. "Besides I did have a grandmother who was a force of nature, and she will be the one to rescue you."

She looked around, half expecting an ancient woman to pop out of the closet. Instead, there was an old trunk sitting in the middle of the bed.

"My grandmother lived a life you would only believe if you saw it on film. She was a courtesan in Italy during Mussolini's reign of idiocy and firmly believed in buying the best. When she got pregnant, on purpose of course, with my father, she convinced her current lover to marry her and take her away from the aftereffects of the war. But, before she did that, she carefully packed up everything she'd had custom designed for her – in case she ever had a daughter that needed it, according to her. I suspect she was hedging her bets, fearing she might need them again. Unfortunately, she had two sons, who had sons. And me, with my love of the theater, became the closest thing she had to a daughter. Hence, her legacy, your windfall."

As he spoke, he had been busy pulling sealed package after sealed package out of the trunk. "Adaelia, my grandmother, had curves all her life." Cecil shot her a sharp glance. "And she used those curves to great effect. Since the majority of the clothing she left me is couture, altering it to fit you should be relatively easy. Well, easy for me and Simon. Theater teaches you to alter almost anything very quickly. It won't hold up to a lifetime of wear. But for a night, you'll look like a princess. Now choose."

She felt like she had fallen into a fairy tale. Stepping towards the bed, her hand trembling, she touched the package of each of the six dresses.

One in white and gold sparkled like a Christmas ornament.

Another in green and gold, so rich and lush it brought to mind the Nile in all its glory.

The third gown in a red so rich she thought of pomegranates dripping juice.

Next cream-colored lace, so intricate and fine she shuddered thinking of touching it.

One in rich purple edged with black caught her attention.

But she reached for the blue. Blue so vivid, the image of the ocean, sparkling with fish, hung in her mind. Hints of silver could be seen through the bag.

"Could I see that one? Please?"

"I was sure you would go for the green. But let me get it out and take a look at them. It is been too many decades since I've looked at them to remember details." Cecil pulled the dress out of the bag and hung it on the door for Ember to look at.

Blue trimmed in silver, a corset like bodice, sleeveless, with blue lace wrapping over her shoulders.

"Ah yes. That will look wonderful on you. No bra needed. That corset should hold you up wonderfully. And she had a mask to match." He pulled out the additions to the dress. A stunning filigreed silver mask and a small purse made up of the same colors.

"Bathroom is there, go try it on."

"You sure? It is so expensive."

"*Liebchen*, things like this are made to be worn, to be admired. And I'm pretty sure my body type will not do it justice."

She snickered at the image and reverently took the dress down and into the bathroom with her. A few minutes later she emerged to see Cecil and Simon waiting for her.

"Oh my, that does look delicious. But it needs a bit of tweaking. The corset means we don't need to adjust through the bust though."

Both men got up and twisted and turned her, marking things with pins while she just felt awkward. In the bathroom, she hadn't been able to lace it up herself, so the bodice sagged. She looked like a little girl playing dress up from her mother's closet.

"This is easy to fix. Give me an hour, and it'll be ready," Cecil declared after stepping back.

"Good. It will take about that for me to do something with this mess." Simon sighed, lifting up a lock of Ember's hair.

"I'm still here," she protested as they talked around her.

"Yes, dear. Just be a good little doll for us. And enjoy the results." The tone and the wink Simon gave her prevented her from being offended, and she didn't have any other options, so she went along with it.

They made her strip, providing her a robe to slip into. Simon pulled her back into the living room, dumping her into an office chair. "Just hold still dear. I'll do a miracle. Trust me."

For the next forty-five minutes, her hair and face were pulled, plucked, tilted, blown, curled, and other things she'd never even heard of before, much less had done to her.

"I'm ready," Cecil called. "And I found the shoes to go with it. What size feet do you have *Liebchen*?"

"Um, about an eight." At this point she felt like she was caught in an ocean current, and her only option was to go with it. Fighting it would be a lost cause.

"Then this should work. A bit loose at eight and half, but

should be okay."

"I'm done with her," Simon called. "I think you'll like."

"Good and I'm done with the dress. Come in here and slip it on. I'll turn my back."

Feeling like she had fallen through the looking glass, Ember headed back to the room, where Cecil held up the dress. "Slip it on." He handed it to her and turned around, his impatience coming through every tap of his fingers.

She let the robe tumble off her shoulders and stepped into the dress, pulling up the zipper to the waist.

"It needs to be laced now."

Cecil whirled around and moved behind her, tightening it up in short hard jerks that almost pulled her off her feet. But then the bodice was snug.

"Reach down and pull up your girls a bit so I can make sure this is supporting you."

Feeling like an idiot, she did that, pulling up each breast until it was snug in the cup waiting for it. "Done."

"Good." He finished lacing. It felt good. Stiff, but her back was supported, her breasts were firmly held, and it was strangely comfortable, though sitting might be more problematic.

"Slip these on."

He handed her two shoes with inch high heels that looked like they were made of silvery glass.

"Are these glass? They'll shatter."

"No, they are plexiglass, with gel insoles. Not exactly period, but they should be comfortable. A designer friend of mine had left them over here as a joke. They should fit you just fine. The slippers that went with that dress didn't fare as well as the dress did."

She slipped them on and took the purse he handed her, which from the weight felt like he had already put her cellphone and ID in it. The shoes felt like they were at least tolerable, if she got to sit occasionally.

Turning around, she looked at the two men. "Well, how do I look?"

Cecil just grinned. "Go to the front door. I have a full-length mirror near it."

Hoping she looked nice, she headed that way and then froze in shock at the image looking back at her.

A woman dressed in blue silk, her hair in an up-do of blond curls, the sapphire and silver filigree mask bringing out platinum highlights, looked back at her. She saw light blue eyes that sparkled and rich lips that she touched to verify they were hers. His grandmother's dress gave her body a true hourglass figure. Her already impressive bosom now was covered with blue silk that had not lost its luster in the last seventy years, and her figure filled it out to perfection. The touch of glitter on her cheekbones made her look like a fairy had covered her in kisses.

"I, I look like a princess."

"Of course you do. Do you think I just work miracles on ordinary mortals?" Simon teased as she stood looking at herself in awe.

"You will wow them all, *Liebchen*," Cecil assured her as she spun, looking in the mirror. "But don't stay out too late." His voice teased her as she looked at the stranger in the mirror.

"I still have to be up by 4:00 AM, so I don't think that'll be an issue." Ember stood staring in the mirror. "I just can't believe that is me. I look like that?" She shot him a teasing look. "You are a fairy godmother, aren't you?"

"Fairy I may be dear, but that would be godfather, thank you very much." Cecil affected an affronted pose even as she giggled at him.

"Thank you for all of this. Not just the dress or makeup, but everything. You've been a true friend through all of this."

"Pfft, it was nothing you would not have done for me. Now stand still so Simon can fix this last bit of hair."

In her heart, she prayed she would have been as giving as he had been if the situation had been reversed. With a sigh she shook off the sober thought and stood still to let Simon tweak her hair.

"Okay, *Liebchen*, run. My friend is driving you there in between his other pickups. Don't keep him waiting."

"Oh, a special friend, huh?" She arched an eyebrow at him as she picked up the white silk stole, her clutch bag, mask, and the all-important entrant copy.

"A gentleman never kisses and tells." He stuck his nose up in the air and sniffed. "Now run along. I'll arrange to get the dress back at a later time. You are still young, so try to remember that?"

"I will." Smiling, Ember headed out of the apartment, and as she stepped outside of the building, an older man with silver hair leaned against an elegant Bentley.

"Your chariot awaits, Madame."

With a sense of glee, she slipped into the elegant car, and her chauffeur for the night closed it behind her. In but a moment, the smooth purr of the engine whisked her to the hotel that Jordan had been working on for so long. Peering out the window, she caught her first glimpse of it all decked out for the party.

The hotel had changed drastically from the bedraggled Mission-style adobe hotel she remembered when she first moved here. She hadn't paid much attention to the changes, what with Mom and Belinda occupying what little free time she had. Nevertheless, it had been transformed into a Mediterranean palace. The changes were subtle, yet sweeping, and she longed to walk the halls, to feel the cool wind she imagined would drift in off the Grecian Sea. Lanterns lit the drive up to the hotel, and soft music greeted them as they pulled up.

The opening of the door pulled her from her daydreams and she grinned to herself. She had to win the contest, get the prize, and maybe the job as chef. The window for her mom's treatment was dwindling.

No, she told herself sternly. Tonight she would be young and responsibility-free. Drink, dance, and wait for the announcement of the winner of the contest. With a smile of thanks at the hand her chauffeur offered, she climbed out of the car and slipped her mask on. The clear elastic band had been an easy addition and it looked like it floated on her face.

"Cecil told me to remind you to forget being responsible. Enjoy being young."

The smile that spread to her whole face hadn't graced it in far too long. "I will, at least for tonight. Thank you again."

"My pleasure, Madame." He nodded and slipped back into the driver's seat, and then drove down the driveway, leaving her standing with all the other guests that were heading into the hotel.

Feeling strangely at ease with her face covered, Ember headed into the hotel, the way to the grand ballroom obvious from the signage and the fabulously attired peopled heading that direction.

Maybe Jordan would be here, and they could steal a dance or two. Surely the owner wouldn't deny his workers a chance to enjoy the celebration of their hard work. She took a breath intended to reassure herself, but it made her more aware of her nerves. She headed in, blending with the other grand-opening attendees.

Chapter Twenty-Four

The taste test had definitely been required and with Clay and Greyson demanding to be involved in tasting the food "their" restaurant would be serving, it had quickly been narrowed down to three a few days ago.

Monica stated she'd made her final decision, and no one else would find out until she announced it. And it all would come out tonight.

Ring walked into the large hall where the ball would be held. They had set up one corner with a parquet dance floor, placing a cash bar next to it. A buffet with the three finalists' dishes had been set up along one wall. The colors had been finalized, and the new tablecloths and carpet would be getting their first showing. He admitted it looked sharp, and the new paint brought out the blue.

He tugged on his outfit a bit, a white linen shirt over black trousers that fit him like a second skin, and knee-high boots in black. His mom had said she had a vest for him that would match her outfit, so he looked around for her and wondered if he should trust Greyson and Clay to show up in acceptable outfits. They had assured him it would be appropriate, but while he might trust Greyson when he said that, Clay was a completely different story. He would show up in a loincloth if he thought he could get away with it.

"Ring, over here."

He turned and saw his mother in a stunning yellow gown that, as he got closer, he realized was a yellow brocade. It fit her perfectly and reminded him of pictures of her and Luke when they were younger.

"Here you go." She handed him a vest made of the same brocade, and he slipped it on, a simple frog at the front securing it. "Ah, good. It looks nice on you and brings out the bleached highlights in your hair."

He shrugged, thinking that wearing clothes was always good, and female approval very good, though right now he wanted the approval from Ember more than his mom. "Everything ready?"

"Yes. Though I realized I overlooked letting the finalists know they are finalists." She sighed. "I just got too caught up in everything else. So I do hope they show up, or they'll miss all the pageantry and we'll be calling them after the fact."

The urge to roll his eyes at his mother was strong but he resisted. "We'll see. You have it all figured out what you are doing?"

"Oh, I'm not the one announcing the winner. That will be you."

"Wait, what? Why me? You did all the judging."

"Yes I did." Her smile was serene and he scowled back, making her smile even more. "Which means when you read the name in the envelope I'll hand you, it will be a surprise to you also."

"Fine, fine. I'll do it."

She chewed on the corner of her lip, and her eyes alighted on Greyson and Clay, who were just walking in. "Ah ha. Just the men I needed to talk to. Will you go grab those two and meet me in meeting room Sicily?"

"And which one is that again?" They had renamed all the meeting rooms, and he still didn't have them all straight.

"The small one we did the initial winnowing in."

"Ah. Okay. Let me go grab them."

He headed over to his friends, who did look rather nice if a bit rakish on Clay's part.

"Hey. Mom wants to talk to us."

"I swear I didn't do it. Whatever it is, I didn't do it, or know about it," Clay protested instantly, guilt flashing across his face.

Ring opened his mouth to ask, changed his mind, and murmured, "I don't want to know. I really don't. Come on."

He caught Greyson giving Clay the eye, and part of him did want to know what Clay felt guilty about, but right now he didn't have the energy to follow up on it.

The three of them traipsed down to the room, where Monica waited for them.

"Shut the door boys and take a seat."

"Oh, boy, we're in for it now."

"Yes, you've been such bad boys." Monica rolled her eyes at them, and for a minute the young woman his dad fell in love with flashed through. "Not quite. Now please sit." She waited until they were all looking at her. "Ring, do you have any desire to run this hotel and restaurant."

The question threw him off balance. What could she mean? "This is dad's legacy. I'm not sure what you're asking."

With a twist of one side of her mouth she asked, "I'm asking, is this what you want to do? If your father were still alive, would you be here now working to repair this place?"

Ring sat back in his chair, and said his thoughts out loud. "I never wanted to be tied here, but when Dad died, I couldn't just let it all fall apart. But besides him dying, and dropping out of school, I've enjoyed doing this. It was fun and challenging. Though a bit stressful." He paused and added, "My friends trying to kill me might have something to do with that."

Monica nodded. She shifted those clear eyes to Greyson and Clay. "And what about you two?"

They looked at each other and shrugged. Greyson spoke up. "We did this to help out Ring. But he's right. Excluding the almost killing him part"—Ring flipped him off—"this has been fun. Hard work, but figuring it all out and getting it done was interesting."

Clay shrugged. "Look, I grew up in the oil fields, but I think that the oil industry is slowly dying. You need a high-tech degree anymore to be competitive. And while I'm sure Dad would find a place for me, I don't have the passion for it he does. Building, repairing things is much more interesting."

She took a deep breath, looked at the three of them. "So what do you want to do?"

They looked at each other, long familiarity causing ideas and thoughts to flash between the three of them without any words being said. Ring spoke for the three of them. "We want to do this again. Repair and revitalize places."

This time she smiled. "Good. I'm bored to tears and I want to feel closer to Luke. So, I'll run this place. I know enough after all the years of listening to him to do it. And what I don't know I'll learn. You three, set up a business. And as soon as I start making money on this place, Ring, I'll repay what you spent to get this place going, while you two will get your net profits."

The idea just felt right to Ring. And there were lots of places that needed the investment. With the three of them, they could get some decent loans to repair and resell places. He turned to look at them, and the excitement on their faces gave him their answer.

"Well then." She stood up. "It is settled. For tonight, we need to find our new chef, and you need to dance with your girl." Monica paused and turned to cast matchmaking eyes on Ring. "She is coming, right?"

"I hope so. She said she was."

"Good. I want to meet her."

He swallowed a bit at that but nodded.

"Now go have fun, and don't get drunk until later. We do have an image to maintain, you know." She grinned, winked at them, and walked out of the room. The boys watching her go.

"You know, Ring, your mom's got a fine body."

Ring just walked out, refusing to respond to Clay in any way at all.

Moving back into the main area, he was surprised at how many people had shown up, and pleased. But his eyes were looking for one person in particular.

Hunger grabbed him and he went to get something to eat while he waited. It had been a busy day. When he turned around, a salmon spinach puff in his mouth, his eyes found her, and he forgot to breathe.

Even with the mask, he knew her instantly. She looked like a goddess that had stepped down from Olympus. And somehow he had been lucky enough to find her. Now if he could keep her. Losing all interest in food, he wove through the crowd of people and darted in front of her.

"You look incredible." His hand reached up to trace down her jaw.

Her smile was thanks enough as it lit up her face. "Thank you. You look rather impressive yourself."

"I'm a guy; I'll wear whatever I'm told to wear. But you, wow."

She blushed and he wanted nothing more than to show her right there how much he loved her. But it wasn't the time or the place. "You hungry?"

"Yes, please. It's been an... emotional day."

"Come on. Grab a plate and load up, we made lots."

He pulled her over to the buffet and she slipped her mask onto her wrist as she took a plate, froze, and asked. "What are these?"

"Food? They are all the entries from the three finalists. We wanted people to taste what our menu would be like."

She nodded, a bit hesitant, and they wove through, filling their plates, then grabbed a small table near a wall. Ember arched her brow at that.

"If we grab a big table, Clay and Greyson will come join. And I want you all to myself for a little bit."

She smiled, and he felt heat rush through him. "I think I can go along with that."

They shared the food, and Ring noticed that her hands shook a bit as she picked up some of the pieces, but mostly he noticed her. The dress was stunning, and all he wanted to do was see it on the floor.

He heard a ting from a glass and glanced up to see his mother standing up there. Time to get back to work.

"I gotta go for a bit. I'll be back. Don't leave?"

"Nope. Have fun?"

She looked curious, but he figured everything would be explained in a minute. Kissing her with a tender brush of his lips, he headed up front.

He did look nice, but what could he need to do here, tonight? Her gaze fell back on the plate and she felt her heart start to race again, but this time from excitement. They were serving her food. Hers. Trying to keep hope from overwhelming her, she went back to watching Ring walk up to the front and focused in on what the woman was saying.

"Hi, everyone. Thank you so much for coming to our grand reopening of the Hotel Del Mar. We hope you are enjoying the new soothing atmosphere and the excellent food. I am sure most of you know me. I'm Monica Jordan and my husband, Luke, ran this place prior to this death."

Ember tilted her head, finding the name combination odd, but she just kept listening.

"When we decided to remodel this place, to make it more competitive in today's marketplace, we knew we needed to update the restaurant also. Lacking any good candidates, we held a contest. The food we are serving tonight is based on the recipes of the finalists. In my hand I have the envelope with the name of the winner."

Ember's focus snapped to that. The possibilities that lay in that envelope made her dizzy with hope. She stood, moving closer.

"But rather than me reading out the winner, I'd like to invite the man who has been the driving force behind this remodel, my and Luke's son, Ring Jordan."

She watched Jordan walk up and take the envelope from the woman, his mother, and kiss her softly on the cheek.

Everything fell into place, and she wanted the floor to open up and swallow her. She'd been calling him Jordan all this time, and instead his name was Ring and he owned the place. Why hadn't he told her?

That thought froze her. His dad had died. He'd come here, he must have dropped out. And he'd needed someone that didn't ask how he was, just like she had. He never pushed her, or she him.

And still he came to see her as often as he did.

The knowledge warmed her, and she let herself hear the words he was saying.

"…so after hours of debate, and many tastes tests, here we are. It is my honor to say the winner of the position of chef for our restaurant is…" He paused and struggled to get the envelope open. After a ridiculous amount of difficulty, he managed to pull out the card and look at it.

She clutched her copy of the plan in her hands tightly.

"The winner is—" An explosion from outside shook the room, and a wave of hot air hit her through the open doors to the patio.

Ember staggered, the sudden heat and noise throwing her off balance. The room went silent, the murmurs and cries arose as everyone looked around. Those in the back of the room gasped. She overheard someone mutter something about fire.

Trying to think of anything outdoors that could explode that way, she moved with the flow of people to look down the hill to see what the issue was. Maybe a tanker? A truck or car? She was pretty sure that only happened in the movies. She pushed through the crowd of people looking down the hill, until she could see the scene.

There was so much smoke that it took her a minute to piece together what she was looking at. The road, the path to the beach, the strip of buildings where the bakery stood – her thoughts faded away as everything resolved.

The bakery was on fire.

The knowledge slammed into her harder than the wave of heat had. The flames engulfed the lower building, and Ember followed the flames with her eyes, staring as she realized the apartment above was wreathed in fire also.

Mom, Belinda. She dug out her phone, fumbling blindly for it. 8:45. Dear god. With hands gone numb, she hit the icon for her mother.

Nothing — it just rang and went to voice mail.

"Oh, Mom, not now. Don't ignore me now." She called again, still nothing. Moving to Belinda, she clicked it and got the same thing. Nothing but voice mail.

Panic grabbed her in an iron grip that didn't falter, tighter than the fear she felt the night her dad died. Trying to keep her heart beating, she headed down the hill, moving slowly at first and then picking up her pace. She stumbled, the shoes on her feet too big and slipping with the fast movement.

"Dammit." She tried to keep moving, and one slipped off. "Fuck it." She grabbed her other shoe and let go of the death grip on the copy of the entry. It fluttered to rest next to her other shoe.

"I don't have time for this." Ignoring the shoe and the

entry, she grabbed the other shoe in one hand and ran barefoot down the hill. The shredding of her hose, the gravel biting into her feet, were faint sensations she barely noted. She tore around the back, headed for the stairs to the apartment. Firemen were already there. Her mind supplied the location of the fire station a few blocks away.

"Stop, you can't go up there."

They grabbed her, preventing her from racing up the stairs.

"I have to. My mom and sister might be up there. I have too." She didn't recognize her own voice, shrill and cracking as she struggled.

"If they were, it's too late. I'm sorry. We tried to get up the stairs, but it is already completely engulfed."

She heard the sympathy in his voice. It didn't matter. Where was her family? They handed her over to a cop who pulled her back to the sidewalk, away from the flames. Ember stood watching the red, yellow, and orange flames dancing in the sky as they devoured everything she owned, maybe everything she loved.

Pulling up the phone, she dialed both of them again and again. No answer. Desperate she called Cecil.

"*Liebchen.* Are you having a wonderful time with your prince?"

"Cecil, call Mom. See if she is okay. She won't answer the phone for me."

"Ember, what is wrong?" His voice was sharp.

"The bakery, the apartment, exploded. They might have come home. Call them please," she begged, willing to give her life for one more cuss word from her mother.

"Okay, okay, hold on."

She heard the odd empty tone of being on hold as he flipped over. A minute later he was back.

"I'm sorry, dear, she didn't answer me either. You know how she gets. She may have just shut it off."

"I'm sure that's the answer. Thank you. Call me if they get

a hold of you." Her voice was dead as she looked at the flames.

Cecil said something else, but she didn't hear him. She hung up and just stared ahead.

She sank down to sit on the ground, watching everything crumble to ash. She couldn't think, couldn't scream, couldn't cry. There was nothing there, her heart a formless puddle of glass in her icy cold chest.

Chapter Twenty-Five

Ring stood with the rest of the people, looking down at the bakery, the flames beautiful in their horror. He scanned the crowd for Ember, desperate for a glimpse of her. She'd be upset. He needed to find her.

"Ring?"

He turned at his mother's voice.

"We should give the guests a few more minutes then get back to the announcement."

He nodded, distracted, still looking around.

"Everything okay?"

"I don't see Ember. I'm worried about her."

"Ah, she did come. You will introduce me this time."

"I know, Mom. But she works at the bakery." He had a bad feeling in the pit of his stomach and didn't know why. "She was here, now I can't find her."

"I'm sure she stepped away to call someone. She did work there after all." Monica smiled. "She's fine."

"Yeah." He wandered back up and gave people a few more minutes. The excitement had gone out of the evening.

When he had everyone's attention, he spoke. "Obviously I was upstaged a bit tonight, so I'll get right to it. The winner is E Verre. Is E Verre here? Please come forward so we can introduce the new chef for our restaurant."

There was looking and head turning but no one came up. He just couldn't ditch the feeling in the pit of his stomach.

"Well I guess the winner will have to be contacted afterwards. Thank you so much for coming everyone and please enjoy."

He stepped away and headed right towards Greyson and

Clay who were coming up from the drive.

"Have you seen Ember?"

"Us?" Greyson glanced at Clay who shook his head. "No, we wandered down to see the damage, but there were so many emergency personnel we couldn't get close. However, we did find this on the way up."

Greyson handed him one silvery glass-like shoe and a copy of one of the entries. "It was on the path down to the bakery."

The entry was the winner, the one that had come with the plan and the resumes. He stared at the shoe blankly, then an image of Ember walking towards him, her sparkly shoes catching the light from the candles, reflecting it back.

"This is Ember's shoe." A bad feeling had risen and wrapped around the base of his throat.

"Call her. Yeesh, you're not thinking much." Clay rolled his eyes at Ring as he took a sidestep to grab something to eat.

He wasn't thinking. Ring dug his phone out and hit her number. It rang. After several rings she answered.

"I'm sorry. I can't talk now, Jordan. No, wait, your name is Ring. It doesn't matter. I can't talk now." There were sirens and people yelling, her voice had no life as she spoke.

"Wait, you thought my first name was Jordan?" He shook his head frustrated. "Ember, what's wrong, where are you?"

"I don't know where they are. My fault. All my fault." The dead tone of her voice terrified him. "Good-bye, Jordan, Ring, whomever." With an odd sigh the line disconnected.

"Ember? Ember," he didn't quite shout, but if he thought it would make a difference he would have.

"Ring, what's wrong?" Greyson looked at him, his head tilted at an angle.

"I don't know. She sounds funny, and there is so much noise, sirens, people yelling." His head jerked up, looking at the conflagration at the base of the hill. "Oh, god. Does she live there?" He always picked her up there, thinking she just didn't want him to see where she lived, but what if that is where she lived?

He took off at a dead run, ignoring the twinge in his side, the yells of Greyson and Clay, and ran down the hill, looking for the blue that had captivated him earlier today. Weaving through the people, a flash of blue and silver caught his eye. He altered his course to find her sitting on the ground, her face blank as the light from the fire reflected off her eyes.

She looked unharmed, at least physically. He crouched down next to her, pitching his voice low. "Ember, are you okay?"

Her head turned towards him like she fought molasses and she blinked, the smallest twitch of her lips. "It's gone. Everything is gone."

Ring glanced back at the flames, then at her. "Ember, did you live there?"

"Room and salary that was the deal. Everything's up there. I can't find them."

"Oh, Ember." Ring didn't know what to say, so he focused on the other part. "Who can't you find?"

"Mom, sister. They should have been home by now, but they don't answer the phone. So where else can they be?"

Ring thought he might be sick. Having his dad die had sucked. But this—losing his family like this—it might kill him too.

"Ember, come on. You can't do anything here. Come stay with me. I'll help you figure it out."

She just shrugged but didn't resist as he helped her up. Greyson and Clay had apparently followed him down as they stood watching him, twin looks of shock on their faces.

He turned with her, getting her to cross the street, when a screech wrenched both of them around.

"EMBER!"

She spun in his arms so fast the metallic trim of the dress scratched him. Like a light switch had been thrown, the vacant empty look on her face disappeared; life came flooding back in.

"Belinda."

A golden-haired girl came limping from the sidewalk, and Ember caught her in a bear hug that looked like it would leave bruises.

"You didn't answer your phone when I called. Why didn't you answer?" The words she screamed were almost drowned out by the noise of the fire and the responders. Ring moved in close, unable to bear not being there for her.

"Sorry, sorry. We were on the way back, and I just didn't want to deal with the guilt about the dress. I'm so sorry."

He recognized the girl; the one who had complained about her sister, blaming everything that had happed on her 'fat, ugly' sister. Ring wanted to slap her. How could she disparage her smart, sexy, beautiful sister? Then he remembered everything she said had happened, and the life that had blown up in Ember's face. Suddenly it all made sense.

She had to be the strongest woman he'd ever known.

They held each other and babbled. He turned to Greyson. "Would you go up and get them one of the suites, and get some sweats and T-shirts from my clothes and leave it for them. It'll be a bit big but at least clean.

Greyson just nodded and headed up to the hotel, and Ring turned his attention back to Ember.

"Ember, we're getting the two of you a room. Okay, so let's go up and get you out of here."

"Thanks... Ring." She stumbled over the name a little bit. "Belinda, this is Ring, he is my... friend."

Belinda looked up at him, and her face paled . He just gave her a look. Belinda looked down, avoiding Ring's eyes. Ember quirked a quizzical look, but seeing life in her face made it better. They began to trudge their way back up to the hotel. Remembering the contest Ring asked, "Ember, what is your last name?"

She looked at him, confused. "Verre. Why?"

Joy and sadness competed. He reached out with one arm, hugging her as they walked. "You won. You're the new chef for the hotel. If you want it."

Ember stumbled to a halt and looked up at him, eyes wide. "I won? Really?"

"Yes, it was your name on the card. I thought you just worked at a bakery and were going to school to become a chef."

She shook her head in answer as she resumed walking again. "No, I've got an AA in culinary arts. I had won the scholarship to Le Cordon Bleu for the master's program. So I could polish up the stuff I put in the application."

"Ah. Well yours was amazing, and the food." He shrugged. "You saw everyone eating it and raving about it. It was delicious."

"Thank you."

Belinda looked at her, a look of surprise on her face. "My sister won? Ember?"

Ring swallowed a snarl and went for polite, though it was difficult. "Yes. She's amazing. I didn't realize how amazing until I saw the proposal. You will take the job, right, Ember?"

She sighed, not looking at him. "An hour ago I would have grabbed with both hands, but right now?" Turning at the crest of the small incline, she looked down at the flames. "Now I don't know what is going to happen, or if my mother is alive or dead." She pulled Belinda into a hug with one arm. "I have to think about her first, and see if she can get strong enough to qualify again."

"Qualify?"

Belinda spoke up. "I was qualifying for the Olympic swimming trials when the accident happened. I can try again in four years, if I can get back in shape by then."

They had reached the entry to the lobby, and Monica came

out to meet them.

"Mom. I'd like to present Ember Verre. Our winner." Monica's face lit up, but he continued. "And the woman I'm madly in love with."

He felt Ember stiffen in his arms and turn to look at him. "You're what?"

"I love you. And finding out everything you've been dealing with just makes me love you more. You're sexy, smart, gorgeous, and as awful as everything has been for you, I'm so glad you fell back into my life."

Chapter Twenty-Six

Ember looked at him, trying to focus on his voice. The numbness from watching her life go up in flames vaporized at the look in his eyes. She listened to his words as her heart raced with fear and joy.

"I, I." She swallowed and for a moment put aside Belinda and Sabrina in her mind. "I love you. When you got hurt it almost killed me. The idea of not having you in my life was intolerable. I want to learn everything about you. But right now Belinda is my priority; I can't walk away from her." She might have screamed, or cried, but she had already emptied the well of tears inside her.

Waiting for his anger or frustration, his laugh confused her. He pulled her into him and kissed the top of her head.

"And that is why I'm crazy about you. I'd never ask you to leave her. Tell me what you need, and I'll help."

"We'll help." Ember whirled to face the woman, Ring's mom. "After all, I can't have my newest employee distracted by other issues, can I?"

Her smile exuded warmth and welcome, allowing some of the weight that felt like it was crushing her to lift.

"Thank you."

Ring kissed the top of her head again and led her to the hotel.

His arms around her kept her steady as they stood watching the chaos below. Where was her mother? The idea of her dying in that fire horrified her. Worse was the niggling thought that life would be so much easier if she was gone.

Ember chastised herself mentally; she didn't want her mother gone. She just wanted her mother back. Fingers itched to pull out the phone and listen to the voice mail once more, but she resisted, instead watching Belinda talking to Jor... no, Ring's mom. That name suited him so much better than Jordan.

"Come on. Let's get you cleaned up and into some comfortable clothes."

His words jerked her out of her daze and she looked down at the dress, aghast at the soot, smears, and even a tear.

"Oh no, I ruined Cecil's gift to me." One more blow. She didn't know if she could take any more.

"Ember." The soft touch of her sister's hand on her arm drew her attention. "He loves you. He would never be mad at you for this. You have to be the most responsible person I know, and Cecil knows that. We will get it cleaned up and see what damage can't be repaired."

Throat tight, Ember nodded. She vaguely heard Ring tell Clay and Greyson to get them all food and meet them in the penthouse suite for now.

"Come on, Ember. We can relax in my rooms and give you a chance to recover. I've even got some whiskey up there."

"Thank god." The mutter came from her heart, and he chuckled as his arm held her tight.

As they headed up she heard a faint voice yelling, "Ember, Belinda?"

She stopped and turned around to see someone pushing through the people, a worn backpack on her back and an even more beat-up leather duffel in one hand. A woman who, except for the short no-nonsense haircut, was a ringer for Sabrina. She bullied her way through the crowd.

"Seri?"

The woman halted to a stop in front of them. "Thank god, you're okay. When I realized the fire was right where you had said you lived, I almost died." She pulled Belinda into a hug, and then her strong arms pulled a stiff Ember into her arms.

"I'm here."

And that was the final blow. Ember yanked backwards, and her inner self-control disintegrated.

"You're here? Where were you two months ago when Dad died? Where the hell were you when I was killing myself to figure out how to support a mother and sister that hated me and blamed me for everything?" She heard Belinda's soft moan of protest, but she couldn't stop the words that flowed from her. "Where the bloody hell were you when I was working sixteen-hour days trying to figure out how to deal with insurance I couldn't afford, and barely having enough money for food? Where the fuck were you when I needed you?" The last words came out in a wail, and Ring pulled her into his arms, holding her as she started to cry.

"I wasn't here. And I'm sorry for that. Maybe we can go somewhere else and talk, rather than providing theater for everyone in the lobby?" Her voice had both sorrow, empathy, and a touch of wry humor in it that helped Ember get control. She stood there for a moment glaring at her, wanting to hold onto the anger, to relish in having someone to lash out at. But with a deep sigh, she released it. There had been enough lashing out in her life, there needed to be something else.

"Come with us. I think all of us could use some food and sustenance."

Fifteen minutes later, dressed in a T-shirt and sweats of Ring's, all of them, Monica, Clay, and Greyson included, were in the sitting area in the penthouse, whiskey in everyone's hands except Belinda, who had mineral water, being underage and doing Olympic training after all.

"So you know I had left to backpack through Asia?" Seri started off, watching Ember and Belinda with dark eyes so similar to her sister.

Ember nodded mutely, her fingers white around the tumbler as she leaned into Ring's supportive arm.

"Well, I made the mistake of accessing my email from

Taiwan, and they hacked it. I just shrugged it off and didn't worry about it. Sabrina and I were never good about staying in touch, and I figured I'd be back in another two months. I ran into a friend in Taipei, and he asked how you guys were handling Richard's death. I had no idea what he was talking about. I spent two days trying to recover my email and respond, but everything I sent was marked as having a virus. I begged a friend to send you a note as I raced here. Between flight delays and dealing with security issues, apparently I looked a bit over frantic. They pulled me out for a security check — twice. I just got in a few hours ago. Ember, I swear to you, had I known what was going on, I would have dropped everything to be here. You and Belinda are my nieces, and I love my sister dearly. Just because we don't talk much when I'm off on my adventures doesn't mean I don't think about you."

Some of the brittle glass of Ember's heart strengthened a bit and she took a sip of her whiskey, concentrating on the burn and the sweet smoky taste.

"Thank you. I'm sorry I vented on you. But it's been a bit of a day," Ember said, still not looking up. Seeing that face, and having it not be angry with her, hurt too much right now.

Seri grinned. "So I see. No worries. I'd have been venting on me too. Ember, you've done amazingly well. And I can't tell you how disappointed I am in most of our 'friends.' I promise, I'm here now."

The conversation drifted to what exactly had happened to Sabrina and Belinda while Seri roamed around Asia. Ember provided more than the bare detail that had been in the emails, as to what exactly had happened to Sabrina's mind. Even as they talked, Ember worried over where her mother could be, compulsively checking her phone every few minutes.

When the room phone rang, everyone jumped.

Ring got up an answered it. "I see. Thank you. I'll be right down." He turned around with a grin. "There is apparently a woman in the lobby demanding to know where her 'worthless' step-nothing is, as she was supposed to be up here, gallivanting around."

"Mom?" Her voice emerged as a harsh whisper, and she coughed as the smoke from the fire caught up with her.

"Probably. Let me go get her. I'll be right back."

Ember stood up and paced the room as she waited, hoping it was Sabrina, wanting her mother with a need that was physical.

When the door clicked, and Ring pushed it open, the grim look on his face told her everything she needed to know. Sabrina strode in after her.

"Mom," Belinda jumped up and ran over to her, pulling her into a hug that Sabrina resisted for a moment then relaxed into. Ember moved to do the same when the vitriol spilled out.

"I see, up here dressed in his clothes like a whore, while our possessions go up in flames. Just shows how worthless you are. Why I ever agreed to raise you, I'll never understand."

The entire room took in a sharp breath, and Ember tried to remember to let it go, to understand it was damage and not her mother. She was rescued before she could respond.

"Sabrina, I always knew you could be a bitch, and took the easy way out of everything. But that was completely uncalled for." Seri stood up and walked over to Sabrina. "And if I ever hear you talk that way again about your amazing daughter, I will hold you down and wash your mouth out with soap. For once in your life, you are going to have to do something the hard way and fight yourself every inch of the way, until the mother that Ember and Belinda deserve is back. And I'm going to be here kicking your butt every time you slide back even a little. Do you understand me?"

Standing side by side, the differences between the sisters popped out. While their features were the same, Sabrina appeared thinner and willowy, while Seri was muscled and powerful. Sabrina bowed her head, and muttered softly. "Sorry, Ember. I'm trying."

"Not hard enough. I'm going to tattoo 'say something nice or keep your fucking mouth shut' on your hand if I have to." Seri turned and flashed a smile at Monica and Ring. "With that, could I possibly rent a room from you? I think my sister and I have a lot of catching up to do."

"But of course." Monica stood up smoothly. "I believe the boys got a room already, but I'll move you three to rooms with a door between them. If you'll come with me, I think we are all ready for bed."

The woman followed Monica out the door, Seri giving Ember a wink as she left. She felt Ring behind her and sagged against him, using his strength instead of her own.

Ring cast a glance at Clay and Greyson, and for once Clay got the hint first. He stood and walked over to touch Ember's shoulder.

"I'm sorry all this happened to you. And completely impressed by what you did. You ever need us, call. We don't believe in fair-weather friendships." Greyson had followed Clay's lead and stood up too.

"What he said. But for now, I think we're going to go downstairs and enjoy the party. Don't expect us back anytime soon."

With that they both left, and Ring pulled her back down to sit on the couch with him.

"Is that what you've been dealing with for the last few months?"

She didn't reply, just nodded, having picked up the whiskey glass from the table, gripping it in her hands, avoiding looking at him. Ring fought the desire to go beat her mother and sister.

"And yet you still had the ability to smile at me in the mornings and be nice to people?" His tone was soothing. She darted a glance up at him.

"Well, sure. I mean, you weren't yelling at me. If you were, I wouldn't have wanted to see you."

Ring chuckled and squeezed her where his arm still lay around her shoulders.

"You amaze me." At her curious look, he shook his head. "If someone was treating me like that, I would have washed my hands of them and been a jerk to everyone. Especially a stepmother."

"She's my mom. I couldn't leave her."

"Even when she treated you worse than a stranger would ever have?"

"Especially then. She's my mother in everything but blood. And she wasn't always like that."

"And that is what makes you so amazing." He gave in and tilted her head towards him, watching for any reluctance, but she moved in to meet him and he kissed her. The feeling of having her in his arms, mixed with the knowledge of just how amazing she was, overwhelmed him. Ring pulled her tight to him, letting his tongue dance with hers. When he pulled back they were both panting.

"Do you? I mean, I'd understand if you aren't up to-" He broke off as she laid a finger along his lips, a gentle smile curving hers.

"Yes, please." Her voice was soft and breathy as she spoke, and his body leapt to attention. Ring stood, pulling her up with him. "I want to pick you up and carry you to bed, but right now I'd tear my stitches. Rain check?"

Her low laugh wrapped around him and raised his pulse

even more. "Deal. Right now, just convince me it will all be all right?"

"It will, cause I'll be here. I'll help you with everything you need. Love means staying here, even when everything falls apart."

Ember turned her face up to him, and the look that resided there seared into his heart. Need, love, hope, and joy. A look he would forever associate with her.

The steps to the bed took forever, and yet, before he could figure out what to do, they were there, tumbling on the bed. His hands rode up under the borrowed shirt, caressing her body. He was thrilled to know she was there with him.

Ring had to fight to keep his hands steady as he pulled the T-shirt off, exposing the beauty that had filled his dreams since that long-ago night at the club.

Starting at her collarbone, he kissed his way down, missing the scent of cinnamon and other spices that always seemed to surround her but enjoying the subtle jasmine she wore tonight.

He still wore the costume from earlier, and her hands undid the frog on the vest and worked on the buttons on his shirt as he kissed down her naked torso. Ember whimpered when he pulled away from the reach of her hands, and he came back up to kiss her deeply.

"Soon. Let me finish worshiping you."

She arched a brow at him, but a soft smile tilted the sides of her lips, and she lay back as he slipped the sweats off of her. A sharp intake of breath escaped his lips as he saw the black lace revealed. Dropping the sweats on the floor, he kissed down the front of the lace, smelling her scent. It went straight through him. The need to be naked, to be touching her with all of his body, couldn't be put off anymore.

Ring pulled back and stood up, his eyes locked on her wide eyes, knowing the hunger in hers matched the hunger in his. His clothes were removed without any thought and left lying on the floor as he moved onto the bed with her. Lying down next to her, feeling her skin against his, he let go of thought and just felt.

A soft breast and the moan of pleasure as he took her nipple in his mouth.

The feel of her tongue licking down his inner hipbone.

The taste of her inner folds as he delved into them with his tongue.

Her mouth wrapped around him, pleasure shivering through him.

Ring roused enough to pull out a condom, but Ember took it and slid it over him, licking and nipping the shaft as she did so, then she rose and seated herself on him. His world narrowed to the woman rising above him, both of them moving in patterns that had come down through time.

Her head tilted back, hair falling loose and cascading down her back, as she hit her peak a moment before him. As the pleasure rippled through him, one thought solidified in his heart and made his pleasure even greater.

This is the woman he would marry.

Ring arched up, thrusting into her as he came, the vision of her in a wedding dress with his ring on her finger floating through his mind.

After they were cleaned up, she in a clean T-shirt of his and nothing else, he pulled her close to him and drifted down to sleep, the image of her by his side leaving a smile on his lips as sleep caught him.

Chapter Twenty-Six

Ember jerked awake early in the morning with a frantic thought. She had never called Ernie to let him know they were all right. Ring slept next to her as she scrambled for her cell phone. Finding it in a small pile next to the shoes and purse, she looked at it and saw a bunch of missed calls. Ember dialed, sitting in a chair, watching Ring sleep.

"Ember?"

There was a bit of panic in his voice, and a wave of guilt hit her.

"We're all okay, Ernie. None of us were there when it went up."

"Oh thank god." She heard the chair creak and the muffled umph as he sat down. "I'm sorry. This is my fault. When I sent you home, I was tired and the pain pills were a bit stronger than I realized. I left the gas on in one of the ovens and apparently it sparked out. The arson investigator has been there all night and let me know what the cause was early this morning. Ember, I am so sorry. I've got full insurance, so I'll work with you and the insurers to get you everything you need. I was so scared."

Relief that they were not at fault soothed her. "Thanks, Ernie. We're up at the Hotel Del Mar for now."

"Good, and I'm sorry again."

She said good-bye and looked up to see Ring looking at her.

"Everything okay?"

"Yeah, I think it will be."

"Good. Come back to bed." He lifted the covers, and she crawled back in, snuggling into his warmth.

They both must have fallen back asleep, as when they

woke, it was almost eleven. She tried to remember what time they went to bed last night but couldn't. It had been an eventful night.

Knocking at the bedroom door forced her all the way awake.

"Yes?" Ring asked as he climbed out of bed, a pair of boxer briefs on. She enjoyed the view as he stretched.

"Morning lovebirds. Ring, your mom asks if both of you could join her in the normal conference room." Clay's voice came through the door.

Ring turned to look at her and she nodded.

"Yep, give us about thirty okay?"

"Will do."

Thirty minutes later they walked into the conference room. Ring had taken her hand as soon as they left the room and hadn't released it. When they got there, Monica and Seri were sitting at the table, talking quietly. Seri looked better, less travel worn, and smiled when she saw them.

"Morning you two." Monica greeted them, and Ember ducked her head trying not to blush. While she had never expected anything to come of Ring and her, that hadn't stopped a few daydreams, and this was never how meeting his family went.

"There are some breakfast items over there. Nothing as good as what you make, I'm afraid, Ember." Monica smiled. "But Seri and I wanted to talk to you, and see if we can get some things settled."

Ember swallowed past the sudden lump in her throat, but the squeeze of her hand from Ring and his smile made it easier. Getting the coffee and a bagel, she settled down at the table with Ring sitting right next to her.

"Ember. Can you give me a full update on the issues with the money, and why you can't get to any of it?" Seri asked, frowning slightly.

"Sure." She laid it all out, pulling up her phone to get to

some of the documentation. Moving everything to cloud storage was the smartest thing she had done. If it had all been in her computer, she would have been in even more trouble.

She laid everything out, and Seri frowned.

"I don't say this to be mean, Ember, but I think you were stonewalled and tricked."

"What?" Dread pooled deep in her stomach, and she hastily put the bagel down.

"So, locking accounts for a short time under mysterious circumstances is normal. But they had cause of death, and any good lawyer should have been able to get them unlocked shortly. The house I totally understand, but your Mom should have still had access to her trust accounts."

Ember shook her head. "What trust accounts?"

Seri blinked at her, a funny look on her face. "Your mom didn't tell you?"

Ember just arched her brow at Seri, and she sighed. "I don't know if she didn't tell you or if she forgot. We are co-signers on each other's accounts, and she hasn't touched hers in about three decades." Another soft sigh. "I am sorry I missed the funeral. If I had known, I would have been here. I swear." She said it again, as if trying to convince herself.

Focusing on her coffee, Ember marshaled her thoughts. "I know. That is in the past. Where do we go now?"

There was silence in the room for a minute.

"Well, first. About your job-" Monica stopped at the knock on the door, and one of the hotel staff stuck their head in.

"Excuse me. There are two police detectives here asking for Ember Verre?"

What little appetite she had disappeared in a flash. She fought not to shake, but her hand trembled anyhow.

"Send them here, please," Monica asked. Ring took her hand in his, looking at her.

"Ember, you're family now. We aren't going anywhere."

His words startled her, and she caught a glimpse of an odd smile on Monica's face as she turned to look at Ring. "But you barely know me."

He responded with laughter. "Ember, over the last few months, I've gotten to know you as well as I know Clay and Greyson. You only know how to give the best, and I know you are the best thing in my life. Nothing can change that."

She just blinked at him, her mind whirling. Before she could come to any conclusions, the door opened and two men walked in. One of them she recognized as Detective Richert, the other, an older man, she didn't know.

Monica, with a regal air Ember wished she could emulate, gestured to the chairs. "Please take a seat and tell me how we can help you."

"If it's all the same, ma'am, I think we'd better remain standing. Hopefully, this won't take long," the older of them spoke. "I'm Lieutenant John Dorschet, and Miss Verre, I believe you know Detective Richert?"

Her muscles were so tight she couldn't even nod. "We've met." Forcing the words out hurt.

The detective shifted, looking down at his shoes, and the Lieutenant kept talking. "I'd like to apologize for my detective. He jumped to some conclusions he shouldn't have. However, because of those conclusions, we took a second look at that accident and discovered a grievous error."

"Error? What error?" She tried to pick up the coffee, but her hands shook too much. Ring took both of them in his hands, holding them tight.

The lieutenant waffled then ran his hand through his hair. "To be frank, both the crime scene techs and my department screwed up. Your father wasn't drinking. The other driver was. Two samples were mislabeled. When the detective here investigated to see if the accident was on purpose, as was insinuated by your mother and sister, this was discovered. At that point, he went back and found out about the damage your mother had suffered. And I, being the father of two teenage daughters, enlightened him as to exactly how"—he cleared his throat and shrugged—"complicated dealing with a teenage girl can be. Especially an angry grieving teenager."

"You mean my niece was being a little bitch."

"I'm sorry, ma'am, you are?" Detective Richert asked, a confused furrow on his forehead.

"Seri Davis. Sabrina is my twin."

"Oh. I was wondering, ma'am."

"So what exactly does all this mean?" Monica asked leaning forward.

The lieutenant set down the manila envelope he'd been holding. "All legal proceedings have been dropped. And insurance has been contacted with the new information. Here is our information. If you wish to file a lawsuit, it is your right. The lawyers for the other driver should be contacting you shortly with settlement information." He said all of this by rote, as he pulled out a card. "Here is my contact information if you need to contact me."

He laid that down on the table also and looked around the room. "Is there anything else we can do for you?"

Ember felt like a skydiver, free falling through the sky. It was over? She shook her head in small jerks, unable to formulate words. The iron grip from Ring gave her an anchor to reality.

"No, thank you, gentlemen. Be assured we will be in contact if we need to." The lieutenant nodded to everyone and tilted his head at his detective, and they headed to the door.

The two police officers left, leaving a silent room. Seri began to laugh.

"So all that, and it is over. I assume with this we can make everything right, get my sister the help she needs, and get Belinda back and ready for the Olympics." She turned eyes, the mirror of her sister's, to Ember. "But what do you want to do, dear? I know you entered this contest as a last ditch effort to save everyone. Well, you've done that. You can do anything, including go to Cordon Bleu, if you want."

Ember jerked her head to look at Ring, who had a carefully blank expression.

"Why would I want to go anywhere? The answer to all my dreams is right here." The smile that lit up Ring's face as he kissed her let her know this man would never walk away from her, or her family. The fractures in her heart melted and healed, forming a solid object, stronger than it had been before.

Epilogue — Six Months Later

Ring walked into the gleaming restaurant. The blue and white calmed him instantly as he made his way back into the kitchen. He leaned against the wall and watched the organized chaos that made up any restaurant kitchen. Ember stood strong in the middle, directing, cooking, tasting, and keeping everyone on task. Once again, her strength and beauty grabbed him.

Her head turned, seeing him, and her face lit up. She handed the pan she was holding over the stove to Karly, as she headed over to him.

"You're back. How did it go?"

"Good, we got the contract. We'll start next week." He had finished his master's. His instructors lobbied for work credit for the effort involved in renovating the hotel. This allowed him to finish all his classwork over the summer and a single quarter. The company he had formed with Clay and Greyson, RGC Vitalization, Inc. had just won its first contract. It had taken a week of proving to the owners they were the right people for the job.

"Wonderful. You staying there or commuting most days?" She leaned into him, and he pulled her close, loving the feeling of having her in his arms.

"I'll drive the 45 minutes. I rather enjoy waking up to you."

"Am I supposed to complain?" She grinned at him.

"I hope not. How's your mom doing?"

"Well, Seri has been great, and the anger is much less, though it is still hard for both of us. Belinda though is blossoming, and finished her therapy. She starts her training tomorrow. But I think she'll do fine."

"Good." He looked around the kitchen, not the most romantic place, but it was so uniquely her that it seemed to fit. "Ember, you know I love you, right?"

She laughed, lifting her face to him. "Yes. As you make sure to tell me every day. And I love you."

A sudden decision – he couldn't wait for a fancy dinner, or anything else. The idea of her ever not being there was wrong.

He dropped to one knee, hiding the wince as his knee hit the tile floor, and pulled out the black box that had been in his pocket for a week now.

"Will you marry me? I can't imagine my life without you in it." He opened the box and held up the ring, rich gold with a pale blue diamond in the middle, almost the color of her eyes.

The kitchen froze like someone had hit the mute button as everyone watched. Ember looked at him, eyes wide. Ring started to think it was a mistake when he saw the tears tracking down her face. She began to nod, a smile splitting her face.

"Yes! Oh yes!"

He slipped the ring on her finger, and the kitchen exploded into cheers. She pulled him up, her strength part and parcel of her beauty, and he pulled her into a kiss, pouring his love into her as the chaos of their lives started back up around them, two glass hearts, protected by their love.

ABOUT THE AUTHOR

Renee Lovins lives in Atlanta, Georgia. She has a
husband and cats. The cats are better trained. She's
been writing for years and has multiple other books
in process at this time.

If you liked this book and would like to know when my
other titles are available, sign up for News& Tidbits at–
www.reneelovins.com